Lady Adel's Captain

by

Loretta C. Rogers

Lady Adel's Captain

Cover Art by *RJ Morris*

The Wild Rose Press, Inc.
PO Box 708
Adams Basin, NY 14410-0708
Visit us at www.thewildrosepress.com

Publishing History
First English Tea Rose Edition, 2014
Print ISBN 978-1-62830-279-0
Digital ISBN 978-1-62830-280-6

Dedication

This book is dedicated to
my grandmother, Adel Frier Wright,
who always said that one day my imagination
would take me to unexpected places.

England

Part I

Miracle

1854

Chapter One

Lady Adel Fitzhugh believed in miracles, but in all her twenty-one years on this sweet earth she had never actually witnessed one. What she needed most on this bleak February afternoon was a true act of God.

Struggling to conceal a fiery panic, nausea welled up inside her. How had she offended her stepbrother so deeply as to find herself discarded like a piece of unwanted rubble?

She placed her finger against the window, traced a single raindrop's path as it meandered down the pane, and envied the water's freedom to blend and mingle at will.

She stepped back as lightning fingered across the sky and thunder vibrated the windows. Lord Reginald Fitzhugh's voice broke the ominous silence that followed.

"Adel, I will not debate the issue."

She clenched her jaw so hard her teeth ached as she turned to face him. He stood with his arms crossed over his chest. The force of his scowl chafed like a windstorm pressing against her skin.

Anxiety and anger laced her tongue. "No, Reggie, for the last time, I will not marry Baron Wishy-Washy."

"You'd do well to hold your waspish tongue, Sister. Since you've refused everyone at court, I'm afraid you are out of eligible bachelors. Besides, Baron

1

Wishingham is quite wealthy. He can afford to keep you in the custom you so richly enjoy."

Adel straightened her posture and jutted her chin forward. "What law is there that states a woman must marry, dear brother?"

"The one that says if you wish to eat, have a roof over your head, and new gowns for the season—that law."

Adel ground out the words. "I have my own money. I will not marry. The summerhouse in Kensington, small that it is, will serve me well."

The scowl on her stepbrother's face deepened as he placed his palms on the desk and leaned forward. "You have no money, *dear* sister."

She swallowed back the sickness building in the pit of her stomach. "What...what do you mean? There is my dowry."

With a long wavering sigh, Reginald smiled rather sadly. "As you well know, I am my father's only child. Although you were a babe in arms when he married your mother, you and I are not blood related. Father did not provide for you in his will. There is only your mother's jewelry, which you hold in your possession."

Adel drew up her shoulders in a small, distressed shrug. "But Father adopted me—gave me his name. Briarwood is as much my home as yours. Why must I leave?"

"It's the sting of your tongue, Adel. I can no longer abide my sweet bride's tears when she tells me you have once again usurped her in front of the servants."

"Then you shouldn't have married a stupid twit with marbles for brains."

A look of distaste washed over Reginald

Fitzhugh's face as he rounded the desk.

The slap rang in Adel's ears even before the pain stung her cheek and tears sprang to her eyes.

She touched a trembling hand to her cheek as her stepbrother's posture straightened stoically. She silently cursed her unbridled tongue as he said, "Enough of your insolence. I will hear no more. Instruct your maid to pack your trunks." He wagged a finger under her nose. "Heed my words, Adel. I will visit the vicar on the morrow and arrange an unpretentious ceremony to wed you to Baron Wishingham in less than a fortnight."

Like a petulant child, Adel stamped her foot. "No, Reggie! I will live out my life with the nuns at St. Francis Convent before spending one night wed to a fat, baldheaded clodpole who has sired seven unruly brats. Why, his poor dead wife probably counts it a blessing that she no longer has to endure his beastly rutting."

Her stepbrother's laughter and cocked eyebrow mocked her outrage. "You know little of the pleasures between a man and a woman, Adel. On the cusp of your twenty-second birthday, and with a tongue as sharp as a two-edged blade, consider yourself fortunate that the baron has agreed to wed you."

Adel reached out and laid her hand on her stepbrother's arm. Her voice softened. "It's only my dowry he wants, Reggie. Why not give me the money so that I may live my life as I please?"

Reginald Fitzhugh released a long sigh. He touched the red mark he'd left on his stepsister's cheek. "You know Father's penchant for the gaming tables and wagering on the races?" Reginald expelled a polite cough, then loudly cleared his throat. "In truth, Adel, Father left us near penniless. With your churlish temperament and the pittance I received from the sale of Sage and Royal—"

It took a moment for his words to sink in. She stepped back, as if avoiding another slap. When she tried to speak, the words nearly locked inside her throat. "You sold my mare and the foal?"

Her eyes held his for a long moment, while she searched that flint gray for some hint of feeling for her as a sister. Her entire body trembled with anger, and without thought she lashed out, returning the blow he'd given her. "You really are quite a blackhearted cur, aren't you?"

Rain pelting against the windows was the only sound in the room until the patter of approaching feet along the corridor beyond the closed office door penetrated Adel's angry silence, followed by a sharp and repeated rap at the door.

Without waiting for her stepbrother to react, she cried out, "Oh, for heaven's sake, stop that incessant pounding. We know it's you, Dudley. Do come in."

The tall, aging butler smoothed the front of his jacket as he entered the room. "Milord, Lady Adel." He cleared his throat as he extended a silver salver. "Travelers, sire. It appears the storm has made the road to Oxford impassable. They seek a place out of the weather. One says he knows you."

Adel reached for the card. It galled her when the old butler offered her a simpering smile as he moved the silver tray toward his master. She watched the taut creases relax in Reggie's pinguid face as he read the name on the small piece of stiff paper. He glanced up. "Make haste with your packing, Adel. I'm certain among your many gowns is one appropriate for a wedding."

She knew she had been dismissed as the butler pushed the door wide. Outside the study's great oaken doors, she looked heavenward and smiled when she heard Reginald say to the butler, "Find Lady Felicity and tell her that Lieutenant Robert Beck and his traveling companion will join us for dinner. And Dudley, after you show the gentlemen to the library, instruct Mrs. James to ready rooms for our guests."

"Very good, sire. Ah—"

"Yes, yes? What is it?"

"Well, sire, there is a small child. Her father does not wish her separated from him."

Standing with her ear against the door, the impatience in her stepbrother's voice was evident. "Then make certain Mrs. James sets up a daybed for the child in the guest suite."

"Most excellent. I should have thought of that myself, sire."

Adel landed on her backside when the butler pushed open the door. He tsked. "For shame, eavesdropping like a common charwoman."

She picked herself up from the floor. As she gave her skirts an indignant shake, she met her stepbrother's frown. "I warn you, Adel, you are no longer mistress of this house. You will not usurp Felicity's authority, and you will go to your room and begin gathering your belongings."

His voice sounded tired when he instructed the butler to show the guests to the library and to make certain to set out the brandy decanter and glasses. "And when you are finished, Dudley, kindly send Tilde to Lady Adel's suite."

Adel gathered her skirts to follow after the butler. She winced when Reginald grabbed her arm. "Where do you think you're going?"

Snatching her limb from his grip, she refused to rub the painful area. "The child may need tending."

His brows gathered in an agitated frown. He leaned over, bringing his face close to hers. His growl came through clenched teeth. "You try my patience, Adel." He extended his arm and pointed toward the stairs. "I don't expect to see you until dinner is announced."

She had pushed too far and dared not ignore his warning. Well, let him be angry. She climbed the stairs as if her whole world had come to an end.

****

Adel paced the length of her bedroom, clothed only in her white linen shift that came to mid-thigh, then flounced into the wingback chair, clutching an embroidered pillow to her chest, and watched the gentle rain streak the windowpanes. Her mind raced with the argument she'd had with her stepbrother. She knew there was much to be done in the next few days before Briarwood became a mere memory.

A knock sounded at the door. "'Tis only me, mum."

The maid entered the room on noiseless feet. Crossing to where Adel sat, Tilde dropped to her knees and gently lifted her mistress's hand into her own. "Why are you weeping?"

"What am I to do, Tilde?" A shroud of doom wrapped its mystical arms around Adel, and she moaned. "Reggie has pledged me to that fat, piggy-eyed Wishingham."

"Aye, 'tis a sorry thing, to be sure."

Adel pressed the heel of her hand against her forehead and railed, "It is bad enough that my own brother no longer wants me under his roof, but worse, he wants to punish me with a forced marriage to that profane old man."

"Meanin' no disrespect, mum, but a stepbrother bain't the same as a blood-kin brother."

Adel looked out the wide window onto the vast yard of Briarwood Manor. The pitter-pattering of rain against the sill added little comfort to her agitated state.

This was her home. She'd never questioned that she belonged; such thoughts had never occurred to her. She tried to console herself by laying blame on Reggie's bride.

Adel spoke the defamation aloud. "Simpering chit!"

"God's lamb," the maid exclaimed beneath her breath.

Adel felt deep resentment toward her sister-in-law. She gave vent to several gutter-born epithets with a voice that was sharp and piercing. "How dare that sister of a whoreson steal away my birthright? Answer me that, Tilde."

The maid gasped at the unladylike words spewing from her mistress's lips. "Beg'n' pardon, mum, but yer language would sear the ears off a donkey."

A moment of silence followed. Adel flung away the cushion and bounded out of the chair. "I refuse to surrender to *any* man."

She stood for a moment, then began her aimless trek across the room again. "I'll make good on my threat. Yes, that's what I'll do."

The maid answered, with a giggle, "You mean the

one about living out your days with the nuns?"

Adel spun around to stare heatedly at her maid. She wasn't in the frame of mind to bandy words with the woman, even though she considered Tilde more of a friend than a servant.

"Were you listening at the door again?"

Tilde's chin came up. "I wasn't listening on purpose, milady. Yours and Lord Fitzhugh's voices were loud enough to wake the dead. Had I known your conversation was meant to be private, I would have gone about me business. But, since I didn't, and I couldn't help overhearin', maybe you'd like a suggestion."

"Such as?" Adel cocked an eyebrow.

The maid stood in front of her mistress. She didn't bother to suppress the giggle. "Such as, you'd better commission the saddle maker to stitch several pairs of thick knee pads."

Adel's lower lip jutted out into a pout. "Pray tell, why would I need such a silly thing?"

"Meanin' no disrespect, mum, but, with your temperament, the Sisters at St. Francis will have you on your knees doing penance every day. Either that or scrubbing floors."

Adel flung herself on the bed and covered her eyes with one arm. "Oh, damn," she wailed. "You're not a bit of help."

"Aye, 'tis a joke, but the truth is, you've put your brother in the uncomfortable position of choosing between love for a stepsister and that of his wife. Only the saints above know why you've taken to belittlin' poor Lady Felicity the way you do. Aye, for certain this is your home, there's no disputin' that. But when a man weds, his wife becomes the mistress of the household. If you ask me, I'm thinking the green-eyed monster has gobbled up your sweet nature."

Adel chose not to comment. Tilde had a way of always hitting upon the truth, and now the truth hurt.

"Maybe I am a little jealous. What am I to do, Tilde? I'm trapped. I can't live on the streets. I'll have to marry Atwood Wishingham whether I like it or not."

"You could apologize to 'is lordship and to Lady Felicity. Mayhap he'll change his mind, if you promise to be nicer to your sister-in-law."

"I'm afraid it's too late. As Mother used to say, I've made my bed, and whether it be thorns or rose petals, I must now lie in it."

Although Tilde was close to five years older than her mistress, her cherubic face and the sprinkling of freckles across her nose made her appear much younger. She had worked in the Fitzhugh household for ten years, the last eight as Adel's personal maid.

"You'll think of something, milady, and the sooner the better. I've no more liking for the beastly man than yerself."

"What is it that you're not telling me, Tilde?" Adel moved as if to touch the maid's arm.

"I… Um… 'Tis only gossip from the scullery maids, mind you."

A spark of hope flickered inside Adel. Whatever her maid was about to reveal, perhaps she could use it as another argument against marrying a man thirty years her senior. "Gossip or no, Tilde, give over."

The maid glanced around the room before lowering her voice. "Well, mum, 'tis said Baron Wishingham romps around like a stallion and doesn't care whose pasture he plays in. And mostly, he likes to break the young ones to the saddle—if'n you know what I mean."

Adel's breath caught in her chest. She stared at her maid. "Girls? Unwed…girls? That's disgusting. If I were a man, I'd take a horsewhip to him."

"Aye, 'tis for certain he is a vile creature."

Tilde went to the armoire and selected a pearl-gray dress with long sleeves. "Mayhap you should wear this to dinner. There's a chill in the air tonight, and not all of it is from the weather."

She poured a basin of water, laid out a towel, and waited for Adel to freshen her face. After helping her into the gown, Tilde brushed Adel's long cord of hair until it shone. Adel sat patiently while her maid fashioned a coronet of braids.

What had happened to her wonderful life and the father she had loved so dearly? Had he not considered her his daughter, after all, to not provide for her after his death? She couldn't help the sorrowful sigh that escaped her.

"Don't fret so, mum. Things have a way of working out. You'll see."

Adel looked at her reflection in the cheval glass, her fingers loosely linked against the pleats of the somber gray gown. In a few short weeks, spring would bring a blanket of green to cloak the hills, and the lavender and daisies would spring into profuse bloom. The breeze would carry their sweetest fragrance across the meadows. She would not be here to enjoy it as in seasons past.

She held no real malice against her sister-in-law. It was just that she had no patience toward people with little starch in their backbone. Felicity was a narrow-hipped, flat-bosomed, simpering twit who'd come to Briarwood with a large dowry.

The dowry. That was it. Hadn't Reggie said Father left the estate near penniless? Adel drew her shoulders up straight. The tears were there, clinging to her lashes.

Her girlish dreams of exploring the world—riding camels in Egypt's Sahara Desert, sailing in a dory down the crocodile-infested Congo, studying animal husbandry and becoming a veterinarian—were like moving pictures inside her head, the dreams of a young girl, dreams that had never materialized. They had been almost as important to her as breeding thoroughbred horses and improving the line at Briarwood...nearly as important as her dear mother and stepfather.

Reginald had sold Sage and Royal—even her prized horses were lost to her. Adel pressed her mouth into a thin line. "Which of my ball gowns is the ugliest, Tilde?"

The maid's eyes crinkled into a frown. "The one that reminds me of a toad with warts—the lime green taffeta with the sheer overlay of pink polka dots."

Adel smiled. "It'll make a lovely wedding dress."

"Mum, you wouldn't dare?"

Sending her thoughts to some far-off place, Adel breathed deeply. "Instruct Edwin to bring the trunks down from the attic. Leave all my ball gowns in the armoire. Pack the rest of my dresses, both summer and winter, and my unmentionables. Leave my wigs. I shall want to take all of my books, and—"

A knock at the door sounded before it opened. Mrs. James, the head housekeeper, stepped inside the room. "My pardon, Lady Adel. Dinner is served in ten minutes. The master requests you arrive on time."

"What guests are we entertaining tonight, Mrs. James?"

"One you are acquainted with, mum. That cheeky lad Robert Beck, now a lieutenant in the Royal Guard, and a Captain Liam O'Shea."

Linking her fingers behind her back, a slight smile curved the corners of Adel's mouth. "An Irish captain? Hmmm. I foresee a rousing joust of politics between my stepbrother and the captain."

The housekeeper remained silent for several seconds. Her words flicked Adel like a whiplash. "You'd do well to bide that fickle tongue of yours, Lady Adel."

She could hardly fault the servant's loyalty to Reggie. "And you'd do well to remember your place in this household, Mrs. James."

The housekeeper sniffed in annoyance. "More's the pity to poor Baron Wishingham when he takes you to wed."

Adel flung up her hand in an impatient gesture. "You may go now, Mrs. James."

Wearily Adel slumped on the settee, hardly relishing the evening meal. She frowned, distressed at the thought of leaving Briarwood.

Chapter Two

The hall clock chimed six musical notes before Adel descended the stairs and made her way to the dining hall.

She greeted the butler as he pulled the massive oaken door open. Bright lights from the chandeliers spilled into the hall and clearly revealed her presence, she knew. Adel looked into the mischievous brown eyes of Lieutenant Robert Beck and noted the rakish grin on his face the instant he saw her. With exaggerated elegance, he bowed low.

She dismissed the temptation to giggle. "Oh, do stand up straight, Robby, and introduce your friend."

Warm blue eyes in a handsome face locked onto hers. Adel felt the hot blush rising in her cheeks as the uniformed man gave her a slight nod.

Robert Beck's brow furrowed, and he heaved a sigh. "Captain Liam O'Shea, may I present the only woman I know who has a tongue sharp as a rapier and doesn't mind hurling a shovel of fresh horse manure all over a man's crisp new uniform."

The color in her cheeks heightened, but she forced a weak smile. "I believe I was fifteen, Robby, and you were trying to steal a kiss."

Robert Beck pressed his hand over his heart. A soft smile teased the corners of his mouth. "And I was twenty and leaving for my first duty station."

Her breath stalled in her throat as both men stared at her. She gathered her composure.

Liam O'Shea's dark blue gaze never left her face. The deep timbre of his voice seemed to rumble in his chest, and Adel barely caught herself from lowering her gaze to that wide expanse.

"My gratitude to your brother for his extended invitation until the storm abates, Lady Adel."

"Stepbrother. Reggie is my stepbrother, Captain."

For pity's sake, take hold of yourself, Adel. She had a sudden desire to race up to her room and change into a prettier gown. Instead, her eyes sought the child in his arms.

What she saw in the little girl's dark eyes bespoke a sadness, as if she, in her own child's way, understood a change was about to take place in her life. Their eyes met, and in that moment was born between them a bond that nothing of this world could touch.

Adel reached out and fingered an auburn curl. "Such pretty hair. The color of a fiery setting sun." She brushed her hand over the child's head. "What is your name?"

The little girl snuggled closer against her father's chest and hid her face against his uniform jacket.

"Mary Kathryn doesn't take well to strangers."

"Are you traveling to meet your wife, Captain?"

"Mary Kathryn is my only family."

Adel had the distinct feeling Captain O'Shea had ingeniously sidestepped the question without truly giving her an answer. She wondered if some secret existed.

Before she could satisfy her curiosity, the sound of rustling skirts and the clack of heels against the hallway's wooden floor caused a frown to crease her brow.

Reginald Fitzhugh's nose twitched as he entered the room. "Damned if the aroma of a rich beef stew on a cold rainy night doesn't tantalize my taste buds."

With a flourish he seated his wife, an indication for the others to take their places at the long dining table. He picked up the bell next to his plate to signal the servants, and ale was brought to fill leather-bound tankards, loaves of crusty bread hot from the oven were placed on the table, and thick stew was ladled into bowls.

After her stepbrother had offered a toast, Adel motioned for one of the servants to come near. "Bennett, do go into the library and bring several large tomes. Mistress Mary Kathryn can scarce see over the edge of the table—even seated on her father's lap. And fetch a clean apron from Mrs. Bliss. We shall create a bib for the child so that she shan't spoil her pretty gown."

As the servant stepped toward the kitchen door, Adel called him back. "I should think a cup of milk, a spoon, and a bowl suitably sized for our little miss will do nicely, as well."

Lady Felicity Fitzhugh punctuated each word with restrained determination. "As usual, Adel, you take too much upon yourself. Perhaps the child isn't old enough to feed herself. After all, it isn't for you to say what Captain O'Shea prefers for his daughter."

Adel's chin tilted upward. Sarcasm thickened her voice. "It's quite noble of you to point out my tactless lack of judgment, Felicity." She shifted her attention to the man and child sitting across from her. Adel softened her voice. "How old are you, Mary Kathryn?"

The little girl straightened on her father's lap. She stretched a timid hand forward with three extended fingers. "I free."

A dimpled smile pulled at Liam O'Shea's handsome features before a shadow of remorse snatched it away. "She has hardly spoken a dozen words since her mother's death. It saddens me that duty calls me away."

"And where is duty calling you, Captain O'Shea?" Adel asked with obvious interest.

A minor disturbance caused Adel and the diners to look around as Bennett entered the dining room, his arms loaded with a stack of large books. The dour butler trailed behind. Dudley placed a chair next to Captain O'Shea, while Mrs. James arranged the place setting. When she'd secured the apron around the little girl's shoulders and tied a tidy bow, she instructed the servant to place the cup of milk and small bowl of stew on the table.

Adel nodded her pleasure as the servants took their leave. "Then you are taking Mary Kathryn to her grandparents while you are away, Captain?"

"As I said, I have no family. Before the storm deterred us, Lieutenant Beck and I were on our way to St. Francis Convent, and afterward to London, where we will meet our troops before sailing to India."

A long wavering sigh escaped Adel. "A convent is no place for a child. Mary Kathryn needs love and nurturing. She—"

Felicity's voice reminded Adel of a whining mosquito. "Heaven take pity, Adel. What would you know of such matters?" Felicity Fitzhugh frowned at

16

her sister-in-law.

Adel's matter-of-fact voice belied her intense dislike of the pale limpid creature she blamed for the ills with her stepbrother. "No more than you, to be sure. And with six months past your nuptials, it appears you are a barren wasteland who may never know what it is to raise a child."

She watched Felicity's face grow scarlet as she wailed, "Reginald, don't just sit there. Say something!"

An aborted laugh escaped Robby Beck as he lifted the linen napkin to his mouth. Adel didn't miss the wink he cast toward Liam. "Maybe we should take Adel with us to India. With the sharpness of her tongue, we could make her an army of one."

Adel cringed inwardly at the remark. Nevertheless, she forged ahead with the idea forming in her mind. "Captain O'Shea, would you not prefer to leave Mary Kathryn in the care of a qualified governess rather than in a cold, sterile convent?"

One bushy brow rose. "I'm afraid, Lady Adel, it's near impossible to find someone qualified on such short notice. Our ship sails on Wednesday next."

His scowl was not reassuring. She had no way of knowing whether her suggestion caused him discomfort. Her voice cracked and was an octave higher than she intended, so she paused to clear her throat. "I am proficient in Latin and French, play the harpsichord, embroider, paint and sketch, and I am well read in the classics. I have a good head for sums and know how to keep household accounts. I'm proficient with gardening, know horses, and I don't mind getting my hands dirty if necessary. If you wish to ask the kitchen staff, I am also a fair cook. I believe my credentials qualify me as a governess."

When Reginald puffed red, he reminded Adel of an enraged rooster. He slammed his hand down on the table. "Enough of this nonsense, Adel." His tone was low and thick with frustration. "Have you forgotten your betrothal to Baron Wishingham?"

The retort came quick and hot. "I would sooner drink poison than agree to marry a fat, fish-mouthed fop."

"I'll thank you to keep a civil tongue in your head and stop this foolery about becoming a governess." Reginald's voice was gruff with threat.

****

Captain Liam O'Shea studied the woman whose pale cheeks suffused with color. If he'd learned anything in the short time since meeting Lady Adel Fitzhugh, it was that she had a mind and a will of her own. The animosity between the two sisters-in-law was evident. He pitied poor Fitzhugh for being caught in the middle of the battle between wife and sister. Yet it puzzled him that Fitzhugh would betroth his sister to a man of fifty-and-three years. Liam knew of Wishingham's reputation for philandering. He'd also heard the whispers that the real reason for his wife's death was not childbirth but, rather, the malady of syphilis.

A sympathetic smile lit the captain's face as he looked at Adel's lovely puckered mouth—as if she'd just tasted something bitter. Leaning in to study her, he found her violet eyes snapping fire at her stepbrother as she reached for a cloverleaf biscuit to place on Mary Kathryn's plate.

And then there was Mary Kathryn, the daughter he

hadn't known existed until eight months ago. Though her mother was a girl on the line, there was no doubting he'd been her first trick. It was for this reason, when she sent a note saying she'd borne him a daughter and was dying of consumption, that he'd rushed to her side. There was no denying the child was his—russet curls, eyes the color of sapphire—a miniature of his own grandmother.

The toddler had stolen his heart, but now duty to the Queen and England called, and he must leave Mary Kathryn with strangers.

In a timid voice, Mary Kathryn said, "Da-dee, milk, peez."

Though the child's voice was but a whisper, it jarred him out of his reverie. He reached for the cup and then smiled as her tiny fingers wrapped around his.

In his careful search for words, his gaze probed Adel's pools of deep lilac. "I have but one wish, Lady Adel: that my daughter be raised in Ireland. My mother was English, my father from Connemara. She longed for her homeland, so we left Ireland when I was ten. I own no property in England. These many years I have called the Guard barracks my home, though I inherited my grandmother's estate in Connemara."

Grinding his teeth in obvious vexation, Reginald Fitzhugh mangled several expletives as he slammed his leather-bound tankard down upon the table. He wrapped a steely grip around Adel's wrist. "The contract is signed, the pittance of a dowry accepted. You dare not make a mockery of me, Sister."

Adel forgot the pounding in her head. Her softening smile was sweetly apologetic. "Forgive me, Reggie," she replied, trying to extricate her wrist from his hold. "Tell Baron Wishingham to go fish in another stream. After all, the storm has delayed your efforts to contact the vicar. You have yet to make any formal marriage arrangements."

Adel could hardly believe her good fortune when the captain intervened. "Lord Fitzhugh, if it is your sister's dowry that concerns you so, I will buy it."

"No, by god, there is a principle at stake, and my reputation."

Liam's eyes seemed to go from warmth to blue ice and his voice as cold as winter. Adel felt an icy wind had filled the room when he spoke. "What brother on the face of this earth would want it known that he is willing to sell his sister to a man well known to have infected his deceased wife with the most dreaded of diseases...which he himself caught from *fishing* in more than one polluted stream?"

The squeak that escaped Felicity's throat reminded Adel of a trapped mouse.

Reginald blustered in some embarrassment. "I...ah...oh, saints preserve us all. I took no notice, thinking it only a nasty rumor."

Adel's expressive eyes reflected the horror she felt. "Reggie, you knew, and still you...? Do you hate me so much?" When he didn't answer, she was struck with a strong aversion to her stepbrother. She brought her hands together as she pushed from the table.

Lieutenant Beck rose to her assistance. She spoke through the tightness in her throat. "I bid you all goodnight. Captain O'Shea, we will discuss the terms of my employment over breakfast on the morrow, and, rest assured, I will nurture Mary Kathryn with much more affection than I've received since my own dear mother's passing." She swallowed hard to keep her voice from cracking.

Turning abruptly toward the door, Adel lifted her skirts and flew up the stairs before her stepbrother found his voice. Though he called after her, she dashed along the dimly lit hallway without giving acknowledgement, snatched open the door to her bedroom, and slammed it behind her, rattling nearby windows with the force of her passage.

Lightning followed by rolls of thunder mimicked the storm that raged inside her, as powerful as the one soaking the countryside. She swiped at her tears.

"Mum, it pains me to see you in such distress. Wot 'appened to cause this misery?"

Adel didn't voice her feelings to Tilde. It would simply invite further comment from the maid, comment Adel was too emotionally spent to deal with sensibly. Besides, the woman had probably eavesdropped on every word that passed in the dining room.

"I'll undress myself. Goodnight, Tilde."

"You must look upon this as your destiny unfolding, mum."

"Were you eavesdropping again, Tilde? If so, I'm too tired to ferret out your meaning." Her voice held no reproach.

"Only a tad bit, mum. I did 'ear your offer to the Capt'n. 'Tis a fine governess you'd be makin', too."

"Stop your gibberish and go to bed," Adel whispered.

"That I will, when I've explained me gibberish." The maid drew a deep breath.

Adel stirred restlessly. "Oh, all right. If you must."

"Well, mum, one chapter of your life is closing and

another is about to open up. Thankfully God has spared you the vile ways of Baron Wishingham, but how will you cope with being all alone and raising a wee child…and so far from home?"

Adel folded her hands against her chest as the enormity of her spur-of-the-moment decision sank in. She considered her words. "It isn't exactly the adventure I'd dreamed of, but it is what it is, and I shall make the most of it." The sad expression on her maid's face pricked Adel's heart. "Don't fret, my dear friend. I won't be alone. You and your Edwin will accompany me to Ireland. Now leave me."

"'Tis downright generous of you, because I've no liking to remain 'ere meself. But, mum, I need to take down your hair, and—"

A hand at her throat, Adel sagged back into her chair. "Good night, Tilde."

The maid stood as if reluctant to leave the room. A smile tugged at the corners of her lip. She curtsied. "So be it, mum. Rest well."

Vaguely aware that she was alone, Adel removed the pins from her hair and unraveled the crown of braids. She picked up the silver-handled brush and pulled it through the long strands, vigorously brushing until her scalp ached. A lump rose in her throat, and she bit back a sob. *Whether a bed of rose petals or thorns, you made your bed and must lie in it.*

I hear your words, Mother. I hear them loud and clear. Adel threw the brush across the room.

Chapter Three

Liam O'Shea smiled down at the small bundle on the cot. Coppery eyelashes curled against the sleeping child's cheeks. "Sweet dreams, my darling daughter." The words were a wisp of a whisper.

Easing through the bedroom door, he left it ajar to listen lest Mary Kathryn awaken afraid of her unfamiliar surroundings.

In the hallway, he rapped on the door next to his room and waited, impatient. "Saw the light under your door, Robby."

"Anything amiss, Liam?"

"May I come in?"

The lieutenant held the portal wide and stepped aside. "I was pouring myself a nightcap. Care for one?"

"I could use something to chase the chill from my bones." Liam accepted the snifter. He paused for a long time, allowing the almond-flavored brandy to warm the back of his throat.

Robert savored his own brandy. "I can tell by the scowl on your face you have something serious on your mind."

"You've an instinct about you, Robby. It's what makes you a fine officer." Liam tossed back the remains of the brandy and set the glass on the table. "I have formed an unhealthy opinion of our host."

Robert Beck slipped the heel of his boot inside the

bootjack and tugged his stockinged foot free, then proceeded to remove the other boot. "Sad state of affairs, I must admit, when a man arranges for his sister's marriage to a veritable scoundrel."

"Do you think Fitzhugh ignorant, or just plain stupid?" Liam asked, looking at the young lieutenant.

"I believe the word *gullible* more defines Reggie."

His voice quiet, Liam said, "Tell me about Lady Adel. Is she someone I can trust to properly care for my daughter?"

Robert seemed to weigh the question before giving his answer. "Had I not chosen the service as my lifelong mistress, I would have pursued Adel's hand in marriage. Though I don't think she would have accepted me."

"You're a fine lad, with a title, and wealth. Is she daft, Robby?"

Robert laughed as he crossed a leg over his knee and massaged the toes on his foot. "Damned tight boots." He smiled up at his friend. "No, not daft, Liam. Admittedly, Adel is a forward-thinking woman. I don't believe marriage is an institution she craves—rather, it is adventure for which she yearns. The few times we were together, she often spoke of traveling to far-off places. I can tell you one thing—she isn't afraid to speak her mind."

Liam cocked an eyebrow. "You mean more so than what she demonstrated at dinner? I'm intrigued. Tell me more."

Robby topped off his glass and took a sip. "We once debated the necessity of war, and it was Adel's steadfast opinion that if the Queen were to commission women into the Royal Guard there would be no more wars." He chortled, then turned serious. "Adel knows what it's like to lose a parent. She was twelve when the fever took her mother. I'd stake my life she would give up her own breath before she'd allow any harm to befall Mary Kathryn."

Still not reassured by the answer, Liam pursued. "Do you think Lady Adel is up to the task of managing an estate? She will, after all, be an Englishwoman in a strange land and amongst people who may well challenge her authority."

"Ask yourself this, Liam. Who will be the better teacher for your daughter—the nuns at St. Francis, or Adel? If you think the nuns, then consider who will love Mary Kathryn more, the Sisters with their daily prayers and strict servitude, or a young woman who needs to give love as much as she needs to receive it?"

Liam patted the young lieutenant on the shoulder. "You make a sound argument, Robby. Perhaps you should give up the Queen's service and become a politician."

"It's something to consider. Mayhap when we return from India." Robert Beck opened the bedroom door. "Good night, Liam."

Emotions twisted inside Liam. "Aye, I've much to think on." His shoulders squared visibly. "I'll have one more question before retiring, Robby."

"And that would be?"

"Why did Lady Adel's mother marry the elder Fitzhugh?"

"Adel was about Mary Kathryn's age when her father was felled during England's battle with China's Quing Dynasty. You can understand the difficulty of raising a child alone, and multiply your knowledge by the difference between being a man and being a woman left in such circumstance."

Without answering, Liam nodded his goodnight.

****

Liam stood in front of the fireplace and warmed his hands. He clenched his jaw until the muscles in his neck and shoulders felt as tight as sailor knots.

When the child whimpered in her sleep, he went to kneel beside the cot. He lifted her tiny hand into his and spoke soft, reassuring words. "I'm here, Mary Kathryn. Your father is here."

Fearing she might be chilled, he removed his uniform jacket and laid it on top of the blanket that covered her. He caressed the indentation on her cheek, a twin to his own dimple.

A heavy feeling plagued his soul. Like his second in command, Liam, too, was married to the Queen's service. There was no room in his life for a wife, and certainly not for a child with no mother. Truth of the matter, he'd never wanted to be a parent, fearing he had no love to give and no nurturing instincts. He'd known, better than most men in the shade of thirty years, the harshness of a cold and domineering mother. He closed his eyes, trying to evoke the image of his father. Liam barely remembered the gentle giant with a boisterous laugh. A man who died before reaching his prime.

For fear of waking his daughter, Liam swallowed the string of oaths building in his throat as he jerked his shirt over his head, then sat on a chair to tug and remove each leather boot. The coolness of the room prickled his skin as he completely undressed. Before slipping into bed, he rubbed the jagged scar that traced across his shoulder. The old wound was a grim reminder of how close he'd come to death, of the rumblings of a rebellion in India, and of his duty to England.

He punched the pillow. The child had unwittingly wiggled her way into his heart. God knew there was no resigning his commission. He had five years left, and his service to the Crown demanded he leave Mary Kathryn behind.

His heart pummeled against his sternum when he turned his thoughts to Lady Adel. Tall, for a female, and slim, dressed in a well-fitted gown of gray, she appeared confident and strong-minded. With hair the color of mink, she was a beauty—fair skin, lips that reminded him of rose petals, intelligent eyes…eyes the color of spring lilacs, that drew him in and made him wonder what kind of magic she possessed to win over his daughter and to cause a fire to grow in his belly.

Unable to sleep, he rose from the bed and wrapped the quilt around his body. He padded to the writing desk and sat down. Pulling paper from the drawer, he dipped the quill pen into the inkpot and bent to the task of writing out a succinct set of instructions for his daughter's new governess.

****

The fury of the storm mirrored Adel's mood as she tossed and turned in a tempest of her own. A blinding flash of lightning bleached the darkness of the night, setting the rain-drenched windows aglow. A sharp crack of thunder trod on its heels, bringing Adel upright with a curse. Her temper had reached its peak. The play of streaking lights beyond the crystal panes lighted the room. With a deep sigh she sank back beneath the heavy coverlet.

She had much to think about. Then, too agitated to sleep, she was out of bed and pacing. And though she believed a woman should choose her own destiny, she knew little of children. Except for those old enough to work in the fields or in the kitchen, her stepbrother's rules forbade the servants from bringing their young ones to the house.

Her senses came crashing down around her. As usual, she had plunged headfirst into a decision without thinking it through. Surely nurturing a child wasn't much different from gentling a foal. Her mind screamed, *No, no, no!* A child wasn't an animal.

Adel climbed into the large four-poster bed and flopped on her back, pulling the heavy quilts to her chin. She passed the next hours trying to recall her own childhood. A warm feeling filled her when she thought about the special memories she had of her mother.

Adel had prayed for a miracle to save her from marrying a man she detested, and by the saints, she didn't intend to turn her back on it.

Excitement surged through her veins, and apprehension, powerful and intense, filled her heart. What if Captain O'Shea changed his mind about hiring her as governess, deciding instead that the Sisters of St. Francis were more suitable for raising his daughter?

Captain O'Shea. If she closed her eyes, she could almost envision the man rising naked, walking across the room, walking toward her bed. At dinner, she'd studied him in the glow of lamps. He had left an impression on her—towering height, broad shoulders tapering to narrow hips, and short hair neatly trimmed against a sun-bronzed neck. He was a man among many.

She let out a loud sigh. Any doubts she had about leaving Briarwood were erased when the image of Liam O'Shea was replaced by Baron Wishingham, with his piggy eyes, bloated cheeks, and lascivious grin. An uncontrollable shiver of revulsion raced down her spine to the tips of her toes. In truth, she couldn't imagine remaining in England if marriage to him was required.

****

Exhaustion caused Adel to slip into a fitful sleep. One disturbing dream seemed to follow another.

She groaned and pushed at the persistent hand that dared disturb her sleep. "Go away. I've just closed my eyes."

Tilde nudged the shoulder of her mistress. "Wake up with your sleepy self, mum. You wouldn't want to keep the captain waiting, now, would you?"

Adel pushed the mop of unruly hair from her face. She felt so disoriented she couldn't remember where she was. "Oh, saints preserve us, Tilde."

She swung her legs over the side of the bed and, in her haste, missed the bedside steps and tumbled to the floor. The maid rushed to her. "Are you hurt, mum?"

Adel expelled an exasperated groan and scrambled to her feet. She rubbed her hands up and down the sleeves of her wool nightgown. "It's freezing in here."

Tilde went to the window and opened the heavy drapes to brighten the room. "At least the rain has stopped." She, too, shivered. She added kindling to the fireplace and used the hand bellows to spark life into the shy embers.

Before Tilde had time to help her mistress, Adel grabbed a fresh pair of stockings and rolled them up her legs. Stepping into a petticoat, she pointed to the armoire. "My blue wool gown with the white collar will do. Oh, there isn't time to properly do my hair."

"Stop flitting around like a drunken butterfly, mum, and stick out your arms."

"Do hurry, Tilde," Adel fussed. Slipping the gown over her head, she fidgeted while the maid's deft fingers worked into place the long row of buttons lining the back of the dress.

"I'm thinking to tie your hair back with a pretty blue ribbon, the one that matches your dress, and leave a few curls to soften your face."

"For pity's sake, Tilde, I'm not courting the man. There's no need to look pretty. I should appear as a governess."

The maid placed her fists on her hips. "Goodness me, did your governess look like a shriveled-up old prune with hair pulled back so tight it made her eyes slanty?"

"Be forewarned, I'm not in the mood for one of your lectures, Tilde."

"You'll be listening, for sure, unless it's your wish Captain O'Shea should take one look at your sourpuss face and decide the nuns are a better choice for his daughter."

"If you weren't my friend, Tilde, I swear I'd trade you for another."

The maid laughed outright. She brushed Adel's hair until it shone, fastening it at the nape with a neat bow. "Aye, mum, with your sharp tongue, you'd be hard put to find a replacement."

Adel tried to look incredulous but knew the maid spoke the truth. She rose from the dressing table and hastened to the door. Tilde's voice called her back.

"Forgetting something, are you, mum?"

Adel glanced over her shoulder. She flung up her hands in an impatient gesture. "No, I don't think so."

Wearing a wide grin, Tilde held forth the blue brocade slippers. "Did you think to meet the captain in your stocking feet?"

Adel looked down at the black-clad toes peeking from beneath the hem of her dress. "Oh, for pity's sake." She slipped a foot into each slipper.

Shoulders stiff and head held high, she gave her skirt an indignant swish and left the bedroom.

She met the housekeeper at the bottom of the stairs. "Mrs. James, has Captain O'Shea come down for breakfast?"

"A while ago. His lordship is showing the Captain and Lieutenant Beck the stables."

"Did he leave a message for me?"

"Who, mum?"

To show her impatience, Adel narrowed her eyes and tapped her toe. "Don't be cheeky, Mrs. James. It's unbecoming. Who else would I expect to leave me a message?"

"Of course. The captain said to enjoy your breakfast, and he would meet you in the library at ten."

"Where is the child—Mary Kathryn?"

"Since you were not about, he bundled the little girl in an afghan and carried her with him. Not a very good first impression for a governess, I'd think."

Not willing to concede the field, Adel said in soft admonishment, "Careful you don't overstep your boundaries, Mrs. James. While you may be the head of staff at Briarwood, you are not the mistress. You would be well advised to remember the reason my stepbrother has banished me from his house. He will favor his insipid little wife over a housekeeper, no matter how long you have served the family."

The housekeeper's face flushed with anger. "If you will excuse me, Lady Adel, I must see that the linens are properly ironed."

When Mrs. James vanished through a door leading to the laundry, a depressing coldness clamped its clammy hands upon Adel as the lump in the pit of her stomach grew weightier. She groaned inwardly at her thoughts. What if Mrs. James is correct? What if I have given the captain the impression I am irresponsible?

Chapter Four

There was a price to be paid for oversleeping. It seemed forever before Adel spotted Captain O'Shea, Lieutenant Beck, and her stepbrother striding across the sodden ground toward the house.

A full head taller than both Reggie and the lieutenant, the captain carried a bundle nestled against his shoulder, and that sparked an idea. Adel opened the library door to search the hallway. "Oh, where is Mrs. James or Dudley when I need them?"

Mumbling under her breath, she lifted her skirts and raced to the kitchen. Mrs. Bliss lived up to her name. Always cheerful, the woman was a miracle worker when it came to preparing food.

"Wot's got ye in such a huff, milady?" Mrs. Bliss offered a rosy-cheeked grin while she basted a lamb shank.

"Captain O'Shea took his daughter with him on a tour of the stables with my brother and Lieutenant Beck."

The cook's eyes widened. "Ye mean he took the wee pumpkin outside—in the cold? Why the dear thing'll catch her death."

Adel came to the captain's defense. "He did bundle her in a quilt."

"All the same, milady—"

Adel cut the conversation short. "Exactly, Mrs.

Bliss. That's why I thought you might warm a cup of milk and sweeten it with a spoonful of honey."

The cook's eyes crinkled when she smiled. "And wot 'bout a scone?"

"Lovely. In fact, a fresh pot of tea and several scones, and a pot of your wonderful gooseberry jam, if you please."

The portly cook fairly gushed at the compliment. "I'll get a tray to Mrs. James in two shakes of a mare's tail."

Wanting to return to the library before the captain got there, Adel called over her shoulder, "I don't know what I'd do without you, Mrs. Bliss."

"Ye could be takin' me with you to Ireland. I've 'bout had me fill of Lady Felicity and Mrs. James." The cook clamped a beefy hand over her mouth. "Sorry, mum. Don't go thinkin' I ain't grateful for me job."

Adel dashed back and hugged the plump cook. "Ever since I was a child, you've always been someone I could talk to." She glanced around at the huge kitchen, with its pots and pans hanging in a tidy row. "I'm certain Captain O'Shea has a full staff at his country estate."

"'Twas afeerd I was ye might say such, mum."

Adel swallowed hard against the knot that had risen in her throat. She scarcely remembered a time when Mrs. Bliss had not been in her life. "I won't make promises I can't keep, but—"

"'Twill be awright, milady. I know you'll send for me and the mister if'n there be a place for us."

Adel chided, "I sometimes think you know me better than I know myself."

Returning to the library, Adel rehearsed all the

things she would say if her stepbrother had convinced the captain to rescind his offer to take her into his employ.

Doll. The word popped into her mind. Every child loved dolls. Certain Mary Kathryn was no exception, Adel decided to have Tilde rummage through some old trunks to find just the right doll for the little girl.

Deep in thought, she plowed headfirst into the butler, nearly knocking him off his feet. His indignant glare almost caused her to laugh aloud.

"My apologies, Dudley. Please send Tilde to the library. And do hurry."

"Have you lost your wits, milady? Always running willy-nilly without a thought in your head except to unsettle the master's home. You are not a child any longer."

"You'd do well to bridle your tongue, Dudley."

The butler looked her up and down. He hissed at her. "Baron Wishingham or a pagan land...you deserve whichever the master decides."

She squared her shoulders against his stinging suggestion. Surely Reggie would see the sense in accepting Captain O'Shea's request that she serve as governess to his child. She shook away the doubt.

She arched an eyebrow. "If your feet have not taken root to the floor, Dudley, I suggest you find Tilde as I have requested."

Before doing her bidding, the old man matched Adel glare for glare. "As you wish, milady. But, first, an unexpected guest waits in the parlor. I must find Lady Felicity and let her know."

Adel stared. "Why was I not made aware of this?"

"I believe Lord Fitzhugh has made clear your

position in this house."

As much as she wanted to slap the smirk from the butler's face, she held her temper. "And who, pray tell, is this unannounced visitor?"

"Why, your betrothed, Baron Wishingham, of course."

****

Fear congealed in Adel's breast and ran its icy tendrils through her veins as she entered the parlor.

Three men stood to greet her. Where was the child? She didn't remember seeing Mrs. James or Tilde with Mary Kathryn.

Her heart labored against the dreadful chill of dread, for she feared what the outcome would be if the baron had successfully goaded her stepbrother into honoring the marriage agreement.

Feeling the trap closing in on her, she suppressed a moan as she entered the parlor. "Baron Wishingham, this is so…unexpected. What I mean to say is—"

The plump, baldheaded baron, in a fine burgundy coat with gold buttons, stood next to her stepbrother. His leering grin reminded Adel of a hungry animal sizing up its prey.

The bane of her existence swept forward. "Fair Adel, your beauty is like the sun gracing this drenched land with its warmth and brilliance," the baron avowed, gallantly sweeping an arm across his chest and bowing low in a courtly manner. He straightened, taking her hand and lifting it to his lips.

Adel inwardly cringed at the odious moisture, and at the clutch that imprisoned her fingers.

Reginald said, "Please, gentlemen, let us sit and enjoy the scones while Adel pours tea."

She swept her stepbrother a grateful look for saving her from the baron's offending grasp.

As she stepped forward to do Reggie's bidding, she wondered why the captain chose to remain standing.

"Cream and sugar, Captain?"

"Neither, thank you."

Wishingham tossed a gleeful smile toward Adel. "Cream and three lumps for me, my dear."

The captain's choice of black tea spoke volumes to Adel. Here was a man of strength and valor, not a limp-wristed, piggy-eyed fop. She had a wicked desire to deliberately spill the hot liquid over the baron's corpulent belly.

Deliberately ignoring the portly man, she served the first cup to the captain.

"I've not had the privilege of meeting many men who prefer to drink their tea black, Captain O'Shea."

Adel stared into the warmly shining eyes and finally, after a lengthy pause, looked away when his lips slowly spread into a smile that softened the harsh lines of his face.

"There are few luxuries in the service, Lady Adel."

Wishingham proffered, "Come, come, Captain. Officers of the Crown are surely afforded such minute indulgences as sugar for tea, are they not?"

Adel shifted her gaze from the baron to O'Shea, expectant of what drama might unfold.

"An officer's worth isn't measured by indulgences, Baron, but rather by the example he sets for the men who serve under his command."

"Ah, *touché*, Captain. I stand corrected."

Though a fire flickered in the massive fireplace, Adel suppressed a shiver at the way the three men stared at her. Was she a piece of prime horseflesh being sized up before the bidding began? Taking a seat on a tufted lady's chair, she let her eyes wander from man to man.

"Captain O'Shea, may I ask in whose charge did you leave Mary Kathryn?"

Her brother's sharp reprimand came without warning. "Adel, you take too much upon yourself. To whom the captain assigns his child is none of your business."

Wishingham interceded. "Dear Reggie, there is no need to scold. Our sweet Adel is merely displaying motherly instincts. She will fit quite nicely as stepmother to my own children."

His gaze swept her from head to toe as he licked his fleshy lips. With effort he pushed his heavy body from the chair to stand behind Adel and lay a hand on her shoulder. "My dearest lady, I value the day I accepted your brother's proposition. It is a fair price we agreed upon."

A rush of disturbing visions filled her head. Bile rushed into her throat. She sent a puzzled frown toward her stepbrother.

"I'm afraid I don't understand. Since Reggie has made it clear that I have no dowry, what is this price you speak of?"

The red glow staining her stepbrother's cheeks confirmed her fear.

Her temper exploded. "How dare you, Reggie! You cannot sell me as if I were one of your horses."

"It is your own fault, Adel."

"Surely you jest. Why, just last night you were present when I accepted Captain O'Shea's offer to become governess to his daughter."

"I did not agree to any such arrangement, Sister. The marriage agreement is signed and, only this morning, the money paid. You have no further say in the matter."

Wishingham nodded, with a leering grin, as he returned to his seat and generously slathered butter and jam on a scone before plopping it into his mouth.

Adel's gaze met and locked with O'Shea's. He looked almost angry. The room went silent. His nostrils flared when he spoke. "Unless your sister is of unsound mind and incapable of rendering responsible decisions, I believe she is of an age to speak for herself. Last night, I was willing to buy her dowry. Today, I am not."

Her heart beat a breakneck rhythm against her ribs. A cloud of doom weighed her down.

O'Shea turned to look at her, his expression grim. He reached inside his uniform blouse and withdrew a document. "These are the terms of your employment, Lady Adel. I trust you will find your wage more than fair. My coachman tells me the roads are now passable. I expect you to be ready to leave on the morrow."

The baron harrumphed, his voice muffled as he spoke with a mouthful of sugary confection. "Now, see here, O'Shea. You overstep ethical boundaries. I have friends in the Queen's Court."

Adel didn't miss the way the captain's dark eyes sparkled with malicious amusement. "And I have the Queen's favor. Do not doubt her reaction when she hears the true cause of your wife's death." He turned to Reggie. "And how do you think Her Grace will receive you at court when she learns that you sold your sister to this loathsome piece of flesh?"

Adel clenched her teeth until her jaw hurt. She surveyed the faces of her stepbrother and the baron and knew her life was about to change forever.

"Reggie...Baron, you are both pompous oafs!" The words escaped her taut lips as she gripped the scrolled document that held her future.

Keenly aware of the captain's gaze on her every move, she said, "You will not have to wait for me, sir. I shall be packed and ready to leave before dawn."

As night draped the land with its blanketing cloak of blackness, lightning began to flicker in the distance, followed by low rumbles of thunder. Another storm advanced in slow degrees, grumbling and stamping its way across the leaden landscape and finally reaching its peak. It seemed bent on thwarting Adel's attempt at sleep, but she could hardly blame her lack of slumber on the thundering crashes.

The fury of the storm again mirrored Adel's mood as she tossed and turned in a tempest of her own. A blinding flash of lightning bleached the darkness from the night, setting the rain-drenched windows aglow. A sharp crack of thunder trod on its heels, bringing Adel upright.

Revulsion shuddered through her as she imagined the repugnant Baron Wishingham's damp, pudgy hands groping and pinching her body.

****

Adel woke with a start. Something was amiss. She felt the gnawing truth of it in her bones. She rose to a cloudy dawn, the chilly bite in the room making her reluctant to leave the warmth of her bed.

Then, below her window, she heard sounds. Voices low and menacing, one of the baritones sounding distinctly like Baron Wishingham. "Adel is mine. I will kill any man who tries to take her from me. Choose your weapon."

Wrapping the silken coverlet around her body, she slid from the massive four-poster bed and raced barefoot across the room, her toes curling when her feet touched the cold floor. The clouded light helped guide her to the window. Hugging the quilt to her chest, fearful of what she might find, she used the edge of the eiderdown to wipe moisture from the panes. Unable to clearly see, she opened the window and leaned forward.

Lieutenant Beck stood stalwart. "Your Lordship, Captain O'Shea is not only an expert marksman, he is an able swordsman with rapier and saber, and quick as a cobra with a dirk. If you persist in this foolish challenge, I will act as my captain's second, though it is not he who will die."

In the morning gloom, Captain O'Shea stood rigid, his voice harsh with anger. "The rashes on the palms of your hands are sure signs of syphilis, Baron. I have witnessed the deaths of men infected with this disease. In the last stages, it eats away at the brain, driving its victims to madness. We both know you are the worst of cowards, Wishingham. I do not accept your challenge. You will not use me as your angel of death."

The baron shrieked, "You are a bastard cur! You and that chit have cuckolded me. I demand retribution!"

O'Shea chortled. "Rather like the pot calling the kettle black. Go home to your children. Spend your last days arranging for their care so they are not doomed to spend their youth in the care of others. Your family will suffer enough for the legacy you leave them."

Liam O'Shea gestured to the coachman. "Assist

your employer into the coach and leave these grounds immediately."

Holding a lacy handkerchief to his nose, the baron glared at Liam, whose eyes snapped with blue fire. He delivered a sneer to his adversary. "The chit is hardly worth an ounce of my blood." Then, to his coachman, "Come, Bevis, let us be on our way."

Liam must have felt Adel's gaze on him, because he suddenly looked up. He was still frowning, but his expression changed. Tenderness came into his eyes, and he smiled at her.

Chapter Five

Adel managed to endure her stepbrother's condemnation. "Not only have you shamed yourself by betraying the baron, you have tarnished the Fitzhugh name."

She swallowed with some difficulty, the genuine tears blurring her eyes. Felicity wore an odd smile that reminded Adel of an impish child who had won a challenge by cheating.

"Dear, dear sister-in-law, can you not see how distressed our Reginald is over your silly behavior? Give up this foolish idea of running off to Ireland. With time, I'm certain my husband will find a suitable match for you."

Fighting the urge to hiss at both of them, Adel blinked to clear her vision. "I have never considered myself *silly*. And I will never yield to a forced marriage."

Reginald stepped forward. He watched Adel with an oddly detached, yet intent, expression. "Since you persist in this childish behavior, I have no other alternative than to banish you from Briarwood. When you tire of this charade of playing governess and return to England, you will not be welcomed under my roof. Pray that you do not come back penniless, for you will find yourself begging in the streets of London before I offer a charitable hand." His fearsome dark brows drew together, his appearance altogether malevolent, and even Felicity shrank back.

A long wavering sigh escaped Adel's lips, as though her spirits deflated.

As accompaniment, the wind whistled over a low ridge that buttressed the hill and wailed a mournful lament as it passed through the trees. The sorrowful sound echoed Adel's dismal mood.

Lord Fitzhugh's pronouncement to Adel rankled Liam. With a snort of irritation, he stepped forward, clearing his throat. "The dray is loaded with your trunks. May I assist you into the coach, Lady Adel?"

"A favor, if you please?"

He nodded his consent.

Though she addressed Liam, her defiance was directed toward her stepbrother. "As I was not born into my title, from this moment on please address me as Mistress Adel or simply Adel."

The dimple in Liam's cheek deepened when he smiled. He lifted her into the coach. "As you wish, Mistress Adel."

"Wait! Woo-hoo…" Mrs. Bliss huffed through the mansion's double arched doors and toward the carriage. She handed a wicker basket to Liam. "'Ere, now, ye can't be leavin' wi'out a bite of food and a pot o' 'ot tea. Ye'll fair starve afore stoppin' for the night. There be fresh bread, boiled eggs, slices of ham, and, for the li'l un, a pint of milk."

Liam reached inside the coach and set the basket on the floor. "We are grateful for your thoughtfulness, kind lady."

Adel stepped down from the carriage. She hugged the cook. "Most of all, I shall miss you, Mrs. Bliss."

"Well, now, go on wi' yerself, or ye'll 'ave me blubberin' like a babe."

Mrs. James and Dudley stood without speaking. Their faces resembled stone. Adel didn't fault them for their loyalty to her stepbrother.

Liam cupped Adel's elbow. "We must make haste. Our ship sails in three days."

Without answering, she allowed him to assist her back into the brougham. She forced a smile as she settled next to her maid.

"Don't be sad, mum. Think on this as the adventure ye've always craved."

Adel shivered. She welcomed the fur lap blanket. "I hope you are right, Tilde. Part of me fears I'll wake up and discover this is all a dream. The other part fears I have made a dreadful mistake."

She looked at the child snuggled in Tilde's arms. "Is Mary Kathryn warm enough?"

"Aye. Snug as a bug, and sound asleep." Ringlets of auburn hair peeked from beneath the little girl's fur-trimmed bonnet. She clutched a porcelain doll adorned in a pink satin gown and with hair of yellow ringlets.

The coach dipped under Liam's weight. He reached up and thumped the roof to signal everyone inside was settled. "For an hour or so, Robby will ride atop with the coachman and Edwin."

"He'll get terribly cold. Can't we make room for him?"

"He's a stalwart soul. Besides, he and I will change places when we stop for a short repast."

Adel scowled out the window at her stepbrother. "I think it's perfectly mean-spirited of Reggie to refuse your offer of purchasing a dray to carry our extra luggage."

"Lord Fitzhugh doesn't care about the wagon, Mistress Adel. He didn't want to part with the remaining four horses on the estate."

She turned from the scene on the front lawn. "He is more like his father than I imagined. A complete wastrel." She tsked. "I suppose I should feel pity for my sister-in-law. Alas, she and Reggie deserve each other."

Adel thought Liam smiled. She couldn't be certain.

All the sounds were acute to Adel: The driver slapping the leathers against the horses' rumps, the carriage springs groaning with strain as the conveyance lurched forward, and the crunch of gravel beneath the wheels as it jostled down the long elm-lined drive.

A strange foreboding filled her. A sudden eerie feeling sent a shiver sinuating down her spine. Doubts clouded her decision. What if she wasn't a suitable governess, what if circumstances forced her to return to England? Reggie's threat rattled inside her head—*I'll not offer a charitable hand.*

The carriage jounced through a deep rut, bumping her head against the back of the seat. She gazed out the window at the massive manor house. No one lingered in the yard. It was as if she had already been dismissed from their lives.

She blinked back the tears as she gazed back at the house, distressed at having to leave Briarwood. Slumping against the tufted seat, she wondered if she would ever return.

The next bump jarred her teeth and wrung an unhappy little moan from her throat.

"Blimey, mum. 'Tis bumpy enough to rattle me brain. And this poor little 'un, too."

Liam lifted his daughter from Tilde's lap and drew Mary Kathryn into the circle of his arms to cushion her against the blows of the road.

Brimming with her tangle of emotions, Adel watched the little girl nestle her cheek against Liam's chest, as if trying to find a comfortable spot.

As the carriage bounced through another rut, he was the one forced to clench his teeth against an exclamation. He rolled his eyes toward the carriage's roof. "Surely the highway won't be as rutted as Lord Fitzhugh's drive."

Tilde complained, "'Twill be black and blue all over we'll be, for certain, if not all ready."

When the child opened her eyes and whimpered, Liam brushed a curl from the downy softness of her cheek. "Shh. Go back to sleep."

"It appears there is much my stepbrother has neglected in the upkeep of Briarwood." Adel sighed and burrowed deeper beneath the warm lap rug. The air grew steadily brisker as they traveled north toward the road leading to London. Remembering the wicker basket tucked beneath the seat, she said, "Tilde, it is hours before we stop for lunch."

"Aye, mum. 'Tis a blessin' Mrs. Bliss thought to include a pot of tea to warm our bones. Poor Lieutenant Beck and me own Edwin, riding atop, need a dram to warm their innards. Devilish cold outside."

While the maid portioned the food, Adel focused her attention on Liam. In her bolder daydreams she had already dared to imagine herself in his arms. She was mesmerized by the chiseled planes of his face and the impressive expanse of his chest. An odd shivery feeling wavered over her as she imagined his strong, masculine hands touching her secret places.

He asked, "Are you cold, Mistress Adel?"

His voice sounded like a husky purr. She closed her eyes briefly, counting to ten. "No, it's…just a shiver." Wishing to redirect her thoughts, she continued, "I have read your directive outlining my responsibilities. All seems quite fair, and the stipend overly generous. I am eager to hear about Ireland and your home."

A nostalgic smile curved Liam's lips. "Since I was only ten when my mother brought me to England, what I recall of the estate is more a figment of my imagination than reality. Though I can scarcely call it home, Mautagh Manor, my grandmother's estate inherited from her grandmother, is in Connemara. Some, such as my mother, say it is a barren and windswept place. I remember Connemara as green and fertile. Mountains of gray granite that reach into the clouds. Fields divided by stone walls. And the ocean, as powerful and fierce as the old clan chieftains. I also remember tramping through fog-shrouded bogs, and in the spring, fields of purple heather much like the color of your eyes."

A blush crept beneath her collar to warm her cheeks. "It sounds quite beautiful. I'm sure there is a perfectly good reason why you have never returned?"

"Actually, I did return once, at the time my *seanmháthair* died." The dimple in his cheek deepened when he smiled. "'Tis old Gaelic for grandmother."

She studied him for a long thoughtful moment, giving him time to continue.

"I was sixteen. Mautagh was much the way I remembered it as a young lad. The house was beginning to show its age, but what does a boy know of such matters?" He seemed to drift for a moment, then wrested himself back to the present. "The fields were dotted white with Mautagh sheep. At shearing time, I'm certain the wool will fetch a fine income."

Her remark came sharper than she intended. "Why didn't you stay? I mean, after all, you were of age, were you not? If such a property were mine—"

A sharp jab to the ribs caused Adel to flinch. She almost barked a shrill scold to Tilde, until the maid's deeply furrowed brows reminded Adel that she needed to bridle her tongue. It wouldn't do to upset her new employer or to have him order the coach's return to Briarwood.

"Forgive me, Captain O'Shea. I am such a lackwit. I didn't mean to sound judgmental. Please tell me about your grandmother."

Liam chuckled softly, as if making light of her comments. He shifted to one side of the coach to make room on the seat, where he settled the sleeping child.

"My grandmother was Maeve Mautagh O'Neill. She married Aengus Liam O'Shea, whose family holdings were confiscated years earlier. Their union produced a son—my father William. Not wanting him to be following the ways of the old clans, my grandmother insisted her son attend school in London. It was at court he and my mother met."

At court? The wheels of curiosity churned inside Adel's head. How did a mere school lad rank an invitation to the Queen's Court? Liam's voice interrupted her musing.

His reply was terse. "It was the old love-at-first-sight story. That is, until he took his wife to

Connemara. My mother wasn't suited for the county lifestyle. I was nine when my father died, and it was shortly after that my mother brought me to England."

He was thoughtful for a moment. "You asked why I didn't remain in Ireland after my grandmother's funeral. I had already committed to serve in the Royal Guard."

A lengthy silence filled the coach. Trying to bridge the gap between them, Adel made an attempt to apologize.

"Forgive me, Captain. I seem to have a penchant toward boldness. It was not my intent to pry into your private life."

Casually he waved a hand as if dismissing her apology, and then closed his eyes.

Chapter Six

The light of late afternoon had been obscured by a slow, misty rain that was more fog than drizzle. Long hours passed in silence.

"It seems the journey is taking most of the day. We are fair chilled to the bone." Adel tightened the ribbon at the top of her white fur-lined burgundy cloak.

Liam nodded to please her. Every time he looked at her, he forgot his own thoughts. Her eyes were a wondrous shade of lilac. She had the darkest and surely the longest eyelashes he'd ever noticed, and her complexion was exquisitely pure. Only a sprinkle of freckles across the bridge of her nose marred her skin, but if it were a flaw he found it pleasing.

He cleared his throat to unscramble his thoughts. As soon as privacy permitted, he needed to unfurl his deepest concerns to Robby Beck.

Shifting his position, he lifted the leather shade and leaned through the carriage window. "Robby, stop the coach. Let us change places so you ride inside until we get to the inn."

"There's no denying it is beastly cold out here, but no need to stop. The Horse and Crown is over the next rise."

"Then I'll spot you to a hot brandy while you toast your feet before a warm fire, my faithful friend."

Wind snatched away the young lieutenant's

laughter. "Only a fool would turn down such an offer, and I'm no bloody fool."

Liam retied the black curtain. The bracing wind had reddened his cheeks. "I calculate we'll arrive within the next twenty minutes, Mistress Adel."

Adel gave a brief nod. "We are all really quite exhausted. Bless Mary Kathryn. We've barely heard a querulous peep from the child. Will it put us behind schedule if we spend the night, Captain?"

Liam's body was stiff from the long hours of jostling. He rolled his shoulders, trying to work out the kinks. He kept his voice low and soothing. "In spite of the fog, we've made excellent time. A hot meal and a night's rest will do us all good."

Robby Beck's shout alerted them. "Look lively, the Horse and Crown just ahead."

"It's past the dinner hour, Captain. Do you think the innkeeper will mind preparing a meal for us?"

"I'm certain that for a coin or two, the proprietor will gladly see to our needs."

After a shimmy and a bump, the carriage rolled to a stop. Liam opened the door and stepped down. It felt good to stretch the muscles in his long legs.

Mary Kathryn scooted from the seat. Her face crumpled into tears. Liam lifted the child into his arms. He shot a puzzled look toward Adel. "Why are you crying? Are you hungry?"

The little girl put her mouth close to Liam's ear and whispered. His eyes widened. "Mistress Adel, it seems we have an emergency. Mary Kathryn—"

As if guessing the problem, Adel offered her hand for Liam to assist her from the coach. "Of course, at once. Tilde, we must hurry. Mary Kathryn is in dire need of a chamber pot."

With the little girl supported in one arm, Adel gathered her skirts and hurriedly picked her way around the puddles of mud and toward the inn's sturdy oaken door.

Tilde followed, carrying the child's small travel bag in the event a changing of clothes became necessary.

****

After dinner, Liam settled deep into a brown leather chair facing the large fireplace. He crossed one leg over the other. The fire snapped and crackled. His conversation with Robby Beck had stopped, each man seemingly lost in his own thoughts.

"You are quiet, Liam. Are you thinking of India?"

"Aye, Robby, that I am."

"If it's Mary Kathryn's care you're worried about, there is no need. Adel is as trustworthy as the truest soldier."

Liam lifted his hand to signal the innkeeper. "If you please, kind sir, two tankards of ale."

A falling log on the fire sent a shower of sparks flying outward onto the stone hearth.

Liam bided his tongue until the heavily jowled innkeeper had bustled forward with two mugs of frothy brew and then returned to his station behind the scarred mahogany bar.

In a long wavering sigh, Liam stared into the fire in thoughtful reflection, wondering about the future. He drew a deep draught of ale, considering his words with care.

"I am not a man who fears death. Now that I have Mary Kathryn's future to consider, the thought of dying plays on my mind."

"Pshaw, Liam, you are a crackerjack shot with pistol and rifle. Not to speak of your talents with a saber. You've nothing to fear."

Sharp talons of dread raked Liam's heart, and his mind began to race. "There are more ways of dying than by sword or bullet, my young friend—cholera, scorpion or cobra bites, heat prostration, just to name a few."

Robby Beck shifted in his chair and gave Liam a quizzical stare. "Spit it out, man. Whatever is stuck in your craw, I'll think no less of you for the telling."

A great weight descended on Liam's shoulders. Of a sudden he was tired, and his mind labored to sort out the realities of this pressing burden. "What will become of my daughter should I not return from India? I am her only legal family. I trust your judgment where Mistress Adel's character is concerned. However, she has no obligation to Mary Kathryn. And what if the child forgets who I am? After all, we have only known each other a few months." Liam spread his hands wide in desolation. "These questions weigh heavy on my mind. There seem no simple answers."

Robby chortled softly. He raised a querying brow. "I believe the solution is as plain as the nose on your face, my dear Captain."

Liam allowed a moment of silence to pass as he studied the young lieutenant. "I'm not a mind reader, Robby. What is this solution you speak of?"

Robby shrugged. "Simple. Marry Adel. Make her your legal wife."

Liam responded with a short, incredulous chuckle. He peered at his companion closely. "Have you gone completely daft? Why, I've only just met the woman."

Robby drew deep from the tankard. He brushed a sleeve across his moist lips. "And a more beautiful woman you cannot deny."

Liam's steely blue eyes bore into the man sitting across from him. "I'm not sure I like where this is going, but for sake of conversation, I will hear this ludicrous plan you propose."

For a moment, Robby stared into his mug as if weighing his words. "You are one of the best strategists I know. Bear me out. My plan is simple strategy. It will work only if you keep an open mind."

With infinite patience, Liam listened until Robby finally said, "And it's as simple as that."

Liam stood. He stretched and yawned. Lord, he was tired. "Nothing is ever as simple as it sounds. Have you considered that Mistress Adel might take opposition to such a proposal?"

"Ah, my friend, you have eyes, but you do not see the way she looks at you when she thinks no one is watching."

Liam placed the tankard to his lips and drained the remaining ale. "While I believe you exaggerate, and while I think your idea is preposterous, I'll give it some thought."

He lifted a lantern from the wall hook and progressed up the stairs and down the hall toward his room, pausing beside a door on his left. He found a small latch securing the door, and tugged, surprised that it gave beneath the light touch.

Though he had opened it no more than the breadth of a hand, he found himself much bemused, for he was standing at the threshold of the chamber occupied by his new governess.

The fire on the hearth had burned low, and the lady herself was sound asleep beneath several quilts spread upon her bed. He pushed the door wide and crossed the room with noiseless tread. Lifting the lantern high, he looked down upon her, feeling as if he had chanced upon a victory of sorts. Her long lashes lay like dark shadows on her fair cheeks, and her soft lips were slightly parted as she breathed long and slowly in deepest slumber. Her hair formed a dark tumbled halo over the pillow, over which an arm rested in a flawless curve above her head, leaving her shoulder and the higher, swelling curves of her bosom naked to his gaze. He allowed his regard to linger on her face and the tempting fullness of her breasts, as one who had chosen to savor a special treat. She was truly a beautiful woman, to be sure.

He leaned slightly closer to study her more carefully. In sleep the lass seemed almost childlike, not so much woman, with her delicate features and creamy skin.

She possessed an uncommon beauty, certainly more vivid and lively than that of most of the transparent women he'd known.

The child next to Adel stirred, whimpered.

Instinctively Adel reached out and touched the little girl as if to soothe her.

He wanted to scoop Mary Kathryn into his arms, to kiss away the dreams that disturbed her slumber.

He wanted to scoop Adel into his arms, as well, to lie beside her, to kiss the pouty curve of her lips.

Liam passed to the hearth, where he carefully laid fresh logs on the coals before silently withdrawing from the room.

Thoughts whispered inside his head. *Only a lunatic would consider such a notion. It might work—it just might.*

Seeking the comfort of his own bed and a warm spot to indulge his slumbers, a knowing smile curved his lips as his thoughts turned back to the vision he had just seen.

****

After settling the child and bidding goodnight to her maid, Adel had fallen asleep a scant thirty minutes after dinner. As was her usual habit, she slept quite soundly for several hours, but promptly at two o'clock in the morning she awakened. She put on her robe, added another log to the fire, and then, careful not to awaken the sleeping child, she got back into bed with a book. She would read in hopes it would make her sleepy.

Sleep eluded her. When her candle guttered, she blew it out and lay on the bed—a comfortable one— and stared into the inky darkness above her. Moonlight trickled through the window so the gilding on the ceiling shimmered now and then, as if a starlit sky arched above her. She wondered idly if someone had planned that exact effect.

Liam haunted her dreams. Every time she closed her eyes she saw his smile. She didn't understand the yearning inside her. Perhaps this was passion. She'd never known passion, so she could not say whether it did or did not exist, nor of what it consisted.

She thought about the way her heart fluttered when Liam looked at her, the way her blood thrummed in her veins and her skin tingled and her senses came alive when he was near.

Captain Liam O'Shea was different from any man she had ever encountered. She shook herself. Whatever was she thinking? He was leaving for a five-year commitment in India. She was his employee. He had hired her as governess to his child.

She sighed and gave up trying to sleep. They'd be leaving in a few short hours. She could nap then, if she chose to, until they arrived at the harbor in London.

She tossed aside the heavy quilt, making certain not to uncover Mary Kathryn. The rugs beneath her bare feet were thick, plush wool, tickling her toes.

She moved to the window and drew back the drapes. Night interested her. Night washed away the uncertainties that awaited her in Ireland. But night did not wash away the memory of how Liam's blue eyes crinkled at the corners when he smiled.

Sighing, she returned to the bed. She could not afford to indulge in such whimsical fantasies.

Chapter Seven

Adel drifted into wakefulness with a hand playing gently in her hair. She kept her eyes pressed firmly shut, luxuriating in the novel sensation. Her stepfather and her very own mother had rarely touched one another, and only in privacy did her mother offer affection by sitting before a fire and stroking a brush through Adel's silken strands.

She had once asked if it was wrong to display love in front of others. Her mother had replied that people of station prided themselves on reserve—to do less was considered indecorous. At such a young age, Adel had truly not understood what her mother had meant.

She sighed at the memory and scooted deeper into the pillow.

A child's hand drifted like a whisper against Adel's cheek. "Del, me go potty."

Her eyes flew open in horror as she realized the hand gently tugging on a curl was Mary Kathryn's.

Sliding from the bed, she lifted the child and carried her behind the privacy screen. "Of course you do. Oh, where is Tilde when I need her?"

The little girl looked up at Adel. "I sorry Del mad."

The child's moisture-filled eyes tugged at Adel's heart. "Oh, my precious sweetums. I'm not angry at you. Never at you."

She kissed the top of Mary Kathryn's unruly red

curls. And then she wondered if, in her haste to escape an arranged but unwanted marriage to a despicable oversized oaf, she had been too hasty in her decision to become a governess. What did she know of raising a child?

Well, the deed was done, and she vowed to make the most of her decision, both for her sake and for the sake of Mary Kathryn. After all, she did have Tilde and Edwin for support.

A forlorn shadow crept across her mind. A few days ago, she had asked for a miracle and received it. Adventure lay ahead of her. Not the adventure she had dreamed of, but nonetheless exciting, and not without challenge.

Doubt crept in. She pondered her mother's favorite saying—*Be careful what you wish for.*

What would happen if Captain O'Shea decided he wasn't satisfied with her services? What if she discovered she didn't enjoy her position as governess and overseer of a large estate? She had no money. Where would she go? Not back to England, for her stepbrother had made it clear he would extend her no charity.

Pushing the uncertainties aside, she tended the child's toilette.

A short time later, pleased with herself, she had fully dressed Mary Kathryn. A light knock sounded at the door and Tilde came in with a tray.

"I thought you might like to dine in the privacy of your room. The inn is fair bustling with travelers, noisier than a swarm of angry bees."

"The food smells lovely. What did you bring Mary Kathryn and me?"

Tilde set the tray on a small table next to the window and pushed back the heavy drape, allowing sunlight to flood the room. "'Tis a lovely day for travel, mum. We have sausages, tea for you, and warm milk for the wee one." She lifted lids to expose a bowl of porridge and a plate of scones.

"Have you eaten, Tilde? There's enough for you, too."

Tilde set about tying a bib around Mary Kathryn's neck. "I've already broke fast with Edwin. Now, go ahead and eat while I pack your belongings and ready the bags for him to load atop the coach."

Almost through the door, the maid turned. "I've nearly forgotten. Captain O'Shea said he wished an audience with you as soon as you've finished your meal. I'll return shortly to tend Mary Kathryn."

Adel watched the child lift the spoon and taste the porridge. Mary Kathryn frowned and spit the mush from her mouth.

Adel's voice was much harsher than she intended. "Mary Kathryn, polite young ladies do not spit out their food."

The chastisement caused tears to form in the child's eyes.

"Oh, dear, mum, now ye've gone and done it." Tilde dipped a spoon into the white gloppy mess and tasted it. "I don't fault the child. It tastes like lard. Our Mrs. Bliss could give the cook lessons on how to make a decent pot o' porridge." She buttered a scone and added a liberal amount of gooseberry jam. She poured a cup of milk and set it in front of the little girl.

Adel reached over and wiped the tears from Mary Kathryn's cheek. "Please don't cry. I didn't mean to scold."

Tilde leaned close and whispered, "You might try hugging the child. Mayhap even cutting the sausage into bitty pieces and feeding her."

Adel squirmed in sudden discomfiture. "I have a lot to learn, don't I?"

"You'll do just fine, mum. Though I wouldn't keep the captain waiting over long. He seemed a bit out of composure this morning."

"Would you ask him to give me one hour? I must finish feeding Mary Kathryn; and Tilde, do come help me with my toilette."

"I've already laid out your traveling clothes, mum. But I'll return in two shakes of a lamb's tail."

****

Liam had fallen asleep while considering Robby's plan. Marriage to Adel? But the more he thought about it, the more he reasoned the idea was workable. He had a well-honed instinct about strategy, and this was as Robby had presented it: strategy.

Now he positioned the same brown leather chair he'd occupied the night before so that he would see Adel the moment she descended the stairs. He listened to the mantel clock ticking. His fingers tapped the arm of the chair, keeping rhythm with each tick.

The moment he heard heels clacking down the wooden stairs, he stood. With a mingling of euphoria and nervous anticipation, he greeted Adel.

His eyes seemed to capture her from head to shoes. At his gaze, she tucked her feet deeper under her skirts and straightened her spine, with a clearing of her throat, in an obvious attempt to appear businesslike.

"Good morning, Mistress Adel. I trust you rested

well?"

"I did, Captain."

"And Mary Kathryn?"

"I'm afraid she didn't much enjoy the porridge. Not that I can blame her."

"She did eat, didn't she?"

"That she did. Every bite of sausage, an entire cup of milk, and a scone."

Her smile caused his heart to knock in panic like that of a green recruit in a dugout with shells whizzing over his head. He needed to bring an end to this mundane chit-chat and get on with business.

"While Edwin readies the coach, will you do me the honor of walking with me? I have a proposal to discuss with you."

At her nod, he cupped her elbow and led her outside. Gravel crunched under their feet as he led her toward the inn's winter garden. The leaves rustling in the trees calmed him, and he inhaled deeply the soothing scent of pine.

"What is this proposal you wish to discuss with me, Captain?"

"I'll get straight to the point, Mistress Adel. Five years is a long time for a father to be away from his child, don't you agree?"

"Yes, of course, but if you're worried that I—"

He held up a hand silence her. "Hear me out before you speak."

Although a frown puckered between her eyes, she nodded.

"Rumor has it there is a war brewing in India. Death is always imminent in battle. I cannot leave without knowing Mary Kathryn has a legal guardian—a mother."

Offering a puzzled frown, Adel said, "But I thought her mother was dead."

"She is. I am Mary Kathryn's nearest living relative. Should something happen to me, she would surely be taken advantage of by unscrupulous solicitors, and as her governess you would have no legal authority to make decisions for her.

"And then there is the question of what would happen to Mautagh Manor. It is my fervent desire that Mary Kathryn has someone who will love her, who will teach her, and who will take care of her interests should I not return from India. You are that person, Mistress Adel."

Liam reached out and placed both her hands into his. "Understand, this is strictly a business arrangement. You are under no obligation to share my bed."

Adel withdrew her hands. A surprised gasp escaped her throat. "I do not understand your meaning, sir."

"Forgive me. I'm mucking this up terribly. In my poor bumbling way, I am asking you to be my wife."

Adel stood silent.

Liam considered saying something. Offering an apology, perhaps. Then he decided it would be rubbing salt into an open wound, and he should leave it be. He'd made the offer. There was no point dwelling on it. He turned to leave.

****

Adel's heart raced and in spite of the damp cold air, her palms grew sweaty. She swallowed hard at the thought of marrying a most suitable man—perhaps, the man of her dreams. She glanced up at Liam's handsome face, noticed the line of his strong jaw, and caught the scent of his shaving soap.

She drew a deep breath, not sure how to reply to his abrupt announcement, nor how to deal with his even more abrupt departure. Still gaping in astonishment, she cried, "Wait!"

He gave her a melancholy look that she wished she could read. Was it an apology for the awkward proposal, or was he predicting his own death?

Her heart quaking, she moistened her lips with the tip of her tongue. "I-I accept your offer."

He nodded at her, and she knew he was passing his duty as a parent over to her. "There is a magistrate in London. He will perform the ceremony. Robby and Tilde can stand as witnesses for us. There is one other consideration you need to be aware of."

She tried to smile to hide the pink flush that burned her cheeks. He had already said she wasn't obligated to share his bed. What more was he about to ask of her?

"Our marriage is in name only. The union will not be consummated. Therefore, if I return to Ireland at the end of my five-year stint, if you wish to petition the church for an annulment I will offer no objection."

The morning sun moved across the sky, leaving dapples of shadow on the still muddy ground. Hot and cold. Exactly the way Adel felt—hot and cold.

There was something intense in Liam's expression, in the color of his eyes, in the set of his jaw. Her heart broke a little at the sight of it. She closed her eyes briefly.

"Mistress Adel, I know this comes as a sudden shock. I have no right asking you to put your life on hold for a child that isn't yours and for a man you've known for less than a week. If you wish to recant your answer, I will surely understand."

"And if I should, what happens to Mary Kathryn?"

He considered a mere second. "I shall relieve you of your obligation by hiring a coach to escort you to St. Francis. After you leave Mary Kathryn with the nuns, you may do as you wish."

He'd given her a way out. She could leave with no further obligations. Yet it was obvious he had given thorough regard to all the details. She had to admire a man who was willing to marry a woman merely for the sake of his child.

"May I ask a question, Captain?"

"Yes, you may ask as many questions as you like."

"Wouldn't it be just as simple to petition the court to make me Mary Kathryn's legal guardian, rather than you and me marrying?"

"It is a valid question, and one I wrestled with most of the night. Once we arrive in London, there will only be a few hours before my ship sails. Petitioning the courts takes time, not to speak of the lengthy paperwork involved. We will not have time for all that is necessary for such a procedure. It only makes sense for you to become my wife, and my daughter's stepmother. As her guardian you are merely that. As her stepmother, you will own all that I now own, if I should die."

Adel considered his explanation. "But are you not afraid that, if you perish in a war, I could become the wicked stepmother, taking all for myself and giving nothing to Mary Kathryn?"

"Ah." He gazed studiously at Adel. His blue eyes softened as he reached out and stroked her cheek. "It is said that the eyes are the windows to the soul. It is not within you to be deceitful or to deliberately bring harm to another being. If I didn't trust you, Mistress Adel, I wouldn't have made the offer."

With nervous apprehension, Adel offered her hand. "Since this is strictly business, I accept your proposed arrangement. Shall we shake on it?"

He smiled down at her as he accepted her hand, giving it a gentle squeeze. "Strictly business."

With unsteady fingers, she withdrew from his grip. "If you will excuse me, I must see to Mary Kathryn, and make certain Tilde has asked the innkeeper to prepare a lunch basket for the remainder of our journey."

She was about to become a wife, a stepmother, and the owner of an estate. It was all too much to grasp. She felt as if she were slogging through a nightmare of her own making.

Just then, the crunch of coach wheels sounded on gravel. Edwin and Robby Beck sat on the high seat. Tilde stepped from the inn door, holding Mary Kathryn by one hand, a large wicker basket in the other.

Adel smoothed her hands down the sides of her burgundy cape. "Shall we tell the others?"

"Unless I miss my guess, and by the wide grin on Edwin's face and the tears in Tilde's eyes, Robby has already divulged the news."

Adel stole a glance at the handsome officer striding beside her. "How did Robby know?"

"Actually, it was his idea."

She bit her lip, visibly composing herself. Then she straightened to her full height, eyes narrowed. "How dare the two of you discuss me as if I were a prize mare up for bid, and decide my future behind my back! If I were a man, I would punch him square on the nose."

"Adel, my apologies. We...that is to say...I... didn't mean to insult you."

She put up a halting hand. "Really?"

Instead of making a snide comment, Liam cupped her elbow, hugging her close. He leaned in low, his warm breath brushing her cheek. "Thank you."

Adele looked into his eyes and surmised he was dealing with his own uncertainties.

Lifting her skirt, she lengthened her stride. Keenly aware of Liam's gaze following her every move, she reached the carriage. Hiking her skirts even higher and grabbing the handrails on either side of the door, she lifted her foot to the step and climbed inside. With a shuddering indrawn breath, she scooted to a corner, turned her face toward the window, and closed her eyes.

The humiliation seared her like a hot iron. She laughed mirthlessly when she realized the irony. She'd made her bed with constant insults toward her sister-in-law, evoking her stepbrother's wrath. There was no returning to Briarwood. A churning dread roiled her stomach. She had sealed her fate. She waited with bated breath for her future husband to enter the coach.

Chapter Eight

Heat laced Adel's face like a slow, painful torture. No one spoke. There was only uncomfortable silence inside the coach. It was the most acrid silence she had ever experienced.

This couldn't be happening...

Dear God, she thought she might be ill.

She was now sitting face to face with Liam, not knowing what in the world to say to him—to this man who was her husband-to-be.

She worked to maintain her dignity while her whole being was winding tight with rage against—whom? Her sister-in-law for taking command of her rightful place as mistress of Briarwood? Her stepbrother for his persistence in arranging unwanted suitors for her? Perhaps Robby Beck for contriving the scheme of a marriage? Or Liam, who had agreed to this humiliating plot?

"I feel like a prize pig up for market." The words were out before she could reclaim them. She clasped her hands over her mouth. "I've made a terrible mistake. I cannot marry you. A governess is no replacement for a mother. I fear it's a difficult transition... I... I..."

"My apologies for the misunderstanding, Mistress Adel. It was not my intention to embarrass you or to cause you unnecessary distress."

Before Adel could answer Liam, Tilde shifted to face the woman she called friend. The ire in her voice was evident. "Ye've been more a sister to me than my charge. So I feel 'tis time I speak me piece. You can chastise me later, if you've a mind." She sat stiff as a statue. "I don't know why you've gone and got your garters in such a bind. Nothing has changed—well, 'cept the marrying part—and ye're gettin' the best part o' the bargain. Ye don't have to marry that 'orrible Baron Wishingham. Ye're 'bout to become mistress of a large estate, and ye're gettin' the independence every woman in England will envy of you.

"Shame on you for the sourpuss face ye be wearin', and shame on you for sending poor Robby Beck and the captain, 'ere, off to who knows what their destiny holds, makin' 'em feel guilty for their good intentions for that wee child sleepin' in 'er papa's lap."

Tilde drew in a deep sigh, expelled a long breath, and crossed her arms over her breasts. "There. I've said me piece. If ye be wishin' to dismiss me from your employment, then so be it. I ne'er thought of ye as a selfish twit, but I've changed me mind."

This was all happening too fast—the confusion, the humiliation, the collapse of Adel's dreams. *But, oh, my, Tilde is right. I am acting like a spoiled child.*

Adel felt shame building up inside her like a rising tide about to overflow. She squeezed her eyes shut, and her bruised feelings rankled all over again. She didn't want to look at Liam's irritatingly handsome face and relive her embarrassing behavior over and over again.

She peeked through her lashes and saw an unyielding conviction in his eyes. She noted the tension around his mouth, and sat there trying to think of a way to apologize for her witless comportment. In truth, she didn't know why she felt so agitated. No, it was time to give up her foolish dreams.

Liam clasped her hand. His touch warmed her in a way that was far too affecting for an employer. "This plan... It goes against all logic. Of that, I am aware. My true concern is for my daughter."

Adel drew a deep breath, trying to gain control over her racing thoughts. "The one thing my stepfather taught me was to never go back on a deal. Tilde is correct, I am being selfish, and for that, I apologize. I suppose I have lived with my ridiculous fantasy of traveling to the far edges of the world for such a long time that I've set myself up for disappointment. It is I who owe you an apology, Captain, and to Robby, too. Thank you, Tilde, for being friend enough to speak your mind even if in fear of losing your employ."

Adel sat up straighter and squared her shoulders. "So, if the offer of marriage still stands, then I accept, and with my solemn promise to love and cherish Mary Kathryn as if she were my very own child."

****

Liam turned his gaze to the fullness of Adel's face and stared at her for a long moment. Her cheeks were delicately carved, her lips full. Her eyes held the look of a young girl whose fascination with a dream had been crushed. She was such a child, yet she had swallowed her pride and done what the most stalwart of men often refused to do—she had owned up to being wrong.

Her husky, sensuous voice shot straight through him. He'd had a few liaisons with beautiful women, but none had touched him as she had. With that thought, a tremor coursed through him.

He tilted his head. "My gratitude, Mistress Adel. I can ask no more for my daughter, and for myself."

"What time will we arrive in London?"

Liam pulled the watch from his fob pocket. "We will stop for about an hour to rest the horses and refresh ourselves from the lunch basket. If we continue making good time, I predict we shall arrive in time for dinner."

"And when will the marriage take place?"

"If it is agreeable with you, tonight. Robby and I will have much to arrange before our ship sails on the morrow."

Liam wanted to wrap his strong arms around Adel, hold her close, hold her dear.

****

Adel sat back in the rolling conveyance, gazing in a detached way at the windswept landscape. The carriage continued down the slope of a ridge and into a thick spruce forest where all was shaded and quiet, save the horses' hooves thumping, and the carriage wheels traveling over the ground, snapping twigs, filling the silence.

Liam was leaving for India tomorrow. An uneasy feeling closed in around her. Ireland was an ocean away from all that was familiar to her. Except for Tilde, Edwin, and Mary Kathryn, she would have no family there. Not that she had any family she could depend upon at Briarwood, either, but at least she knew the country. God forbid Liam should change his mind and demand she share his bed. What if she became with child? If Liam didn't return from India, how would she manage with two children? Worse, what if the people of Mautagh Manor refused to accept an Englishwoman as their mistress? She twisted her gloved fingers together.

Fear chilled her more than the brisk February weather.

"Are you all right, Mistress Adel?" Liam asked, surprising her.

She'd thought she was more proficient in hiding her feelings. She'd have to do better.

"I am fine, Captain."

"You don't look fine."

She drew in a deep breath, not sure how to reply. "I was just thinking…" *That I've never felt more alone in my life.*

"You were thinking about what?"

She huffed in frustration. "That I wish you would stop referring to me as Mistress Adel. It makes me sound like an old spinster."

The silence settled again, prickly and obvious. She tried to study the shapes of the clouds, the shapes of the trees, but the colors and forms swam before her, a spinning kaleidoscope.

She sneaked a glance at him. He seemed utterly at ease with the silence. So many people were uncomfortable with it, rushing to fill it with whatever sprang to the tongue. How many times had meaningless flirtations sent her in search of a hiding place? Now she herself was digging for words, searching for a conversation that sparkled and intrigued. And yet he always answered effortlessly, without any trace of the stultifying shyness that often afflicted those who preferred silence. "What about a marriage license? We don't have time for the calling of banns."

His voice was low, pitched as if making an intimate declaration. "I am a soldier about to go to war. I believe my friend, Magistrate Oxley, will arrange for a special license and will agree to perform the civil ceremony himself."

She sighed deeply. "Oh, of course."

"Do I detect a hint of hesitation?"

"It is a hurried and unusual circumstance. I was hoping there would be time for me to freshen up, perhaps change into a different gown and have Tilde rearrange my hair."

"That is a most reasonable request. Robby will arrange for rooms at the Claridge while I make arrangements with the magistrate."

"Blimey, mum. The Claridge. 'Tis a grand place, or so I've heard."

Adel opened her mouth to scold her maid for such impudence. Instead she wondered how a mere captain in the Queen's Royal Guard could afford the price of a room at London's most regal hotel.

At noon, Adel perched on a fallen tree branch in front of a small fire, warming her hands while Tilde set out sandwiches filled with thick slices of ham. Liam assisted Robby Beck and Edwin with unhitching the horses and leading them to the fast-flowing stream to drink.

Adel watched Mary Kathryn sitting quietly. Liam had set the child on a tree stump with instructions not to move. Although his command was kind, and not in the least threatening, it seemed unnatural for a child, even a little girl, to not let curiosity get the better of her and scamper off.

Adel wondered what had happened to the child's mother, what had caused her death. It wasn't until Tilde spoke the second time that Adel roused from her deep mental meandering.

"Just think, milady, in a matter of hours ye'll be a

married lady, a mother, and mistress of a large estate. 'Tis fair exciting, if you be askin' me. I feel like me and Edwin are livin' our own adventure—thanks to ye and the captain."

Adel picked at the thick crust of her sandwich, tossing the bread to the ground. She watched a brown squirrel scamper down a tree and snatch up the treat before escaping once again to its hiding place among the branches.

"To be perfectly honest, Tilde, I feel like a huge human blunder."

Tilde bit into her own sandwich and chewed thoughtfully. She spoke now as Adel's friend, as she often did in privacy. "I don't understand yer meanin', Adel."

"Let's face it. I'm a penniless spinster." She sighed, woeful. "You have Edwin to love you. Your mother and father loved you, did they not?"

"Yes, but—"

"I don't think anyone has ever truly loved me. Except my mother. Now, I'm to become the wife of a virtual stranger. I keep making silly, impetuous decisions. I'm blundering my way through life. That's what I mean, Tilde. It isn't so difficult to understand."

Now that Adel had made her confession, the very words she'd spoken pierced her heart. She had never been bothered by her life before, at least not deeply. She'd not permitted herself to be concerned over her actions, and she was always firm when it came to keeping her emotions in check. She could sweep away the most painful moments with a mental wave of her unfaltering will. On that account, in childhood and adulthood, too, she had crushed any interest in wishing for or competing for the kind of attention she craved from her mother and stepfather, or even from her stepbrother.

Today, for the first time, she felt the sharp claws of melancholy digging under her skin. She swallowed hard over the lump that had suddenly risen in her throat. The bread from her sandwich seemed to thicken, threatening to choke her. She tossed away the remains.

Tilde clasped Adel's hands in her own. "I wish I had knowledge of fancy words to say that would heal yer hurts. It pains me to see you so down on yerself. I do know this much. Life has a way of righting itself when it gets all out of kilter. Ye just wait and see."

Adel loosened her hands and wrapped her arms around the maid—her only true friend. "You don't need fancy words, Tilde. I'm feeling better already."

Scooting from the branch, she held her hand out to Mary Kathryn. "Come, let us take a little walk in the woods and relieve ourselves before it's time to get underway again."

The child clasped Adel's fingers. She looked up. "Del sad?"

She didn't want the little girl to know she was disappointed or unhappy, so she offered her a smile. "Sometimes when grownup ladies get tired, they get grumpy. I'm not sad, but a little grumpy."

Mary Kathryn frowned. "Me grumpy, too."

"Why?"

The child shrugged her shoulders. She offered no other words.

Adel decided with firm conviction that Mary Kathryn would never feel shunned, never feel like an outsider, especially in her own home.

****

Liam brushed bread crumbs from his jacket as he approached the carriage. "Time to travel on, ladies." After assisting the women, he lifted Mary Kathryn into the coach. Then he placed his boot on the wheel hub and with agile ease climbed to the carriage loft. "I feel the need for a bit of fresh air. Robby, you've been a sporting lad. You should keep the ladies company until we arrive in London."

"If it's all the same, I'll ride atop with you and Edwin."

"It is only a foolish man who turns down an opportunity to socialize with three lovely females."

Robert Beck raised one eyebrow, coolly confident. "I would rather face a firing squad than have to find answers to the many questions written all over Adel's face. Questions she will surely plague me to answer. You forget, I am familiar with her temper."

Liam laughed heartily. "It's not a firing squad you'll face but the tip of my saber, if this scheme of yours backfires. What if she decides to hold me to the marriage contract instead of petitioning the church for an annulment upon my return from the East?"

It was Robby's turn to laugh. "Then my friend, you are stuck with a fine-looking woman who will no doubt give you a brood of lilac-eyed daughters who will either treat you like a king or make your life miserable."

Liam struggled not to grin as he recalled Adel's luxuriant hair, her bright face, and the curves hidden beneath her purple cape. His stomach tightened. His breath seized. Desire slammed into him like a cannon blast.

****

Late evening was fast approaching, threatening to steal away the light, by the time Edwin halted the carriage in front of a red brick building with a shingle boldly printed, "Office of Magistrate, The Honorable Filbert Oxley."

Liam alit from the carriage. He brushed the sleeves of his heavy coat before opening the carriage door. "Robby will escort you to the Claridge and secure rooms for the night, Adel, and I will call for you within the hour."

He watched the reluctant smile touch her lips. "We shall be ready, Captain."

His insides careened. In their few short days together inside the coach, he'd come to believe that beneath Adel's sometimes polite, sometimes astringent exterior was perfection. How could he feel so connected to her?

He stared after the coach until it turned the corner and out of sight before entering the office to secure a special license for marriage.

Chapter Nine

Adel waited next to a window in a large salon with a great fireplace and walls of dark green brocade wallpaper. The Turkish rug was soft under her shoes. Urns with tall palms adorned two corners of the room. A silver vase filled with a dozen or more pink rosebuds sat in the center of a long table draped with a white watered-silk cloth. The table was set for seven. The odd number puzzled Adel, and she was about to ask Tilde what she made of it when they heard the front door crash open and then close again.

Footsteps pounded over the wide floorboards in the center hall and stopped in the doorway. Somehow recognizing the sound of Liam's boots, Adel turned, pressing her hands to the nervous sensation in her stomach.

Liam, flanked by Robby Beck, was followed by Magistrate Oxley and Edwin. Adel heard the hitch in Tilde's breath, for neither of them had ever seen Edwin dressed in such finery, looking every bit the distinguished gentleman.

"God's lamb, Adel. I fair believe I'm dreamin'. Ye'd best pinch me."

Adel whispered, "Look at how Edwin stares at you as if you were the bride and not I."

"I feel like a bride. Thank you for lending me one of your beautiful gowns. I'm s'posing Lieutenant Beck provided the clothes, for he and my Edwin are most the same size."

Liam stepped to the center of the room, faced Adel, and clasped his hands behind his back. "I realize you've barely had a chance to settle in." He smiled. "You look lovely."

Distracted, she gazed into Liam's deep blue eyes. He cut a striking figure; his scarlet tunic, with blue collar and shoulder stripes piped with white, hugged his masculine torso, set off by cuffs of dark blue and white, and his dark blue trousers, a red stripe down the seam of each leg, were cinched by a white leather buff belt around his waist.

"Thank you, Captain."

He leaned close and whispered, "You are about to become my wife. Do you suppose you might call me Liam?"

She acknowledged his request with a bland smile.

Magistrate Oxley cleared his throat. "Shall we begin?"

Liam spoke his vows and then removed the Claddagh ring from his little finger. "This ring belonged to my grandmother. I ask you to cherish it as I cherished her." He smiled at the child Tilde held in her arms. "Someday we will pass the ring on to Mary Kathryn."

Adel felt as if she were slogging through a nightmare of her own making. The man standing next to her was no fairytale prince. She had read the desires in his eyes. He was a man of flesh and blood. He would not settle for a chaste kiss on the cheek.

She had planned never to marry, but here she was standing before a magistrate reciting the vows as if she were a puppet with someone else pulling her strings.

She accepted the ring. "Yes, I will wear this ring until the day Mary Kathryn is old enough to treasure it."

****

The marriage vows spoken, Liam sat at the long table, trying very hard not to look at Adel, because every time he did the urge to stare at her was something close to crippling. He couldn't explain it. He didn't want to stare. He wanted all these desires to go away. After all, he had promised the marriage would not be consummated. Unfortunately, instead of feeling nothing, he felt everything. To be in her presence, here, tonight, made him feel almost short of breath.

She sat at the head of the table. Her pale cream gown of watered silk, adorned with a green fringed shawl embellished with clusters of delicately crocheted rosebuds, highlighted the color in her cheeks. She dabbed her lips with a damask napkin.

Her rich sable hair was pulled into a simple chignon at the nape of her neck and secured with mother-of-nacre combs. She had tucked a single pink rosebud behind her ear.

"What arrangements have you made for our travels to Ireland, Liam?"

Silverware clinked against china plates, the clock ticked audibly, while a hush fell over the room as if awaiting his answer.

He tried not to let his stare wander downward, for that would lead his eyes to her neckline. He felt uncomfortable with the sudden awareness of her décolletage—and the fact that he was curious about it, for he should not be noticing anything like that about this woman whom he was about to leave and not see again for five long years.

He labored to bring his attention back to where it should be—answering her question about travel arrangements.

He gazed at her drawn expression and the way she pursed her full lips. "It is more than two hundred miles by coach to Liverpool. A week's travel, at best. With the poor weather and the possibility of attacks by highwaymen, I dare not risk your lives. I have booked passage on the *SS Mapleton*."

"God's lamb, Capt'n, we be goin' to Ireland by sailing ship?"

Adel's cheeks pinked at Tilde's forwardness. "Thank you for thinking of our comfort."

"Aye, a ship is much more comfortable than traveling by carriage over bumpy roads and in inclement weather. After setting sail, you should arrive in Cork within a fortnight." He nodded toward Edwin. "I have given Edwin purse to pay passage on a local ship from there to Galway's port and to hire a coach for the remainder of the journey. He has directions that will carry you to Mautagh Manor."

Liam pushed away from the table and stood to his full height. Looking at Adel with an intensity that bespoke of a predator eyeing his prey, he asked, "Will you walk with me, Adel? I would like to spend a few private moments with you."

Adel politely stood. "Of course. Tilde will ready Mary Kathryn for bed."

"If you please, I wish my daughter to accompany us."

She moved from her seat at the table, measuring

each step until she stood next to him, then blinked up at him as if confused.

Liam smiled at his guests. He shook hands with the magistrate. "Thank you, Filbert. I shan't forget the favor. Robby, I will meet you at the barracks. Good night all."

Adel accepted his proffered arm. "Where are we going?"

"It's a surprise. I hope you will enjoy it."

****

Relief washed over Adel, leaving her weak-kneed. Apparently Liam wasn't planning to ravish her, at least not with a child in tow. Yet curiosity consumed her. Though she was not schooled in wedding night happenings, she had listened to the giggles and twitters of the housemaids as they recounted the events of their nuptial nights. She was also not ignorant of how breeding took place, for she had often watched stallions mount mares, and bulls with heifers.

They strolled past the hotel's music conservatory and stood for a moment listening to a beautiful waltz played by someone at the harpsichord.

"Where are we going, Liam?"

"It's not far. Just around the corner."

Liam set Mary Kathryn from his arms. "Take Adel's hand."

The child did as her father instructed.

He grasped the large pewter handles and pushed two heavy oaken doors wide. "I didn't have time to shop for a wedding gift. This will have to do for now."

Adel gasped in pleasant surprise. Tears clung to her eyelashes as she led Mary Kathryn forward into the glass-domed atrium. In the center of the room a statue of the water goddess Pantesia stood holding two urns, each with water flowing into a circular pool filled with fish in varying shades of red and gold.

A stone path created multiple walkways to various themed seating areas. Liam led Adel and Mary Kathryn to a summer gazebo centered in a garden of roses—reds, yellows, and whites. A pool filled with lily pads gurgled pleasantly over black shiny rocks.

Like a happy child, Adel clapped her hands together. "It's like something out of a fairy tale. Oh, Liam, this is most generous of you. The perfect gift."

Mary Kathryn trundled to the pool and bent over the edge to sweep her hands through the water. She giggled. "Frog."

Adel joined Liam's laughter as Mary Kathryn reached for the frog statue spewing water from its mouth. Liam captured the child before she tumbled headfirst into the shallow expanse.

A waiter dressed in a crisp white jacket approached. He wore white gloves and carried a tray, which he set on a low table inside the gazebo. "The tea and petit fours you ordered, sir."

Liam offered a nod of thanks. He indicated with a sweep of his open hand that Adel should join him. "It has been a long day. I felt a pot of Darjeeling might help you relax more so than a glass of champagne."

She nodded while trying to ignore all the questions dashing through her brain. Trying to ignore the way her skin erupted into cold prickles just from the mere sound of his voice and the way he looked at her.

She forced her hand not to tremble as she filled the gold-rimmed demitasse cups with steaming amber brew. She found herself wishing he were a crotchety old man with bad teeth and a balding pate rather than a man with finely chiseled features. For want of conversation, she said, "I fear Mary Kathryn is about to fall asleep."

"Then I shall hurry with what I have to say."

After a pause, he cleared his throat. "Mary Kathryn, I have to go away, for a long time."

The child snuffled against his tunic. "No go, Dah-dee. Peez."

The child's crumpled face and teary eyes crushed Adel's heart.

Liam placed his thumb under Mary Kathryn's chin so that she had to look at him. "I have a special gift for you."

The little girl's eyes brightened.

"I have a new mommy for you."

She looked around as if searching. "Where is she?"

"Adel is your new mommy."

"No, my mommy in heaven."

"Yes, she is. But she doesn't want you to be lonely. That's why Adel is your new mommy. She will love you and take care of you while I'm away."

"Where you go, Dah-dee?"

"Far, far away, to a place called India. When you are old enough, Adel will teach you all about elephants and monkeys and tigers. She will also teach you the alphabet, so you can write to me."

"You come home to me?"

He hugged the child close. Adel's heart fair broke when she spied the tears in Liam's eyes. And yet he did not try to hide them. She didn't see his display of emotion as a weakness, rather a strength that most men in her experience didn't possess.

"If it is within my power, my precious child, I will come home in time to celebrate your eighth birthday."

Her face lit with curiosity. She held up three fingers. "This many?"

Liam gently unfurled her fingers. "Count with me—one, two…"

He was so fatherly, so courteous, and so elegant. How handsome he looked as he helped his daughter count to eight.

Adel made a move to stand, but Liam clasped her hand. His gaze swept over her face and settled on her eyes. His voice grew quiet. "The transport ship sails in a few hours; long before the cock will crow. We will say our goodbyes tonight."

Suddenly an unexpected sadness moved through her. She should be overjoyed that she had accomplished her dreams—independence, of a sort. "Please don't worry about Mary Kathryn, and I shall manage Mautagh Manor to the best of my ability."

"Of this, I have no doubt."

She could have sat there and watched him for the rest of the evening. He was rugged and strong, like the Celtic nobles of his ancestors. Then she began to entertain the most indecent thoughts. She imagined him alone in his bedchamber, removing his shirt in the candlelight as he readied for bed. What would his bare chest look like, and what would it feel like to touch? What would it be like to share a bed with him and feel those large hands caressing her body? She imagined they would feel calloused and rough, yet gentle and warm at the same time.

His voice shook her out of these improper thoughts. The atrium seemed unduly warm, and she longed for air to cool her flushed skin. "I, ah, what were you saying?"

As if reading her thoughts, he flashed a seductive smile, and then grew serious. "In the morning, Magistrate Oxley will deliver the official copy of our marriage certificate, among other important papers. Fourteen years have passed since I last visited Ireland. It is doubtful if any of the staff will remember me. Should anyone question your rightful place at Mautagh, the documents will prove you are my wife and the legal proprietor of the house and lands, and of my other holdings."

For a moment it seemed he had slipped inward, recalling long-ago memories. "I have never felt the call of Ireland more than I have these last few days spent with you. I remember my grandmother saying to love the land, to hold it dear to your heart, and that way you would always be close to home. I have a foreboding, Adel. Like a dark shadow, a premonition."

Welling with emotion, Adel wrapped her arms around Liam, encircling the child who now slept in his arms. A rush of new feelings coursed through her. God! Now that she knew him, now that she had seen the beautiful person he was, he was leaving.

She trembled with grief. It was as if someone had died, for she had to remind herself that he might never return, and that theirs was a marriage of convenience.

At last she managed to grapple with her feelings and drew away from him. She swept her hands wide. "Thank you for two beautiful gifts—Mary Kathryn and this place. I am sorry that I have nothing to give you in return."

"You've given me more than you know, Adel."

She tried to laugh, even though she felt as if her insides were being ripped out.

Liam reached to brush a few loose strands of her hair from her face. His touch was gentle and loving and filled her with an agonizing longing. He looked deeply into her eyes. "It's late. Let me escort you to your room. I must ready my equipment and see to my men. The transport ship sails in two hours."

****

At the door to her hotel suite, Adel turned the knob and stood aside as Liam shifted Mary Kathryn into Tilde's waiting arms.

"God speed, Capt'n. Ye and Robby Beck'll be in me daily prayers."

"Thank you, Tilde. We can ask for none better."

The maid turned and left through the room's adjoining door.

Emotions shimmered in Adel's eyes, and his feelings all twisted up inside of him. He swooped, hard and fast, his mouth coming on hers with fierce, unerring speed, so sudden Adel emitted a startled yelp of shock quickly swallowed up in his kiss.

Her mouth opened—of its own accord or because he'd nudged her lips apart? He didn't know. They kissed as if they'd done so a hundred times, like lovers who'd been apart for too long and were finally together once more, who didn't know if this would be their last meeting and so were determined to wring every drop of pleasure from it no matter the price.

His arms came around her. Her back was narrow, almost fragile, the line of her spine bumping against his palm, yet she didn't resist his arms. Thin like a willow whip, misleadingly frail-seeming, tensile and limber and so much stronger than appearance told.

His embrace tightened and the kiss intensified for a long, blissful moment. His brows gathered in a pained frown as he set her from him.

"I must go. I am glad you were in my life, even if for a short time."

"I…" Adel touched his cheek and released a long shuddery breath. "I will write, often."

He drew his hands around her sides, smoothing the fabric of her bodice beneath his palms. The material was silky, her body warm and elegantly lean. His thumbs brushed the sides of her breasts, a gentle, barely there curve that yielded to the slightest pressure, and he heard the quick intake of her breath. His own breath was gone—she'd stolen it from him along with whatever good sense he'd once possessed.

"Liam?" she asked, uncertainty breaking on his name. He felt her fingers tentatively brush the nape of his neck.

He couldn't look at her. *Couldn't*. What would a woman who'd never been kissed assume when the man who'd finally done so would leave her standing in the middle of a hotel suite while he left to travel halfway around the world to an unknown destiny?

If he caught one glimpse of those wide lilac eyes, that lovely mouth, he would never find it possible to pull away again—his career and her future would be damned.

Without speaking a final goodbye, Liam turned on a boot heel and shut the door behind him.

Chapter Ten

Adel awoke to a soft pattering of rain against the windowpane of her bedroom. In spite of the logs that crackled in the fireplace, she pulled the comforter tighter about her shoulders to ward off the chill.

She yawned and realized how tired she was after the long journey, and the disappointing end. She hadn't felt like eating during last night's dinner. Even now, all she wanted to do was drift into a deep, rehabilitating sleep. Then she could wake up and feel ready to begin her new life.

Her heart tripped against her chest. Liam was gone. Tears rose fresh on her eyelids. She had wanted so badly to tell him she loved him...but she had kept her silence. Her heart crumbled and the tears came harder.

As she looked around the bedchamber, noting the dainty writing desk set next to a window to catch the light, she found herself, at this moment, unable to pick herself up, dust herself off, as she usually did.

A sharp and urgent rap sounded at the adjoining bedroom door. Adel groaned and pulled the covers up so that only her eyes peeked over the edge.

Tilde whisked into the room as if she had a definite purpose. She held a note forward. "Blimey, Adel, Magistrate Oxley has sent a note requestin' you meet him for tea."

"Why are you so excited, Tilde? Surely he doesn't

mean now."

The maid shoved the note into Adel's extended hand. "'Tis after eleven. 'E's ordered tea and is waiting for you in the drawing room."

Adel shoved the covers aside and swung her legs over the edge of the bed. Her voice squeaked. "Here? In the suite's drawing room?"

"Aye. The one beyond that door."

"How uncivil of him. His position doesn't give him the right to barge in and assume I will be at his beck and call."

Her voice filled with patience, Tilde gently scolded. "Don't be gettin' yer knickers all in a wad, mum. If ye'll stop fussing long enough to slip the gown over yer 'ead, we'll 'ave you dressed in two shakes of a lamb's tail. Besides, it wouldn't do to get on the wrong side of 'is lordship, now, would it?"

Adel fidgeted while Tilde's deft fingers fastened the row of pearl buttons lining the back of her gown. Sitting in front of the cheval mirror, she raked her fingers through the long braid to loosen the strands, and while she brushed her hair, Tilde bent to the task of rolling thick winter stockings up Adel's legs.

She gave herself a last look in the mirror. "I think I'm presentable. You may announce me to his lordship, Tilde."

Adel swept into the drawing room with all the grace of her former station as Lady Adel Fitzhugh of Briarwood Manor.

She thought there was an odd familiarity about the magistrate, but she shook it off as having met him last evening. A slender man in his fifties, he was immaculate in a black coat and burgundy-striped waistcoat, his crisp white cravat folded with artistic precision.

An apologetic smile graced his face, and he spoke with a certain amount of humility. "Forgive me for calling at such an ungodly hour, Lady Adel, but I have important business to attend for the remainder of the day. As your ship sails early on the morrow, I felt it necessary to see you have this packet of documents to take with you."

She offered a polite smile as she spread her skirt and sat across from him.

He cleared his throat, the only indication of his impatience. "I took the liberty of ordering petite sausages and scones to go with our tea."

A blush rose to her cheeks when her stomach emitted a loud grumble. She lifted the silver domes from the trays of food. "Perhaps I could eat a bite or two."

"Excellent. Then I shall join you." He leaned forward and piled a generous serving on his plate.

Pleasant moments passed while they enjoyed their meal. Wiping her lips, and taking a last sip of tea, Adel said, "Thank you, my lord, for your thoughtfulness."

He reached for the bell pull and, within seconds, Tilde entered the room to remove the trays.

Oxley faced Adel, his expression stern. "May I assume from the shadows under your eyes that you did not rest well last night?"

It was a simple question. A question asked out of concern, a question that should not have ruffled Adel's temper. The words tumbled out before she could draw them back.

"I was married and then separated from my

husband, all within two hours. I am neither wife nor widow. I became an instant mother to a child I've known for exactly three days, I'm traveling to a country I know nothing about, whether it is civilized or barbaric, and"—she swept her hands wide—"and I find myself penniless. I will probably spend the rest of my life in Newgate, for I have no money to pay for all this luxury." She buried her face in the napkin she had twisted in her hands.

"There, there, Lady Adel. Do not take on so. No one has threatened to lock you away, and no one shall."

She dabbed at the tears. Her insides were stretched tighter than harp cords. "Why do you address me as 'Lady'? Do you not know that I forfeited my title when I left my stepbrother's house?"

The magistrate's sudden burst of laughter caused Adel to open her mouth for an angry retort, but she thought better of the notion.

She heaved a sigh. "'Tis no laughing matter, my lord."

"Of course not. Please forgive me. My nephew is overly zealous when it comes to protecting his privacy."

"Your nephew? I'm afraid I don't know who you mean."

"Why, Liam, who else?"

"No, you must be mistaken. He is a commoner who had the good fortune to rise to the position of captain in the Queen's Royal Guard."

"Pshaw, Lady Adel. I assure you that Liam's father was of royal Celtic blood. Had the man outlived his own father, he would have become the O'Shea of Connemara."

93

Adel caught her breath in shock. "And how are you Liam's uncle?"

"His mother was my sister. Though she had not a loving bone in her body, she was nonetheless my blood kin."

She regarded the amused twinkle in the magistrate's eyes. His were the same cobalt blue as Liam's, warm and tender.

"Why did Liam keep this a secret?"

Oxley lifted the teacup for Adel to refill. "If you please."

He thanked her and drew deep, as if quenching a long thirst. "My sister rarely had a kind word for the boy. When she sent him to military school, she enrolled him as William Oxley Kent. The other boys shunned him, accused him of getting preferential treatment because of his name. Most lads would have folded under such harsh circumstances, but not our Liam. At first he had to use his fists to prove he was no coward, and then he used his intellect, but only after he reclaimed his father's name—O'Shea. Liam asked no favors then, and he asks no favors now. He is content to earn respect—not have it given to him because of his title."

Adel drew a deep breath and willed her body to stop trembling. Gripping the dainty porcelain teapot, she was astounded the handle didn't crumble in her hand. "But, the Queen's name is—" She set the teapot aside for fear of dropping it. "*Kent,*" she whispered.

"Yes, the Queen and I are first cousins."

"Oh, dear, I don't know what to say."

"It is a lot to take in, Lady Adel. However, I regret that I must bring an end to our tête-à-tête."

He held forth a leather case. "Inside is a copy of your marriage certificate, along with documents written and signed in Liam's own hand giving you power of authority over the ministrations of all his holdings in Connemara and elsewhere. I have duplicate copies in my vault for safekeeping. You will receive a monthly stipend for Mary Kathryn and for your personal needs, as well as a stipend for the running of Mautagh Manor and the estate lands. It makes for boring reading, but all you will need is inside the case. Guard the documents well. There are also personal letters addressed to you and to Mary Kathryn."

Adel's thoughts were scattered as she stood and accepted the leather case that held the credentials to her new life. "May I ask a foolish question, Lord Oxley?"

"Of course you may, my lady."

"Does this mean that as Liam's wife I am a…countess?"

Oxley's voice softened. "Don't go weak-kneed and faint. I detest women who swoon over the least little nothing. Yes, your official title is Countess of England. In Ireland, Liam is Laird of Connemara. He is the O'Shea."

Adel's grim humor faded. She curtsied as Viscount Oxley bowed deeply and then continued, "I fear Liam and I have been lax in communicating with the solicitor in Connemara. Just know that if you need anything, or have any problems, send your man, Edwin, to me."

He reached inside an inner pocket of his coat and withdrew a pouch. "Coin for your travel. There is also a cheque which you can draw on the Bank of Dublin."

"Thank you. I am most grateful."

When the viscount stepped toward the door, Adel

said, "My lord, may I ask one last favor?"

Oxley's expression remained impassive. "As countess, you may ask anything you please."

Adel stepped to the bell pull and tugged. Tilde immediately entered the room.

"You require my services, mum?"

"Not exactly. More like a request."

She took Tilde's hand in her own and gave it a squeeze. "Tilde has been with me since I was eleven years old. She is but five years my senior, and is more of a sister than a lady's maid." She met the magistrate's gaze. "Sire, I have no blood family, and, except for Edwin, Tilde has no family. I wish to adopt her as my sister. Is such a thing possible?"

A cry spilled from Tilde's mouth. "God's lamb, Adel!"

When Oxley didn't answer, Adel said, "I will not have Tilde enter a new land and begin a new life as a servant."

He nodded his understanding. "As you wish, Countess. Although this is highly irregular, I will draw up the documents and have them delivered tonight. What name shall I place on the adoption papers?"

For a moment Adel's mind went blank. She was legally a Fitzhugh. Her stepfather had adopted her when she was but a babe in arms. She knew no other name.

"Tilde's married name is Trumble. She shall be called Tilde Fitzhugh Trumble, adopted sister of Adel Fitzhugh O'Shea, Countess of England."

"God's lamb, Adel. I'm not fit. My language is pure cockney. I will be an embarrassment to you."

"I don't give a fig about your manner of speaking, Tilde. Just say you will do me the honor of becoming my sister and Mary Kathryn's aunt."

"Do I swear an oath?"

Adel's eyes implored Oxley to understand that for Tilde swearing an oath meant more than signing a piece of paper. "Yes, she must swear an oath, mustn't she, my lord?"

It seemed like ages before he spoke, and Adel feared he might change his mind and walk out of the room.

He stared at them for a long moment, and then, locking his fingers together, he rocked on his heels. "Indeed, she must swear an oath. Please place your right hand over your heart. Tilde Trumble, do you accept Adel Fitzhugh O'Shea's request to become her lawfully adopted sister, and accept as your legal name Tilde Fitzhugh Trumble?"

Adel listened as the words spilled from Tilde's lips. "I do, milord. I mean, my lord."

"Then by the power invested in me by the Court of London, and as Magistrate, I declare you and Countess Adel Fitzhugh O'Shea as legally adopted sisters. May you bring each other much happiness."

The two women giggled and hugged each other. And then Adel held her head high. "Thank you, Viscount Oxley."

After the viscount had departed, Adel eased into the nearest chair. *Oh, Liam, I don't deserve all you have given me. How shall I ever repay you?*

Loretta C. Rogers

Ireland

Part II
The Challenge
1854-1857

Loretta C. Rogers

Chapter Eleven

Adel stood with her hands tight on the rail, her feet braced apart on the rolling deck of the *SS Mapleton*. The icy wind whipped her skirts and cloak, and salty spray chilled her cheeks. She closed her eyes to breathe in the moist, clean scent of the sea and listen to the ship's heavy keel slicing through the frothy waves below.

It wouldn't be long now. Her heart did a little dance in her chest as she tried to recall the images Liam had described of Mautagh Manor.

The ship had passed by the mouth of St. George's Channel some time since. An occasional flurry of white flakes drifted down in the hushed silence of the still day, more a reminder of the season than any real threat of a storm. They had made good time despite the weather and the prevailing winds, but stopping at several English ports along the way had made their progress annoyingly slow.

When at last the ship approached the quay at Cork Harbor and seamen rushed aloft to reef the sails and secure the lines, the cold air penetrated Adel's warm cloak as she stood with Mary Kathryn in her arms, next to Tilde and Edwin, all waiting for the ship's landing and the signal to disembark. When word came, she held the child to her tightly and crossed the gangplank, with Tilde close behind. Edwin and five deckhands followed, each grasping an end of one of the steamer trunks filled with all their earthly possessions. On the dock, Adel and her entourage merged with the bustling activity. All around them vendors hawked their wares in a language she could not understand, while eager merchants haggled for the cargoes that had been brought in, yet the lightly falling snow muffled the variety of sounds and seemed to bring a softer note to the cloudy day.

Edwin had taken the lead through the milling throng, but now he faced her. "If you please, mum, wait here while I hire a conveyance and inquire about a reputable inn."

She accepted his logic. There was no need to go charging about in a strange city where the language was barely comprehensible. She scanned the surroundings. "We will wait for you by yonder lamp post."

"Aye, mum." Escorting Adel to the place she had indicated and there leaving her with Tilde and the child, he hurried off down the street.

A squat, rosy-faced woman had built a small fire beside her cart for the preparation of her wares, and its cheery flames promised the warmth Adel sought for Mary Kathryn. Drawn to its heat, she stretched her icy fingers toward the fire, and almost immediately the jolly, rosy-cheeked woman greeted her. Speaking in her thick brogue, the vendor pressed her to take a short sausage on a stick. The woman pointed to Mary Kathryn.

Adel was reluctant to refuse the purchase, for fear she would be forced to leave the fire. She reached into her handbag and laid a coin in the woman's hand.

The vendor gave the jovial reply, *"Go raibh maith*

agat," and handed Adel the juicy tidbit.

"I'm sorry, I don't understand." She turned to Tilde, who shrugged her shoulders.

"Bain't ye Anglis?"

"Oh, praise be, yes, we are English. Do you know how far to Connemara?"

The woman mutely nodded and pointed to the west. "'Tis better ye catch yon'er ferry to Galway 'arbor an' on to Connemara by road." She held up the fingers of one hand. "Be there in this many days. By wag'n, a for'night, ma'be. No good for ta wee un."

Encouraged by her own appetite, Adel bought three more sausages on a stick. "Thank you, dear lady. We shall heed your advice." The old woman chortled with glee when Adel pressed another coin into her outstretched hand.

They had more than enough time to finish the sausages while they waited for Edwin to return, and Adel had another question for the woman.

"Dear lady, do you know of Mautagh Manor?"

The woman's stare moved to slowly rake Adel. "Onct Connemara was me 'ome, t'was. Wild and 'aunted by 'ems ghosties of 'e old lairds. Some say Mautagh Manor be cursed."

Adel expelled a snort of irritation. "Come, Tilde, let us move away. I will not have Mary Kathryn frightened by such foolish prattle."

It was some time before Edwin returned with a small cart. The poor short-legged donkey didn't look sturdy enough to pull a wagon laden with four heavy trunks and one smaller one, but they were nevertheless loaded on while Edwin related his difficulty in finding a more suitable conveyance. In two bites, he finished off the sausage Tilde handed him, and then said, "The Cork Inn is suitable and away from this rabble, mum. It appears clean, and the lady wot owns it is from Bristol. I made the arrangements."

Though it was early afternoon, low leaden clouds continued to dull the western light and deepen the gloom beneath the trees. Spitting snow stung their faces and left traces of white on the cobbled street where they walked.

The short caravan traversed the winding streets of Cork, crossing a stone bridge over a wide canal until they gained the outer limits of the city. "'Tis there, mum, at the end o' the street."

The poor donkey looked even more miserable than Adel felt as she dragged the sodden hem of her cloak inside the pleasantly warm inn. Mary Kathryn whimpered as she set her down.

"Cheerio, m'ladies. I've sent ewers of 'ot water to yer rooms to freshen yerselves. 'Ere be a rich lamb stew for supper, fresh soda bread, and ginger cakes with clouted cream."

A falling log on the fire sent a shower of sparks flying outward onto the stone hearth. The crackling fire reminded Adel of home, but instead of bringing relief, the orange flickering flames added to Adel's tired tension.

She accepted the keys from the smiling innkeeper's wife and made her way toward the stairs. "We thank you for your hospitality."

****

The next day, Adel and her new family boarded the boat bound for the port of Galway. Early on the morning of their fourth day aboard, they landed in

Galway's bustling harbor.

In farewell, the captain said, "Godspeed on your journey, milady. Connemara is wild as the Irish Sea, but in the spring and summer the heather is beautiful as yer eyes."

Adel squirmed with a sudden discomfiture. "Do you know of Mautagh Manor?"

The ferry captain fell silent. When he at last spoke, his words snapped like a whip. "What I know is the young O'Shea gives 'is loyalty to England and 'as forsaken his mother country."

Adel's chin came up in a gesture of unswerving tenacity. "If you are referring to Liam O'Shea, he gives his loyalty to the people he protects, for he serves his countrymen, both English and Irish, in India. And for that you should be grateful."

"You speak as if you know the O'Shea personally."

"I do. He is my—" Adel did not know what instinct cautioned her to remain silent about her recent nuptials. Perhaps it was the subtle anger in the man's eyes. "Captain O'Shea is my employer, and this is his daughter. We have come to live at Mautagh Manor."

The captain offered a snappy bow from his waist. "Then more's the pity for you, milady. We are about to cast off. I suggest you go ashore."

The boat's lurch caused Adel and Tilde to lift their skirts and hurry down the gangway.

"God's lamb, Adel, wot do ye suppose 'e meant by that?"

Adel shivered. "Pay him no never mind, Tilde. I fear this is a country fraught with superstition."

"I 'ope ye be right. I surely 'ope so."

Before them, Edwin pulled a carriage to a halt.

"'Tis sturdy, mum, with strong horses. The 'ostler said the road is a bit bumpy but leads straight to Connemara. 'E gave me good directions to the O'Shea land, that tally with Captain O'Shea's. There be an inn between 'ere and the estate."

"Did he say how far?"

"Aye, most of a full day. Will we rest at the inn?"

"I think not, Edwin. According to Liam, there is a full staff at Mautagh. We shall rest and replenish ourselves in our new home."

"Do you wish me to send a messenger ahead to alert them to our arrival, mum?"

"I am certain Liam dispatched a letter with instructions to expect us." She refused to show her trepidation. "Let us be on our way."

Edwin stepped down from the carriage loft to help Adel and then Mary Kathryn and Tilde inside. Within minutes, he had whistled up the horses to a canter.

The future was in her hands, all of their futures. Adel had grave doubts about her ability to carry forth. The rising wind caught her breath and sent shivery blasts coursing beneath her woolen cloak. Catching the flaring garment and tucking it securely around her, she settled Mary Kathryn between herself and Tilde as they huddled within its warmth.

"Why did ye not set the boat captain in 'is proper place by tellin' 'im who you really be?"

Adel considered Tilde's question. "Did you see the coldness in his eyes, and hear the contempt in his voice? In an instant I was reminded of the old vendor woman's foolish warning. It might be to our advantage if we appear as who we truly are: a governess hired to raise a child and to manage the estate until her employer completes his military duty and returns to Ireland."

Tilde ran her hands up and down her arms as if warding off a chill. "'Tis an eerie feelin' I 'ave."

Adel watched the fine lines across the other's brow deepen into a troubled scowl and was quick to give comment. "Oh, come now, Tilde. Don't tell me you believe in such rubbish as…as"—she cut her eyes toward the child curled between them and then mouthed the word—"*spirits*."

"I bain't ne'er seen such. Still, there be those wot 'ave."

Adel shrugged to show indifference to Tilde's words. "It is all superstitious rot. Besides, what can happen in a house filled with people?"

Adel settled back against the seat, her throat suddenly dry as bone meal.

Climbing gradually from the lowlands, the carriage rolled through a thinning forest and around large tumbled rocks that became increasingly plentiful. The wheels splashed through water-filled ruts pockmarking the road. So far the laboring horses were holding their own. Then the wagon lurched drunkenly as the right wheel dropped into a hole cut into the road. It came with such force and suddenness that both Adel and Tilde screamed, but the carriage righted itself as the horses pulled onward, and they continued the journey.

"Surely, we are almost there?" Adel's thoughts were ahead of her fears.

The wind whistled over a low ridge that buttressed the hill to their left and wailed a mournful lament as it passed behind them through the trees. The last question hung in the air between Adel and Tilde. It was apparent the two of them shared a common curiosity as to what awaited at the path's end. As for Adel, she was anxious to see her new home, whether house, hall, or fortress.

Edwin's voice struggled through the wind. "S'thin' ahead, mistress."

The carriage topped the ridge, and to Adel's amazement she found their path led to a burned-out ruin nestled on a low bluff a short distance away.

Oddly truncated trees stood like giant, black-bodied mourners around a crypt, posting a threat to anyone who drew near the house.

Gray and bleak as the wintry sky overhead, the outer walls rose from a jumbled pile of jagged rocks near an elbow of ice-crusted stream. Dry tufts of withered grass randomly pierced the clumps of snow that covered the embankment. A low bridge constructed of stout timbers provided access across the stream to the dark, gaping maw of the gatehouse, where a rusted portcullis hung askew over the upper part of the entrance, held there by one chain that still secured a corner. A wooden gate lay in a broken heap across the passage and was covered with a fresh dusting of snow.

Adel leaned out the window. "Edwin, stop the coach. Surely this can't be the right place."

As soon as the coach halted, Adel didn't wait for assistance. Instead she opened the door and jumped to the ground. Edwin seemed mortified. "Milady, tain't decent for a lady of yer station to be—" As if lost for the correct choice of words, he added, "Well, wouldn't want folks here 'bout to think I'm not doin' me rightful duty to ye."

Caring not a whit for her lack of decorum, she reached into the carriage for Mary Kathryn. "First,

Edwin, there is no one around to question if you have breached protocol; and second, we are all equals here."

"As you say, mum."

"And stop calling me 'mum.' You are my adopted brother-in-law, Mary Kathryn's adopted uncle. You must refer to me as—Adel."

"I'll try, mum...er...milady."

She sighed, knowing Edwin would never use her given name.

"'Twill be dark soon, Adel. Mayhap Edwin should drive us to the inn we passed a ways back."

Adel considered Tilde's suggestion. "The horses are tired; the way is rocky, and as steep going down as driving up. I won't risk our lives—as they would be, should one of the steeds falter and cause us to go careening over a cliff."

She lifted her skirt. "Come; let us use what daylight is left to investigate. Perhaps we will find a warm place to rest until morning."

Picking their way around the fallen gate, the three, with Tilde toting Mary Kathryn, passed through the gatehouse and entered the courtyard. Adel found little to assuage her anxieties. The desolation was shattering. There was little but emptiness and black ruins, and the occasional caw of a rook. The stable had all but collapsed.

The stone walls of the manor house were still intact, but most of the shutters and some of the windows on the second and third level, along with the roof, were charred and in need of repair. A few windows stood open, as if to welcome the birds that fluttered about them.

Adel stared agog at her snow-bedecked

surroundings. Without a word she climbed the front steps to the arched doorway of the house. The large, heavy portal gaped open, offering little protection from the blustery winds that whipped about them. Peering into the gloom of the inner chambers, Adel moved cautiously inward. She had no knowledge of what creatures, human or otherwise, might be lurking within the shadows of the great room, and she was alert to any sudden movements. No ferocious beast sprang upon her from the darkened corners of the hall; there was only the assailing attack of her senses by the filth of the place. Years had apparently passed since the manor received the care and attention of a human hand.

Huge, grayish shreds of long-abandoned cobwebs hung from the darkly timbered, rough-hewn trusses that braced the ceiling. The webs spanned doorways, corners, and other nooks and crannies, while tiny droppings gave evidence of the comings and goings of small rodents. As Adel moved about the room, her skirts raised dust from the tapering ridges of dirt that stretched across the stone floor, marking where strong drafts had long invaded the hall. A large table lay on its side in front of the huge hearth, and several high-backed chairs and benches were piled in a jumbled heap beside it, some broken in pieces as if used to feed a fire of more recent time. The soot-coated interior of the open hearth bespoke a lengthy age of roaring blazes and smoldering coals.

A brick oven had been built close against the side of the inner wall, indicating this area had been utilized as a kitchen. A large iron kettle still hung on its bracket above the ashes, and from a beam overhead assorted pots and utensils hung, covered by a thick mantle of dust.

Stone stairs ascended in a flight to the second floor and were buttressed by stout wooden balustrades on either side. A landing existed on the upper level and led to another flight of stairs.

Adel's sigh was as weary as her entire being. This tumbledown ruin could not possibly be where they were going to live.

"Yer pardon, mistress," Edwin mumbled, his face skewed into a frown. "I fear this be Mautagh Manor." He held forth a fire-scorched family crest; he had used the sleeve of his heavy tunic to rub across the surface and found the insignia *O'Shea.*

Adel's bewilderment did not diminish. The journey had taken its toll, but Edwin's discovery nearly rent her soul. Her eyes chased wildly about the room. "Are you saying"—her tone was flat and frigid—"this…pigsty is the wonderful place Liam praised?"

Edwin scrubbed a toe across a mound of dirt. "Are we returning to London, then, mistress?"

As much as she yearned for the beauty and comforts of Briarwood, she smothered the sobs building in her throat. The burden in her breast seemed unbearable, and a ragged sigh did not ease the pain. Her voice was weak, and she could put no force behind her words. She was suddenly bone-tired, weary, and racked with despair at the thought of having to search out even meager comfort in a den fit only for vermin. "I think not. Find a place to shelter the horses from the wind." She shrugged her narrow shoulders. "Perhaps we can make the house livable with a good cleaning."

Tilde stared at her as if in stunned disbelief. "Mum…Adel, ye have more than a pence to yer name, and a title, too. You needn't be afeered o' being 'omeless or turned away by yer stepbrother."

Adel glanced about in growing dismay. She had held a vision of a wealthy estate where she would find a bath, a good meal, a private chamber, and a down-filled tick upon which to rest. She had been unable to sleep during the night, knowing they would soon be docking. The long wait in the cold during the hustle of the landing and the wearisome ride that followed had done nothing to ease her discomfort.

She stared dumbfounded at the blackened pieces of brick and burned timbers that littered the ground.

"This was Liam's home. He envisioned the manor and lands as it was when he last saw it as a boy of sixteen years. He gave this place to me to cherish for Mary Kathryn. I do not know what happened to cause such a terrible fire, or who is lining his pockets with Liam's coin while Mautagh decays to the ground, but I will not disappoint him, nor will I give my stepbrother cause to gloat by running back to Briarwood like a whipped dog."

Tilde set Mary Kathryn from her arms with instruction to stay close. She then stood, hands on hips, to ask, "Are ye plannin' to bend yer hands and knees like a common charwoman to scrub the floors?"

Adel placed the fingertips of both hands together as she delved into her store of determination. "Until they gleam. We will scrub the hearth and repair the door, and mend the windows and peg up the shutters, sweep the chimney, dust the rafters, and find a weaver to spin wool for mats to warm these stone floors. Yes, Tilde, whatever it takes, we will rebuild Mautagh Manor to its former glory. Meanwhile, on the morrow I must make an accounting of what coin we have left and what needs be done first. As for tonight, we will have to make do with what little comfort we can find."

Tilde commented dismally, "A mighty task, to be sure, mum."

"Are you reverting back to my servant, Tilde, to call me mum?"

"I bain't. 'Tis takin' some gettin' used to you as me sister."

A chilly draft swept through the hall. Mary Kathryn wrapped herself in the folds of Adel's heavy skirts, and Adel felt the child's shivers. "A fire would help, and perhaps something to block up those windows that cannot be closed."

Edwin stomped in, his arms loaded with wood. "I've settled the 'orses, mistress. Once a fire is goin', I'll bring in the trunks, then see what's ta be done ta mend the windows an' shutters."

He hurried out, and Adel lifted her gaze toward the higher level, wondering if the upper chambers were in any better condition than the hall.

"Stay with Mary Kathryn, Tilde."

"Where ye be goin'?"

"Up there."

"Do be careful, Adel."

Gathering her skirts, she slowly mounted the stone stairs until she reached the second level. There a short hallway jutted off from the landing. The floor consisted of only two rooms, a tiny one that would be suitable for Mary Kathryn, and a larger chamber. The door of the latter stood slightly ajar, allowing a shaft of the light filtering in through the windows to pierce the gloom of the hall. The hinges creaked in rusty protest as she pushed the door wider and, in sharp repugnance, brushed aside the cobwebs to enter. Within the bedchamber, the floor was covered by a thin layer of dirt.

Several narrow windows allowed light to fill the room. A few stood open, allowing birds and persistent drafts to enter, while beyond them the sagging shutters flapped and rattled in the wind. Crudely chiseled beams supported the ceiling, and from these, thick cobwebs swept downward, gracing the remains of what may have been a canopy bed.

Tattered shreds of a feather mattress covered the rough planks of a box. Another canopy of sorts, constructed of copper and wood, sheltered a large, circular copper tub, which stood in the corner between the fireplace and the windows. Its once-elegant hangings were now merely long shreds of rotted cloth fluttering in the errant breezes. Deeply carved buffets, chests, armchairs, and armoires completed the furnishings that were untouched by anything other than dust and time.

What had caused the fire? Was it deliberate or an accident? Why hadn't one of the servants or someone from the village contacted Liam? Such questions would have to wait until another day for their answers.

Chapter Twelve

Tilde's concerned voice called, "Adel, 'tis gettin' dark. Come down afore ye hurt yourself."

Adel drew in a deep breath and nearly choked on the dust. "She was once a grand house. We are staying, Tilde. We will bring Mautagh Manor back to her former glory."

A pair of low stools, thickly crusted with dirt and grime, squatted before a large fireplace at the end of the chamber near where she stood. On the same wall, nearest the door, a huge tapestry hung from ceiling to floor, covering a section of wooden panels. A grayish layer obscured the needlework, and Adel reached out to examine it to see how well the fabric had withstood the ravages of time. Her hand raised a thick cloud of dust from its surface. Noticing a tasseled cord hanging beside it, she tugged on it, curious as to its purpose. The cord refused to yield to her small inquisitive jerk, and finally, in exasperation, she gave it a mighty yank. A screech of rusty nails tearing loose from dry wood suddenly splintered the silence, bringing her head up with a snap. Without pause, the tapestry, the rod on which it hung, and the carved wooden valance that covered both began a majestic descent as one mounting after another gave way, spilling a billowing cloud of choking gray dust in advance of their ponderous fall.

Adel gasped and stumbled back, barely noting the

doorway that had a moment earlier been hidden by the tapestry as the weight of the cloth brushed heavily against her. In the next instant the air was filled with a growing swarm of small, chittering, black creatures that flitted about her head in swift, staccato swoops and dives.

The horror of the attack seized her, and she gave vent to an undulating scream as she twisted this way and that, flailing her arms to ward off their darting flights.

Rapidly thudding footsteps sounded in the hall, and Edwin burst into the chamber, the heavy tree limb he carried held at the ready. It was apparent he had come to do battle with whatever fierce assailants Adel had encountered, be it wild dogs, highwaymen, or apparitions.

"Bats!" he bellowed as he skidded to a halt in the middle of the room alive with hundreds of the swarming creatures. He swung the bough as a weapon with mighty sweeps and let out a roar in blood-red tones. "Get yerself to safety, milady. I'll 'old 'em off!"

The stout branch fairly whistled as it cleaved through the air, doing little damage to the flying beasties.

Adel crouched as she crept to the doorway. When her breath returned and she peeked around the door, she noticed Edwin had gallantly cleared the room of the winged creatures, and with such astounding success that no sight of the bats remained.

"Edwin, stop. Cease your attack."

He halted abruptly, his feet braced wide and the bough still at the ready, his eyes rolling wildly in search of further attack.

He panted, "Nasty demons, they be. Fair suck the blood right out of ye whilst ye sleep."

Adel gave a nod toward the panels of leaded glass. "For the sake of caution, you'd best latch the windows against their return. We would not want them to visit us again—especially while we sleep."

"Aye, milady, to be sure."

Behind her, Tilde drew in great gulps of air as if she had sprinted up the stairs, and Adel turned to see Mary Kathryn, pasty-white with fear, with her tiny arms locked around Tilde's neck.

Tilde cringed as a stray bat swooped past and flew out the open window. "God's lamb, Adel. Yer scream scared ten years off me growth."

Adel tried to appear casual. "It gave me quite the fright, too."

She smoothed a gentle hand over Mary Kathryn's hair. "There's no need to cry, my sweet child. See, Edwin has protected us. You will be my brave girl, won't you?"

The little girl snuffled and hugged Tilde even tighter.

Adel pinched her nose between her thumb and forefinger against the stench. "This corner will need a thorough cleaning." She indicated the filth the bats had left.

Tilde sighed. "'Tis no small task. It 'pears they've lived 'ere for years."

The dung clung to the walls and mounded the floor.

Gazing at the droppings, Adel agreed. "Yes, we will need stiff brushes and sudsy water to scrape the walls and floor before the room is fit for occupancy. As for the tapestry, I wish to salvage it as part of Mary Kathryn's heritage, though it will need careful cleaning."

Adel was most curious about the panel door hidden behind the tapestry. "I wonder if this is a secret passageway. Where would it lead?"

A myriad of emotions flitted across Tilde's face, fear the most predominant. "Remember wot the old woman in the village said about"—she cut her eyes toward Mary Kathryn—"you know, them wot bain't no more of this earth. Mayhap we should wait 'til morning to go explorin'."

A fresh wave of curiosity rose up to claim Adel. "Superstitious rot. The bats are gone. Let's see what is in the room, in case they have a secret way of getting back inside. Besides, there's safety in numbers."

Edwin straightened his jacket. "Aye, mistress," he agreed heartily. "'Tis best we stay together."

With Edwin's help, Adel gathered the heavy tapestry into a long roll. "Ye want I should open the door, milady?"

Adel glanced from Edwin to Tilde. A pulse thrummed at the base of her throat. "No, just keep the branch handy in case we encounter…" Her voice trailed off. She refused to allow the old harpy's words about ghosts to frighten her.

She gripped the latch and shoved. The door didn't budge. "It's stuck."

"'Ere." Edwin handed her the tree limb. "Let me 'ave a go at it."

He placed his shoulder against the solid surface and shoved. A shower of dust rained down on him as the door swung wide. Brushing grime from his hat, he stepped aside.

Cobwebs adorned the room beyond, in lacy folds. The pungent stench from years of bat feces at its entryway threatened to upend Adel's stomach. She placed a hand over her mouth and nose to inhale the sweet aroma of her cologne instead.

Sun rays filtered through a begrimed, cracked window pane, but lent enough light to allow Adel full view. Her eyes widened. She gave a snort of disbelief.

"God's lamb, Adel. Wot is it—a secret passage?"

"It's…nothing. A small, empty room. Odd that it was hidden behind the tapestry."

Edwin cleared his throat. "Don't be thinkin' me a know-it-all, mistress, but I've heerd tell that in the olden days, such rooms was built as hidin' places to keep ladies and children safe from hooligans. Mayhap this is such as that."

Adel nodded. "I believe you are quite correct in your deduction, Edwin." She took another look. "The space is large enough for a child's room."

Adel stepped into the hallway and swept her gaze upward, wondering what the higher chambers would offer for accommodations and just what she might find there. She was not yet ready to face another such adventure as she had just experienced. "I agree there is safety in numbers. Come," she bade Edwin and Tilde. "Let us explore the rest of the manor. Should we have occasion to meet other beasties, I would prefer not to face them alone."

Willingly the two women, with Mary Kathryn in Adel's arms, followed Edwin up the wooden stairs, which turned in long flights to an upper-story hall. On the left, large windows strategically placed every few yards in the solid stone allowed sunlight to flood the corridor. On the right, the hallway led to a pair of doors, the larger of which sagged from its hinges. The smaller opened onto a room obviously meant for a servant, with its stark furnishings and tiny dimensions.

Edwin tried to appear casual, but Adel noticed that the stout tree limb preceded him as he poked warily at the sagging door to push it wider. Tentatively thrusting his head through and finding no immediate danger, he put a shoulder to the thick plank and heaved the portal aside to allow Adel easy entry.

Adel glanced about the room. The quarters were comprised of a huge bedchamber, a dressing room, and a privy. "Look at the size of that bed. Apparently these were once the old laird's chambers."

"Be ye takin' this room, Adel?" Tilde wanted to know.

Adel surveyed the ample area. The bedchamber might have once been habitable, but a gaping hole in the roof allowed a large expanse of sky to show through where the tiles gaped awry. Snow had accumulated in a small mound on the floor beneath the opening, and its chill pervaded the chamber.

Adel shivered. "Considering my choices, for now, I shall take the bedchamber below for my own, and Mary Kathryn shall sleep in the smaller adjoining room. Adel's small, tight smile readily conveyed her feeling for their present situation. "There are many repairs to make this place habitable for us. For tonight, we shall make ourselves as comfortable as possible. Tilde, I believe there are sandwiches left in the hamper."

"Aye, and we 'ave tea leaves to brew. I will look for a teapot and cups in the larder. Edwin, when you were gathering firewood, did you notice a serviceable well to draw water?"

"I did. There be one near the stable and another in the courtyard, but 'ere be a free-flowing spring wot runs through the estate."

Adel laughed, surprised she could still manage the feat. "At least that is one advantage we have. We will need a fair amount of water to clean this heap of stone."

Edwin cast a worried glance at the hole in the ceiling as if unsure of where his own priorities should be, but Adel gave him little space to dwell on the matter.

"I leave the task of hiring workmen to your good judgment, Edwin. Time enough for that tomorrow. Do you think we are safe here for the night?"

"Though poorly treated, the old house is sturdy built, and safe enough, milady."

"Very good. Repair the hinges on the front door as best you can. Tilde and I will start with the sweeping, dusting, and scrubbing. Hopefully there is enough light left to aid us in making some improvement to this place before full night befalls us. Afterwards, we shall enjoy a meager meal, and then rest."

The woolen cloak billowed out around her, swirling up small puffs of dust on the stairs as Adel began her descent.

Hours later, she wavered on the brink of complete exhaustion when she retired that evening. She had thrown herself into a frenzy of activity as she sought to improve the state of their circumstances before the fall of evening. Only a little progress had been made, and considering the monumental task laid out for them, their efforts that afternoon were comparable to trying to drain the ocean dry.

For the moment, she felt defeated, and then she collapsed weakly to her knees before the hearth and stared into the flames in a dull stupor. Tears glistened on her heavy lashes as memories of Briarwood came stealing upon her, and the agonizing questions roiled up. Why did she always leap before thinking things through? Why hadn't she tried harder to befriend her sister-in-law? Why had she agreed to marriage and coming to this place?

She closed her eyes, spilling the overflow of tears down her cheeks, and from the dark recesses of her mind a vision took shape, that of Liam. His once elegant uniform was torn and filthy. With vacant eyes, he stared at the blank stone of the opposite wall; his lips moved slowly in unintelligible words.

She sniffed loudly and, wiping her face with the hem of her skirt, drew a quavering breath as she struggled for control. Her mind labored to sort out the realities as she slowly came to herself again, and the illusions disappeared in a vapor.

Adel pressed her face in her hands and quietly sobbed as if her heart would break. She wanted desperately to be gone from this place.

Chapter Thirteen

For once, in all her years, Adel wanted to act as if life was made just for her and the world was at her feet waiting to be recognized. Alas, it was not so, and might never be.

Her youth yearned for a lighter, gayer side of life, of adventure and exploring the world.

Mary Kathryn snuggled beneath Adel's arm. "Why Del cry? Mary Kathryn not being bad."

She cuddled the child inside her cloak and whispered, "Of course you are not bad. Remember when I told you that sometimes grownup ladies get grumpy?"

Though Mary Kathryn didn't answer, Adel felt the nod against her ribcage. "Sometimes grownup ladies cry because the sad-fairy has visited them."

"Sad-fairy visit me."

"She did? When?"

"When my mommy go away to heaven."

Tears sprang anew to brim Adel's lashes. "My mother went to heaven, too."

Mary Kathryn shifted so that Adel felt the child's breath tickle her cheek. "Her did?"

"Uh-huh. When I was a little girl like you. Now, close your eyes and think happy thoughts."

"Del?"

"Yes?"

"Are you weelly my new mommy?"

Adel's breath caught in shock at the question. She hadn't realized the little girl had actually understood what Liam had meant that evening in the hotel's solarium. She pondered how best to answer the question.

"Your daddy would never fib to you."

"But your name is Del."

"Yes, it is. You may call me Del for as long as you like. You will know when to call me Mommy, and when you do, it will make me very happy. Now, do as I say, and go back to sleep."

Mary Kathryn stretched up and kissed Adel on the cheek.

Adel heaved a shuddering sigh. She raised her head to stare at the sleeping child, and then about the room. Through lingering tears and in the glow from the large hearth, the room was still filthy. They had swept the floor, washed the wall, and cleaned a spot large enough for them to create pallets from their lap blankets, in front of the fire, but this was reality, this cold, dirty, barren place of pervading musty odors and chilling breezes that whistled through every crack and crevice. And she was here of her own undoing rather than aboard a steamer bound for Africa or even India. Oh, how at this moment she envied Liam and Robby their freedom, as men, to do and travel as they pleased.

Taking firm command of her emotions, she brushed the tears from her cheeks. A long, calming sigh escaped her as she continued to peruse her surroundings. With a few minor repairs, a thorough cleaning, fresh ticking for the beds, and several bolts of cloth, the upstairs chambers could be made into rather pleasant rooms. All she would need was a great deal of strength, wit, and patience to see it changed.

In the morning, Adel's newly formed resolve nearly crumbled. In full daylight the room did not reflect the hours she and Tilde had spent scrubbing and sweeping.

Espying the trunks Edwin had set near the front door, she reflected on her stepbrother's meanness in reminding her that all she owned was purchased with Fitzhugh money and that it was only by his generous nature that he allowed her to leave with more than the clothes on her back.

She had arrogantly retorted that she was gainfully employed and didn't need his handouts. Now, on silent feet, she rose from the pallet she shared with Mary Kathryn and padded toward the five chests—two for her, one each for Tilde and Edwin, and one smaller trunk that held Mary Kathryn's belongings.

Reaching down to the first of her travel chests, she loosened the hasp and lifted the arched lid. She plucked at the clothing she was presently wearing. "What a foolish dolt I am."

"Ye made sensible choices in the gowns and unmentionables, and even the boots ye packed. Ye be no puddin' 'ead, Adel, and that be for certain."

Adel gasped, her hands clutching the base of her throat. "Oh, Tilde, you gave me a start! Where is Edwin?"

The way Tilde twisted her hands together concerned Adel. "What is it? Has Edwin met with harm?"

Tilde's small firm chin jutted forward. "There be only one way to say this, and that be to spit it right out.

Well, Edwin and me was born into servitude. Lord Fitzhugh 'ad a rare kind word for Edwin, though 'e worked 'ard to please the master. Ye must be patient wid 'im for no callin' ye by yer given name. 'Tis not 'is way. He bain't meanin' no disrespect. He will never consider 'imself equal to the gentry, but Adel, 'e will always serve you well. We both will."

Adel acknowledged the statement with a dispirited smile, while outside the sunshine gave way to a gray, cold mist, leaving her feeling as dismal as the weather. "I've done it again, haven't I? Charged full ahead, making decisions without discussing them with the people whose lives they affect." She hesitated. "You are my best friend in the whole world. Forgive me if I have dishonored you or Edwin. I only meant to free you from servitude by making you an equal. Oh, Tilde, tell me you feel as I do about our sisterhood."

Tilde reached out and clasped Adel's hands and held them firm. "'Tisn't blood or a piece of paper wot makes a family. 'Tis wots inside of the 'eart. Ye've always been me sister. But ye and me bain't ne'er to be equals."

Loud stomping caused the women to separate. Edwin stood on the bottom step scraping mud from his boots. He snatched the tam from his head as he entered the room and then reached inside a coat pocket and proudly displayed the contents he held forth. "There be chickens runnin' wild, mistress. Where there be chickens, there be nests. Don't know which eggs are fresh and those not. There be a tool shed, too. Sorry to say looks like thieves stole most, but I found a 'ammer and tacks, and repaired the old coop."

Both Adel and Tilde squealed with delight. Tilde

lifted her apron to form a pouch. "Fresh eggs for the morn. 'Tis grand, bain't it, Adel?"

"It is. What else did you find, Edwin?"

He reached into the other pocket and withdrew two kittens, a calico and a gray-striped. "For the wee lass yon, if ye don't mind, mistress."

The women both cooed over the mewling tabbies, and Adel said, "It is lonely here for a child. Mary Kathryn will adore them. But they are barely weaning age. Where is the mother?"

"Wild dogs, mum. 'Twasn't a pretty sight."

"Oh, the poor orphans. We'll need milk. After we breakfast on the eggs you've provided, we shall travel to the village and buy a milk cow. Come, Tilde, we'll need a fair flood of supplies to clean this heap of stone. We'll need brooms, buckets, soap, rags, and capable workers, though we will need to be frugal, I suppose, for there is scant coin left in my purse. I do have the cheque. Edwin, I don't remember a bank in the village. Did you see one?"

The man gave her a woeful smile. "Not that I can say, mistress. 'Tis certain we've a need to go back to Galway, or maybe Cork."

After breakfast, Adel opened the trunk that held her gowns. Her choices were limited to the dress she was wearing now and the woolen ones in rich browns and grays, greens, and blues. Her fingers lingered over the one plush gown she had brought. She selected the gray dress, though it was trimmed in ebony velvet.

She wrinkled her nose with repugnance at the black grime beneath her fingernails. It would take a scrub brush and soap to get them clean. Thank goodness for gloves, she thought.

As she sifted through the layers of clothing, her hand struck a solid box. She folded all the gowns forward and attempted to lift the medium-sized metal case. She puzzled over it, for it was not hers.

"Tilde, come quick."

"Did somethin' 'appen to Mary Kathryn?"

"No, she's by the hearth, playing with the kittens."

"Then wot be the emergency?"

"Did you pack this metal box?"

"The magistrate, Lord Oxley, gave it to Edwin and instructed I should pack it with your belongings."

"Why did you not tell me?"

Tilde shrugged. "Wid all the excitement and travel, and gettin' 'ere, it plumb went out o' me noggin."

"Did Lord Oxley say what is inside?"

"Not to me."

"By its weight, I cannot imagine what it contains, for I cannot lift it. Help me."

Each woman grabbed an end handle and strained under the weight. Tilde shouted, "Edwin."

He skidded into the room. "Wot, more beasties?"

Adel laughed at the incredulous look on his face. "Did Lord Oxley say what is inside this container?"

Edwin blushed to the tip of his ears. He dug around inside his coat pocket and produced a small key. "'Is lordship said to give ye this key onct ye discovered the box. 'E said to keep me lips buttoned tight. That if anyone knew wot was inside, it would bring danger to us all."

"God's lamb. 'E said that?"

Somewhat wary, Adel inserted the small key into the tiny keyhole. Edwin and Tilde's undivided attention rested on her. She turned the key and the small click seemed to echo off the walls of the great room.

Adel's insides quaked as she lifted the metal lid. Like a heavy cloak, silence draped the large space. A quick peek caused her to slam the top shut. Her breath seemed to stop inside her throat.

Adel lifted the metal lid for another look at the pile of gold coins that seemed ready to spill from the box. "Oh, my mercy. It's…it's…oh, my mercy."

Tilde and Edwin hovered over her shoulder, their breaths warming her neck as they leaned forward to see what caused Adel's discomposure.

Adel gave them a smile despite her consternation. "Not one word of this. Do you hear me? Not a peep from either of you. Lord Oxley was correct in his warning. The contents of this box puts us all in danger."

"God's lamb, Adel. I've ne'er in the whole of me life seen so much mon…" The rest of the word drifted off into silence.

Adel lifted a finger to her lips. "Shush, not a word." Her glance darted about the room, from wall to ceiling to floor, and then to the faces of Edwin and Tilde.

"Blimey, mistress, 'tis all I kin say."

The time had come for serious investigation of the house. "We cannot go to the village without first finding a place to hide the box. A place where no miscreant will ever think to search. For it may be the very reason someone ransacked this house and then set it afire—praise be the fire did not do so very much damage—that person was looking for money. Lots of money."

Adel pivoted slowly around and surveyed the room. The remains of a log settled in the fireplace, sending a shower of sparks up the chimney. The flames dwindled, and it was as if a sneaky, insidious chill encroached upon the three of them. She mentally shook herself as she realized her mind was wandering. Taking hold of her emotions, she said, "Edwin, I'll leave you to explore the ground floor rooms, I will take the next floor, and Tilde, you the top. Search every nook and cranny."

"What be we lookin' for, mistress?" Edwin wanted to know.

Adel tapped a finger against her lip. Even she wasn't certain. "A place that is obvious, but not."

Tilde bunched her brow into a frown. "Me feeble mind bain't knowin' what ye mean."

The large tapestry hanging askew above the fireplace gave Adel the answer. She pointed. "Look, it is obvious someone thought they might find a vault behind the arras, and over there where the floor planks were pulled up."

"'At's bloody good thinkin', mistress. Now me knows what ta look fer."

Tilde agreed. "Shall I take Mary Kathryn with me?"

Another conundrum. "Mary Kathryn, you stay near the fireplace where it is warm. Take care of the kittens while we explore the house. If you get frightened or need me, shout as loud as you can, but do not leave this room. Will you do that?"

A shadow of fear brushed the child's face. She clutched the tabbies close to her chest.

A chord pinged in Adel's heart. Everyone who mattered in Mary Kathryn's life had left her. She bent and kissed the top of her head. "I'm not leaving you.

I'm just going upstairs."

"You come back?"

"Yes, and when I do, Edwin will drive us to the village for a bit of fun."

A tenuous smile quavered on the child's lips. "Yes."

Adel traced her steps up the wide stairs until she reached the second level. She shivered against the chill that pervaded the long hall. The morning sun had failed to warm the chambers with its rays, and Adel contemplated dashing downstairs to the great hearth to lay more kindling and logs upon the glowing coals. Gathering the woolen cape closer, she delayed that action while entering the room that adjoined the one she had claimed for herself.

A thin layer of rime from last night's rain had frozen into a coating over the windows that glistened and twinkled with the light of the morning sun. The chill turned Adel's breath into vapors of frosty white.

For the first time in her life she felt the need to wallow in self-pity. She had always been rather self-sufficient in the matter of her own needs, or so she thought. Now she realized the servants at Briarwood Manor had provided a multitude of comforts, both reasonable and frivolous. Stoking up a dying fire, cooking delicious meals, carrying pails of water to fill a tub for her bath—these were but a few services she had once taken for granted, but now with their absence she felt the loss. And although she could fend for herself quite adequately, she would make certain in the future to do her fair share of the work long after Mautagh Manor was returned to its former glory.

Stifling a sneeze with a slender finger until the urge

passed, she moved to a mammoth tapestry of the Celtic cross, feeling the roughness of its heavy ribbed fabric, the patterns of deep maroons and heather greens no longer rich, brilliant colors but now worn and faded from time and harsh elements. She repeated the Latin phrase tooled beneath the cross, "Fiat Lux," *Let there be light.*

She recalled Liam saying his mother despised living in Ireland, and wanted him educated away from his barbaric Irish relatives, and wondered if she had known the metaphorical meaning of *Fiat Lux*—to dispel ignorance.

Adel decided his mother, though born into British high society, must have been a mean-spirited, lame-witted woman.

She lifted aside the edge of the heavy wall hanging, and to her delight it also concealed a narrow but intricately carved and ornate door. Her curiosity piqued, she hoped whatever passage lay behind the portal had windows to help light her way. She made a mental note to purchase tapers from the village candlemaker. Then, almost lightheaded with excitement, she closed her hand around the arch-shaped metal handle. When the door didn't immediately open, she placed her shoulder against it and shoved. It inched open.

Wary of another encounter with bats, she did not expect to hear screams.

Chapter Fourteen

"Del, bad man! Bad man…get me, Del!"

Mary Kathryn's beseeching cries ripped razor-sharp claws through Adel's heart. Breath stilled in her throat and the secret door hidden behind the tapestry was forgotten.

Adel's feet flew as she ran into the hall and, swinging around the balustrade, half-stumbled, half-slid down the stairs. Her heart kept pace, and when the blond-bearded giant stepped toward a wide-eyed Mary Kathryn, Adel refused to betray her own trepidation.

Her brain seemed to chant—*A weapon…I need a weapon.* Frantic for any object to use for defense, she spied a wooden pail sitting at the base of the stairs, still filled with dirty water from last night's scrubbing. She and Tilde had been too tired to empty its contents.

Thinking only of protecting the child, Adel in one fell swoop grasped the handle, drew back, and let the sooty liquid fly. She had reared back her arm and swung with such force the momentum yanked the rope handle from her hand and, with an ominous thud, the pail found its mark square against the man's chest.

He expelled a pain-filled oath.

The sight of the colossal giant spitting and sputtering as grimy liquid covered his face and then dribbled from his beard was both comical and frightening. Adel didn't know whether to laugh or to find a place to hide. Instead, she scooped Mary Kathryn into her arms and skittered away from the man.

The growl emitted from deep in his throat reminded Adel of a caged bear she'd once seen at a traveling circus. The fierce scowl in his deep-set blue eyes did little to calm her nerves.

Panting for breath, she tried to curb the stammer in her voice as she glanced toward the large trunk that held her gowns, and the money box tucked beneath the dresses. "I-If you are a thief, we have little more than the clothes on our back."

The brusque timbre in his voice spoke of his irritation. "Are ye daft, lass, to attack a man without first askin' his name? And were I a thief, I would not strike in the broad of light, nor without my hooligans. 'Tis you who are the criminal—trespassing on private land."

It seemed foolish to challenge an irate man when it was highly probable he could accomplish whatever he might threaten to do.

Red-faced and huffing for breath, Edwin skidded into the room. He strode to Adel's side. In an authoritative voice, he said, "Who be ye, fellow, and wot be yer business?"

With Tilde standing at the landing, brandishing an ancient broom that looked as if it had seen its better days, Adel's nerves allowed her to take in the man who, though past his prime, stood like a massive oak, his stance that of a warrior, hands clenched against his broad thighs. The quality of his clothing indicated he was no peasant, his pants and jacket of the softest leather and, draped over his shoulder, a mantle of checked maroon and heather green. A sprig of holly was attached to the brat.

"Sir, I can now see by your attire that you are no laborer. However, that does not excuse you from barging into my home and frightening my stepdaughter."

He clasped a hand around his gray-streaked, tawny beard as if to wring it dry. He spoke low from his throat, his tone dark and foreboding, like that of a judge pronouncing sentence upon criminals. "I am the O'Neill, and the lot of you"—he extended his arm—"are trespassing. 'Tis sorry I am to frighten the wee *cailín*, but ye've had your night's rest. Now be on your way, or I'll be forced to oust you."

As was her wont, Adel rose to his challenge. She gave the child clinging to her neck to Tilde and then drew herself into a regal stance.

"I, sir, am Lady Adel Fitzhugh O'Shea, the wife of Captain Liam O'Shea, grandson of the late Maeve O'Neill Mautagh, and this is Mary Kathryn O'Shea, Liam's only child and my stepdaughter." Her voice trailed off at the recognition of the name O'Neill. Surely Liam had no ties to this surly knave.

The warming fire seemed to give her courage, and she returned his unwavering glare unflinchingly. "I presume you have a first name?"

He acknowledged her reply with a bland smile. "Ahern. And I presume you have proof that you are legally wed to the O'Shea?"

"I do not understand. You are the second person to call Liam the O'Shea, and you refer to yourself as the O'Neill. What does that mean?"

"I will not banter with you, lass. Prove who you are or get off the O'Shea's land before nightfall."

She tilted her chin a bit higher. "Or you'll do what?"

Without as much as a flinch, his stormy blue eyes met her challenge. He leaned forward. "I'll set the hounds on you."

A vision of snarling, slathering jaws tearing at Mary Kathryn gave Adel pause. His threat caused a chill to ripple down her spine. Folding her arms across her breasts, she tapped an irritated tattoo on the stone floor. Of a sudden, she broke her stance and pushed past him to open her portmanteau. She closed her fingers around the leather wallet that held her marriage certificate, the letter of instruction from Liam, and the cheque. She removed all but the latter.

Thrusting the papers at Ahern O'Neill, she said, "I hope you do not question the official seal of the Magistrate of London."

Without a word, he perused the matrimonial document, then focused on Liam's letter. Adel thought he took an inordinate amount of time, as if reading every word.

He folded the papers and held them until Adel shoved her hand forward. She stared, trying to interpret the shifting expressions on his face. Crow's feet lined the corners of both eyes, evidently from long hours of squinting into the sun. She imagined him on a magnificent steed, leading the charge into battle.

The resemblance was definite—both blond, both blue-eyed, both powerfully built and with a commanding aura. There was no doubting that Ahern O'Neill was a more mature version of Liam.

His voice was quiet, almost contrite, and Adel sensed the difficulty of his apology. "Your pardon,

Lady Adel. We had no word of you, or your planned arrival. We have had no word from Liam since last he visited, upon the death of my older sister, his grandmother."

"Then you are Liam's uncle."

"Aye."

Adel looked around the room for a suitable chair. "I'm afraid we haven't much to offer in the way of comfort. At least not until we hire craftsmen to make new furniture. Can you tell me what caused the fire?"

"Aye, there is much to tell—another time. My home is but a half-day's ride. If we start now, we will arrive by nightfall. 'Tis shame I bring upon the O'Neill name to not provide comforts for the O'Shea's family and servants."

It was almost as if Tilde read Adel's mind. Before allowing the girl to retort, she laid a hand upon Adel's arm and gave the slightest of nods toward the travel trunk. Adel heeded Tilde's warning. "We would be most grateful to accept your hospitality. Edwin will hitch the horses to the carriage."

He glanced about the room. "Are there more trunks upstairs?"

Adel placed her hands behind her back and, like a naughty child, crossed her fingers for telling a fib. "There was not much time to pack before Liam's ship sailed for India. Out of necessity, we had to pack light in order to make good travel time."

The plight with her stepbrother was no one's business but her own.

Ahern O'Neill hefted one large travel chest upon his broad shoulder and grasped the other as if it weighed nothing at all.

Adel and Tilde exchanged covert glances. They had not had time to find a hiding place for the money.

****

Before accepting Edwin's offer to hand her into the carriage, Adel viewed the scene around her. The crisp salty air poured into her lungs. Hugging her cloak tight against the morning chill, she smiled at the landscape's breathtaking beauty. The splendor that had been shrouded in darkness upon their late yester-evening arrival no longer appeared ill-omened.

"Except for the damage to the house, it is the most glorious place I've ever seen. Look at the cliffs, Tilde." Adel spread her arms wide as if to embrace the whole world and everyone in it.

The wind whipped across the majestic crags. Golden beams of sunlight slanted down from the west, polishing the patches of snow into glittering flecks of gold, and the surf beat upon the escarpment's stone walls.

Adel fingered away strands of hair that tangled with the lusty wind and brushed across her eyes. Laughing aloud, she turned to Ahern O'Neill. "Liam said the sea was as wild and savage as the old Celtic warriors. I believe I shall like living at Mautagh Manor."

"Aye, lass, but there are times when the sea is unforgiving, much like the chieftains whose blood gives life to the land they fought to tame and to keep. Mautagh Manor needs new blood. New life."

Adel breathed in the intoxicating sea breeze. "Is it not glorious? I should like to sketch Mautagh as it is, and each step of progress, as a history for Mary Kathryn and perhaps her children."

Wearing a wistful smile, Tilde agreed. "Aye, and once the house is rebuilt, 'twill be a grand place for Mary Kathryn, and for the captain when he returns from India."

The mention of Liam created an awkward silence broken only when Ahern O'Neill's deep voice commanded, "We've a long ride. Let us be on our way."

Giving the snow-stained meadows and the sun-swept sky one last look, Adel accepted Edwin's assistance and clambered inside the carriage, followed by the child and Tilde.

Mary Kathryn cried, "Del, my kitties…my kitties."

Adjusting the child in her lap, Adel beseeched Edwin. "Oh, the poor dears are too young to survive on their own. Edwin, if you please."

Without hesitation he jogged up the steps and into the house. He returned to the coach and gave custody of two mewling tabbies to a smiling Mary Kathryn.

With every jolting, grinding turn of the carriage's wheels over the stony roads, Adel lost a little more of her infatuation with the landscape and again questioned her sanity in becoming an independent woman. To add to her suffering, every dip and jerk of the conveyance seemed to mock her growing discomfort.

"God's lamb, Adel, I fear there shan't be a place on me poor body that isn't bruised from one end ta th' other."

Adel tried to offer a comforting smile, which ended on a groan. "The O'Neill said we would arrive after dark. The stars are out. Surely we won't have to bear this torture much longer."

She paused and then leaned forward, her voice a

mere whisper. "We must not allow any of the servants near the trunk."

"Bain't ye worried 'bout that. I'll see that nary a one sets a hand on it."

"Tilde, I plan to tell the O'Neill that you are my adopted sister. I don't see the necessity of secrecy."

"No, ye mustn't. We're strangers to this land. We bain't know 'ow these folks think on such things. Why, 'is Lordship Fitzhugh would fair 'ave a conniption and fall in it were he to know. Be patient, Adel."

Tilde then offered a crafty smile. "'Sides, servants live to gossip. Ye ne'er know wot secrets I might find out 'bout Mautagh Manor."

Adel admitted she loved a good intrigue. "Oh, but you are a sly one, aren't you? I like the direction of your thinking."

By full nightfall the spring snow had thickened, settling like downy white feathers on both sides of the roadway. As the darkness deepened, Adel peered out the carriage window. There was no sign of an inn, a cottage, or even a barn. Only the sound of Edwin snapping the reins on the horses' backs and the crunching of the carriage wheels on the road broke the silence.

Edwin called down, "The O'Neill has ridden ahead to alert his household of our arrival."

Mary Kathryn whimpered. "I hungry, Del."

Adel commiserated with the child. Benefits of the surprise bounty of eggs Edwin had discovered earlier that morning, scrambled by Tilde for their breakfast, had long disappeared. She listened to the grumbles in Mary Kathryn's stomach. "I'm certain the O'Neill's home isn't much farther. As soon as we arrive, I will request a glass of warm milk to hold you until we sit at the table."

Without further word, the child snuggled closer to Adel, as if accustomed to bouts of doing without.

In answer to her unspoken prayer, a long blast from a ram's horn sounded eerily across the night, accompanied by the onset of howling and baying dogs. Ahern O'Neill's earlier threat about setting the hounds on her formed knots in the pit of her stomach.

She drew back the leather curtain and was greeted by what appeared to be a swarm of flickering fireflies.

She gathered the child closer. "I hope he has a keeper to call the dogs before we alight from the coach."

Mary Kathryn's voice trembled. "Dogs get my kitties, Del?"

She smoothed her hand over the child's head. "We'll keep the kittens safe, my sweet girl."

The coach halted, and all those inside waited for the door to open. Ahern O'Neill held high a torch. Next to him stood a slender woman, near equal his height. In the firelight, she appeared neither young nor old.

Her smile inviting and genuine, she nodded slightly and then swept her hand toward the house. "Welcome to Cathmor. I am Eveleen O'Neill. Our home is at your disposal until Mautagh Manor is made livable. Now come, the table awaits, and if your appetites are like the O'Neill's, then you must all be famished."

"We welcome your hospitality, my Lady Eveleen. If you please, may I request a glass of warm milk for my stepdaughter? She is but three years of age and has not eaten since we broke our fast this morning."

Eveleen O'Neill called a servant forward and asked

that a request be sent to the kitchen for a glass of warm milk, sweetened with honey.

"Ahern did say there was a wee one. I hope you do not mind a bit of sweetening for the *cailín*? Now come, the house is much warmer."

The darkness hid the nervousness on Adel's face. "The dogs, are they dangerous? I mean, is it safe for us to depart the coach?"

Her voice brisk, Eveleen commanded, "Ahern, call the blasted dogs. Would you frighten our guests half out of their wits?" Without drawing a breath, the Irish woman said, "Once they get to know you, the dogs will become more of a nuisance, always under foot. But 'tis wise to keep a few about."

Eveleen lifted her skirts, and Adel, with Tilde carrying Mary Kathryn, followed up the stone steps.

Inside the great hall, wall sconces perhaps twelve feet apart provided light along the rounded wall.

Succulent aromas teased Adel's senses, and her stomach squeezed with hunger. At one end of the grand hall a table, long enough to seat a small army, sat laden with food. She did a mental count of the chairs— fifteen. In front of each chair sat stoneware and goblets. Another mental count—with the four of them, the O'Neill, and his wife, the count came to six, but as servants, Tilde and Edwin would dine in the kitchen. Then who were the others? She scanned the room and seeming apparitions appeared from the shadows. Tall men, chattering women, and children from ages of youth to near adult came to stand one behind each chair as if it were a designated place at the table.

Eveleen said, "This is my daughter-in-law, Mada. She will show your lady's maid and manservant the kitchen."

Adel protested, "But they are not my…"

Edwin stepped forward with the heaviest of Adel's trunks. "Afore we take our sup, would ye be pleased to direct me to my mistress's sleeping quarters? Me wife would like to see to our lady's necessities."

He winked at Mary Kathryn. "I'll take care of the kittens, too."

Adel gathered Mary Kathryn in her arms as she watched Tilde and Edwin climb stairs that led to the upper level. Once again they had saved her from her own impetus.

She started at the slight touch on her arm. Eveleen's smile was genuine as she directed Adel and Mary Kathryn to empty seats at the massive table. "Come, meet your family."

"I beg you forgive my ignorance, Eveleen, but a question, if you please."

"You may ask anything and I shall try to answer."

"What does it mean when Liam is referred to as the O'Shea and your husband as the O'Neill?"

In the brighter lights Adel didn't miss the glint of pride in eyes that reminded her of emeralds. There was a hint of laughter in Eveleen's voice. "Each county in Ireland has its own clan leader. Of royal bloodlines, he is like a king or a monarch. In our country, he rules by his name. Only the firstborn son inherits the title. Now do you understand?"

This was another surprise for Adel, another discovery about her husband. He was royalty in two countries. She wondered why he would give it all up to be a mere captain in the Queen's service.

"I have much to learn about the ways of Ireland.

May I depend on you for guidance?"

"As if you were my own daughter. Come, let us satisfy our appetites."

After a hearty meal of roasted lamb, boiled potatoes, soda bread, and ale, Adel was shown to her room. She lay propped against the pillows in a bed large enough for three adults. Next to her, Mary Kathryn was curled in a ball, soundly sleeping. A smile curved Adel's lips as she held her graphite instrument above a sheaf of parchment. The room bright from tallow candles, her hand moved with rapid but precise strokes as she sketched the child's image. Satisfied with her accomplishment, she powdered the paper to keep the carbon from smearing and then set it aside.

She then dipped a quill pen into the bottle of ink. She pondered a moment before writing.

3 March 1854

Dear Captain O'Shea,

We have arrived safely in Connemara. Presently, we are residing at Cathmor, the home of your uncle, the O'Neill. It saddens me to say that Mautagh Manor has fallen on hard times. There was a fire and then hooligans stole many treasures, and what livestock they did not slaughter was apparently sold. The O'Neill caught and duly punished the thieves and retrieved many of your family heirlooms. I fear the house needs extensive repairs to make it habitable.

There is a mystery about the fire. No one seems to know if it was deliberately set or caused by an accident. The other mystery seems to involve the yearly stipend you send.

Ahern and Eveleen believed you had deserted responsibilities to your heritage and were dismayed when I informed them otherwise. I have already penned a letter to Magistrate Oxley making him aware to send no further funds to the barrister charged with receiving the money for the upkeep of Mautagh Manor.

Though your aunt and uncle welcomed us into their home, we are, nonetheless, strangers. It is for this reason I tread with caution before making accusations of duplicity toward the barrister.

Mary Kathryn endured the trip to Ireland quite well for a child of such youth. She thrives but is still rather timid, though I believe meeting her cousins will help free her from the shell she hides in.

I do not write this missive to cause you consternation. You have charged me with a grave responsibility, and I feel it is my duty to keep you apprised of all details, from smallest to largest. Never doubt that I will honor our agreement until you arrive home.

As I am not familiar with Ireland's method of posting mail or how often the mail ship runs, I shall send several letters in one package. And as I do not know the postal situation in India, I shan't expect to hear often from you.

Please extend my regards to Robby. I wish you both good health.

Your faithful servant,
Adel Fitzhugh O'Shea

Staring at her marital name, she ran her tongue across her lips, trying to recapture the taste of the kiss she had shared with Liam. A kiss that had made her feel more like a courtesan than a demure wife. She closed her eyes and sighed, hugging a plump pillow to her chest and feeling as if she needed to cool her fiery cheeks with a splash of water.

Inhaling to release the tension from her body, she carefully folded the letter and the drawing of Mary Kathryn and tucked it inside a leather sachet.

Her last thought before sleep overtook her was how it would feel to lie in Liam's arms, to have his hands touch her private places.

Eyes closed, she envisioned the planes of Liam's face. Tomorrow she would sketch his likeness before it faded from her memory.

Chapter Fifteen

The aroma of eggs, sausage, and baked bread wafted from the breakfast room. Adel's stomach churned, not from hunger but from anticipation of her new role as the wife of the O'Shea. How would she be looked upon—with respect or hatred? Instinct told her she would need to remain firm but fair to earn respect.

Tilde's signature knock at the bedroom door alerted Adel. The child cuddled under the covers opened her eyes and offered a sleepy yawn. She crawled from the quilt and whispered in Adel's ear.

After a brief hug, Adel assisted Mary Kathryn to the chamber pot while Tilde laid out fresh garments. "Is everyone up and about, Tilde? I shouldn't want Lady Eveleen to think I'm a lay-abed-laggard."

"The O'Neil and his sons broke fast early this morning. Edwin is riding with them to Mautagh to assess the damages and estimate the repairs. Her ladyship's maid is dressing her lady now."

Tilde tended Mary Kathryn while Adel slipped into her own gown and waited for assistance with the long row of buttons up the back. "Did you and Edwin rest well last night? Were you warm enough?"

"Don't you be frettin' yourself on our account. The O'Neills treat their staff as if they were family." She offered a reassuring wink. As she fastened the dress, she leaned close so the words she spoke were for Adel's ears only.

"Edwin has figured a way to hide the...the, you-know-what."

Adel expelled a small gasp. "Do tell me—where?"

"'Tis as you said. 'Twill be right under your nose, but nobody will ever know, and be at your fingertips, too, when needed."

Adel twisted to face Tilde. Curious, she whispered, "You look like a cat toying with a mouse. Don't keep me in suspense."

Again, Tilde whispered. Adel's eyes widened, and she smiled as she put her hands together in a silent clap. "That is perfectly ingenious. Oh, Tilde, Edwin is a real treasure. But when will he undertake this task? Surely not here?"

Adel's newly adopted sister paused, her gaze sweeping the room toward the largest of Adel's travel trunks. "No, not here. Afraid it'll draw suspicion for him to ask for the necessary wood to build the false bottom in yonder chest. It can wait 'til we return to Mautagh Manor."

Adel patted the key that hung suspended from a ribbon around her neck. "In the meantime, I shall keep the trunk locked. And the"—she mouthed the word—"*coins*, will be hidden at the bottom, with winter dresses and cloaks piled on top. No one will be the wiser."

After brushing her long silken strands and securing them in a neat chignon, Adel took Mary Kathryn's hand. "Join us for the morning meal, Tilde."

The woman met Adel with a stern gaze. "Be patient, Adel. When you are mistress of your own house, then ye can make the rules. 'Tain't the proper thing to do when yer the guest under another's roof."

Sighing in profound frustration, Adel deferred. "As usual, you have much more foresight than I."

Taking her leave, she hesitated at the bottom of the staircase, letting her gaze sweep the room. Lady Eveleen sat at the head of the long oak table. "I am quite alone," Eveleen offered. "Your manservant has ridden with my husband and sons to take stock of what repairs are needed to make Mautagh Manor livable, and the older children and my daughters-in-law are attending their own duties, with one of them in charge of the youngest members of the family."

With a sweep of her hand she invited Adel to partake of the food laid out on the table. Nodding, Adel seated Mary Kathryn in her lap and filled a plate.

Eveleen dabbed her lips with a crisp linen napkin, settling her gaze on Adel. "Tell me about Liam, and what type of man he has become. I scarce remember him, for he was very young when his mother took him to England."

A lump formed in Adel's bone-dry throat. She stumbled over a few possible replies, none of which would do. How could she explain that her recent marriage was a business arrangement and not one born of love?

She felt Eveleen watching her, studying her. Waiting for an answer. Adel refused to look at the woman. How could she? She was afraid Eveleen would see the guilt in her eyes. She swallowed over her heart, now thundering in her ears.

Eveleen's gaze made her uncomfortable for what seemed like a long, agonizing moment before she finally nodded and reached for a cup of tea. "I sense that all is not as it seems, Adel. Arranged marriages are not always perfect. But I am curious. You refer to the child as your stepdaughter. Then Liam is a widower?"

Adel cleared her throat. She didn't want to talk about this—not with Eveleen. Not with anyone.

The older woman touched her hand. "You are not very skilled at hiding your emotions. I see the subject is difficult for you."

Adel shifted in the high-backed chair, her nerves stretched taut.

Eveleen's voice was quiet. "Whatever is causing you such distress, be assured that no one who lives under this roof will pass ill-judgment over you."

Adel nodded hesitantly as she tried to sort through all the recent events in her life, events which had brought her to Mautagh Manor. She mentally shook herself and realized her mind was wandering. Taking a firm hold on her emotions, she related her stepbrother's intentions of marrying her to a man of more than fifty years in age, a man infected with the dreaded syphilis. She told of how she had planned to spend the rest of her life with the nuns at St. Francis, and how a storm had brought Liam to Briarwood. When he explained he was taking Mary Kathryn to live with the nuns until his return from India, she saw the opportunity to escape the dreaded marriage by offering her services as governess to the child.

Her hands clasped in a knot and her eyes focused on the empty plate set in front of her, Adel continued. "Liam feared that, if he never returned from India, a mere governess would not have legal authority to protect Mary Kathryn's financial interests. So you see our marriage is merely a business arrangement. It was never…consummated."

Eveleen was quiet for a moment. "What about the child's mother?"

Mary Kathryn, who had remained silent, carefully set her cup of milk aside. She looked up at Adel and said, "My mommy is in heaven with Del's mommy."

Adel kissed the top of the child's head. "She's very astute for one so young."

"That she is. Oho, your lady's maid is here."

Adel twisted in her chair and watched Tilde descending the stairs. The woman smiled. "If Mary Kathryn is finished eating, I thought she might like to play with the younger children."

Adel lifted the child from her lap. "Would you like that, Mary Kathryn?"

The little girl rewarded her with a dimpled smile and reached to clasp Tilde's hand. As soon as the two were out of sight, Eveleen said, "Tell me about the child's mother."

With a dispirited sigh, Adel continued. "I don't know much about her. Liam never spoke her name. All I can tell you is she was a poor girl from the slums and unable to find quality employment. Her family had fallen on difficult times. To help earn money, she worked in a house of ill-repute. When Liam discovered that he was her first customer," Adel's voice dropped to a whisper, "and that he'd stolen her virginity, he was mortally ashamed. After that first time, Liam never saw her again, nor heard from her, not until a few months ago, when he received a note from the girl saying she was dying, and that she had borne him a daughter. By the time he arrived, the consumption had claimed the girl's life. Liam formally adopted Mary Kathryn to make certain no one could ever dispute her as his legal heir."

The jewel-blue eyes that stared back at Adel were filled with compassion. "How could Liam be certain the child was his?"

"I asked the same question. His answer was, 'You have only to look at Mary Kathryn. There is no disputing I am her father.' "

Eveleen seemed to consider Adel's answer. She broke into a wide smile. "Indeed, Mary Kathryn is the image of all the Mautaghs. And if you look at my sons, and grandchildren, they all possess the red hair and blue eyes of our ancestors, as well as the trademark dimple. Aye, Mary Kathryn is truly of our bloodline."

Adel made a move to stand, but Eveleen clasped her hand. "Set your mind at ease, Adel. No matter the circumstance that brought you and the child to us, I believe God ordained it, and what God ordains, we accept without question. With Liam away, you are his representative and will serve as the O'Shea of the Connemara Mautagh clan. The title comes with a weighty responsibility."

An overwhelming uncertainty moved through Adel. She chastised herself for those feelings. She had accomplished what she had set out to accomplish. Yet she'd found another situation. Doubt overshadowed the joy she wanted to feel. "What do you mean, I am the O'Shea? I don't understand."

Eveleen filled Adel's plate with scrambled eggs and sausage. She filled her cup with tea. "As lady of this house, I command that you eat. You cannot fulfill your duties without strength, and make no mistake, the duties are endless."

She pointed to the fork and made no move to speak further until Adel finished every morsel on the plate and then held her cup out for a refill.

Eveleen's regard turned to Adel. "As the present O'Shea, you are the ruler of your clan, much like a queen. The people are like your children. You will tend to all their needs—food, shelter, clothing, education. You will oversee matchmaking, weddings, birth of their children, when sickness strikes you provide for their doctoring. When disputes arise, you settle them, and when a misdeed is committed, you enact the punishment according to the severity of the crime."

Adel shoved aside the hopelessness waiting to surge through her. "I saw no people. What happened to them? And most of all, how does a woman gain the respect of those who will hate Liam, thinking he has abandoned them?"

When Eveleen rose from the chair, she hugged Adel. "You stood your ground against your stepbrother, you boldly asserted yourself and assumed the responsibility of a small child, and then you traveled across land and water only to find the magnificent home you envisioned a ghost of itself. Did you run away? No, you set about cleaning and looking for a way to rebuild."

Eveleen stopped long enough to laugh. "And when you thought my Ahern was a hooligan, you dared to pick up a bucket of dirty water and clobber him."

Adel clasped her hand to her mouth. "I am mortified at my actions, but I must say the look of surprise on his face was priceless."

Once she gained control of her laughter, a look of admiration was evident upon Eveleen's face. "You are a woman of strength. You are intelligent, and you are not afraid to face the uncertainties. Rest assured, problems will arise, and there will be those who will challenge your authority, especially because you are a woman. Always rule with a firm but fair hand. In time, the respect will follow. And as for the people, some joined our clan, others scattered to find work. Don't worry, Adel. Word has already spread far and wide. They will come home."

Adel rested her cheek on Eveleen's shoulder. "I can count on you and Ahern for support?"

Eveleen pulled away. Her smile was genuine. "We are family. Does that answer your question?"

Adel drew herself up; a sense of duty and honor, and distress, filled her. She met the answer with a deep curtsey. "More than you know."

Chapter Sixteen

Days later, Adel stood in the kitchen alongside Mada, the eldest of the O'Neill daughters-in-law. "Promise you and the other sisters will visit when I return to Mautagh. I shall miss all of you."

Before the woman had time to answer, Eveleen appeared at the door. "Adel, come into the great hall. There is someone who wishes to speak with the O'Shea."

Little worms of apprehension curled in Adel's stomach. "Oh, dear, what must I do?"

Mada laughed. "The first thing you should do is wash the dough from your hands, and remove the apron from your gown."

Still flustered, Adel turned in a complete circle. "Yes, remove the apron, wash my hands. Eveleen, who is it? What does this person want?"

"Calm yourself. The lad poses no threat. He warms himself before the hearth. Remember, firm but fair."

Adel shook her head in wonder that someone had actually requested an audience with her. She rinsed the floury dough from her hands and then removed the apron and hung it on a wall peg before following Eveleen into the great hall.

A young lad stood close to the hearth. He looked as if a strong wind might pick him up and blow him hither and yon. Behind his deep brown eyes, he bore the expression of someone older than his years. Someone who had not known an easy life.

Adel rubbed the palms of her hands down the sides of her skirt. She drew a deep breath. This was merely a scrawny boy, not a bearded man wrapped in furs waiting to challenge her authority.

She walked forward. Her diminutive stature barely reached the lad's shoulder. "I am the O'Shea. Who might you be?"

The boy snatched the woolen tam from his head. "Me name be Shamus Murphy, mum."

Adel motioned for him to sit. He shook his head in refusal. "Well then, Shamus Murphy, what can I do for you?"

"I heard the O'Shea were a woman. Din't believe it." Then, as if realizing he had over-spoken himself, he hurried on. "I was born at Mautagh. Me da was smithy. 'E's been waitin' for the O'Shea to return, so we can return, too. I am a fair 'and wid 'orses, mum."

Adel cut her eyes toward Eveleen, who gave a near invisible nod of approval.

"Where is your mother, Shamus Murphy?"

The boy twisted the cap in his grimy hands. "Her died when I was but a wee lad. There be just me and me da. We're both hale and hearty. We don't 'spect no money, only bread and bed, and mayhap a roof. T'would be welcome, if ye can spare it. We'll work hard for our keep, me ledy."

Though he was not begging, the silent plea in his eyes tugged at Adel's heart. She thought of what life might have been for Mary Kathryn had Liam not rescued her.

"When was the last time you ate, Shamus?"

He shrugged. The cloth of his shirt was threadbare enough for Adel to imagine how the boy must suffer during the cold nights. His silence was answer enough.

Adel looked at Eveleen. "May I?"

"As long as our larder is full, we will turn no one away."

Adel smiled. "Follow me to the kitchen, Shamus. I can't have my first clansman trekking to Mautagh Manor on an empty stomach."

While he savored a cup of milk, Adel buttered two slices of bread and cut a hunk of cheese. She then wrapped more buttered bread, slices of cold mutton, and cheese in a cloth. "This is for you and your father. I wish to charge you with a grave responsibility. Are you up to the task?"

"Anything, mum. You are the O'Shea."

"Good. I am in need of a cook, someone with special skills for creating tasty meals. I will also need a gardener, a herdsman, and someone who can spin wool. Do you know of such?"

"Aye, mum. I do."

"If they are dishonest, or sickly, or laggards, or rabble, do not bring them to my door. I will not tolerate those who create trouble, nor those who expect handouts without giving an honest day's work." She placed her hands on her hips and stood firm. She looked him square in the eye. "I am placing my trust in you, Shamus Murphy. Do not misuse it."

"I won't, mum. You can trust me and me da."

"Finish eating, then. I need to pen a message for you to take to Master Edwin Trumble at Mautagh."

Adel hurried from the kitchen and up the stairs to her bedroom. She quickly wrote a note to Edwin explaining the duties she had charged to Shamus.

He appears to be an honest lad. Go with him and use your good judgment in deciding if the people he chooses are worthy of employment at Mautagh. I have informed Shamus that you have the last say.

Tilde sends her love. We are both anxious to see the improvements to the house.

She signed it simply—*Adel.*

A few minutes later she returned to the kitchen. "I've arranged for the loan of a good horse. Mind you do not abuse the animal. Ride to Mautagh and give this letter to Master Trumble. He is a trustworthy man, and my longtime friend. He will accompany you on your rounds to locate the people who used to live on Mautagh land. If he questions your judgment, do not take offense. He is wise and knowledgeable in the way of humans and animals. As you have asked me to trust you, I ask you to do the same with Master Trumble. Do you have any questions?"

Shamus brushed crumbs from his mouth, then finished the last drop of milk. He gathered the cloth-wrapped bundle of food and stuffed it inside his shirt. "You din't say you needed a smithy."

Adel placed her hand on his shoulder. "Although I am not in immediate need of a smithy, would you know of a craftsman skilled in furniture making?"

"Oh, aye, mum. Me da is the best there is. If ye can draw 'im a picture, 'e can make it."

Adel lifted her eyebrows in question as she glanced toward Eveleen.

Eveleen pointed toward an ornate corner cupboard, a cradle, and a rocking horse. "The boy speaks the truth about his father's talents."

Adel studied the pieces, not replying at first. "How old are you, Shamus?"

She watched him count on his fingers. "As close as I can remember, I have seen sixteen winters."

"Well, then, Shamus, I would not separate a son from his father."

The boy's wide grin was reward enough for Adel. "Be off with you. It is a long ride, but mind my words: do not ride the horse into the ground. Not if you expect to be the master of my stables."

The boy's smile broadened. "I will treat him as if he were me own prized 'orse, my ledy."

She watched the boy race from the room. "He is very young. I hope I have judged his character well."

With a familiarity no woman, save Tilde, had ever shown her, Eveleen hooked her arm through Adel's and preceded toward the kitchen. "Respect from your people is most important. Never fear that Shamus won't spread the word. You've just earned your first trust."

The smile slid from Adel's face. She sobered her expression. If she had truly earned her first trust, there was no better time than now to test it.

"Eveleen, is there a sheriff in the village, or is Ahern the law?"

"There is a sheriff. Why do you ask?"

"Do you know a barrister named Fiske Barclay?"

"How do you know Barclay?"

"I believe he is a thief."

Eveleen's expression, her eyes, her entire demeanor confirmed Adel's suspicions. Anger throbbed with each pulse beat against her temples.

"This is a serious accusation, Adel. Why do you

make it?"

"While traveling from my home to London, Liam recounted how he had arranged with Magistrate Oxley to send a yearly stipend for the upkeep of the house and to issue payment to those who worked the lands. This person was to also collect the rents from the tenant farmers and use the money for other necessities pertaining to the estate, as well as pay himself an agreed-upon amount. The man charged with this responsibility is Fiske Barclay, Barrister and resident of Connemara. Now do you understand why I call him a thief?"

Eveleen's eyes widened as if surprised by the vehemence in Adel's voice. "This is most disturbing, Adel. Barclay returned to England a few days after the fire. He said there was no more reason for him to remain in Ireland, especially since he had an opportunity to expand his law practice."

Adel spoke through gritted teeth. "Indeed! And on Liam's money. I'll wager Fiske Barclay saw an opportunity to fill his pockets, shirk his responsibilities, and leave Connemara with no one being the wiser. And while I'm wagering, I believe it possible the loathsome scoundrel either set fire to Mautagh himself or hired someone to do the dastardly deed for him."

Eveleen's eyes widened another fraction. "Aye, 'tis possible, all that you say. I remember Barclay's eyes were cold, and black as peat. You can never trust a man with eyes like a serpent's. Innis Foley is the sheriff in Clifden. He has distant ties to the O'Neills, and he is an honest man, but a force to be reckoned with when a crime can be proven. What do you plan, Adel?"

Adel compressed her mouth into a straight line. "If

Barclay has returned to England, then there is nothing the sheriff can do. But I can. One moment." She raced to the back door and shouted to young Shamus just as he rode from the paddock. "Shamus, a word, please."

The lad walked the horse to where she stood. "Somethin' be the matter, mum?"

"I'm so happy you hadn't left yet. Forget the message that you are to give to Edwin Trumble. Instead, tell him it is urgent he return to Cathmor. Listen to me carefully, Shamus. I must send Master Trumble on an important errand. He may be gone for several days, perhaps weeks. You've said I can trust you. Prove it by carrying out the duties of bringing me honest workers. Can you do that?"

She bit back her own smile as she watched the boy struggle to contain the grin that threatened to spread from ear to ear.

"Aye, me ledy. You can trust me and me da to do right by ya."

"Then be off. You've a good day's ride ahead of you. Mind what I've said about winding the horse."

Shamus grabbed a hank of mane and swung easily into the saddle. "Aye, mum." He gave a last nod.

Adel stood in the yard watching him canter the sturdy Connemara pony in the direction of Mautagh Manor. With Eveleen's words playing a most ominous tune in her mind, she massaged her throbbing temples as she climbed the steps to the kitchen and walked to the great hall.

Tilde was immediately at her side, concern etching her features. "Wot be your plan, Adel?"

Adel's dark brows drew over narrowed eyes. "My personal preference is to see the rogue hang from the gallows. If that isn't possible, then I plan to see that Fiske Barclay spends the rest of his miserable life in Newgate Prison."

"If ye ask me, 'angin's too good for the blighter. I 'ear tell the rats in Newgate is big as tomcats. Maybe whilst they be chewing on 'is sorry hide, he'll think twice 'bout living off the backs of the honest folks 'e's cheated."

Eveleen smiled, and not the kind of smile reserved for her family. This one held a trace of ire. "Pray he never return to Ireland, for there will be no rock big enough to hide him. Ahern has a special punishment for the likes of Barclay."

The urgency of Adel's situation had her mind working furiously. "If you will both excuse me, I need to pen a letter to Magistrate Oxley, posthaste."

Eveleen said, "Barclay is a barrister. What if the courts show favoritism toward him?"

Adel shrugged. "There will be no favoritism, I assure you, for Magistrate Oxley is Liam's maternal uncle."

"Liam's mother was…stand-offish. There was little she liked about our country, or us as her family. I hope the uncle is not as churlish and will come to your aid."

Adel choked back a sardonic laugh. "I've known Lord Oxley only a short time, and yet I have faith that when Fiske Barclay stands before the Court he will rue the day he decided to embezzle from Liam. Lord Oxley favors his nephew greatly."

She lifted her skirts and raced up the stairs to her room. With her thoughts barreling back and forth like a runaway carriage, she wrote a letter to the magistrate, sparing no details.

A thousand words of explanation sprang to her lips as she pulled another sheet of paper from the leather portfolio. Dipping the quill pen into the inkwell, she battled with whether to inform Liam now or wait until Fiske Barclay was caught and punished.

Her head bent to the task, the scratching of the pen seemed unduly loud in the quiet of her sitting room.

Chapter Seventeen

As Edwin digested Adel's words, he came straight up in his seat, his hands finding the curved arms of the chair. Though his voice was laced with venom, he spoke softly. "Whatever it takes, milady, the bugger will pay if I 'ave to hunt 'im down meself."

Adel handed him a list of supplies to fill while in London, and a pouch of gold for the trip. "Stay as long as needed. I've requested that Lord Oxley provide you with room and found, a request I am certain he will honor. Explain that I have written my suspicions to Captain O'Shea."

As she made to leave, she turned back. "And one last request. I promised to bring Mrs. Bliss to Ireland if I had need of a cook."

Edwin grinned. "'Twill be like 'ome wid Mrs. Bliss and her mister at Mautagh. That be for certain."

She looked over at Tilde, watching as a soft blush feathered her adopted sister's cheeks. "I'll leave the two of you to your farewells."

Ahern O'Neill had sat as a quiet observer throughout Adel's explanations to Edwin. His brows furrowed in anger, the sound of his fist slamming into the palm of his hand caused Adel to jump in surprise. "I am to blame for not listening to my instincts about Barclay. Were he here, I would lop off his head and hang it from the tip of my spear."

Adel countered, "Unless you are a mind reader, Ahern, you cannot fault yourself. What was destroyed, we will rebuild. The house, though it may not be as grandiose as in her glory day, will be comfortable and welcoming. We will work the land, and I shall purchase a stallion and two mares from the Arab country. We will raise blooded horses such as the world has never seen. Mary Kathryn and Liam deserve no less."

Ahern's large calloused hand lay gentle on Adel's shoulder. She was very conscious of the compassion in this giant warrior's eyes. "And you, too, Adel." He folded her into a bear hug. "We are proud to call you family."

****

The days seemed to pass rapidly as Adel settled into the O'Neills' daily regimen. She no longer felt like a stranger and had come to enjoy her daily walks with Mada and with Eveleen's other daughters-in-law. She thrilled at Mary Kathryn's giggles when playing games with her cousins. But while the little girl blossomed Liam was missing many precious moments with his child, so Adel chronicled the daily events in her journal, sketched miniatures of Mary Kathryn, and wrote letters to Liam which she kept together with a neatly tied bow. She would post them on her next trip into the village.

Life was good.

Almost.

Where was Shamus? A fortnight had passed without his appearance and without word from him. She rationalized that perhaps the boy could neither read nor write. Yet, was there no one he could send to Cathmor with a message to speak of his progress in locating reliable souls to work at Mautagh Manor?

Today, thick fog settled over the countryside, obscuring the distant hills until they became vague, dark shapes. At times they disappeared altogether, consumed by a mass of whitish gray. Gazing out from her windows, Adel had an eerie feeling that she was marooned atop a mist-shrouded pinnacle set apart in a faraway universe and she would never again know the comfort of England and home. England—home—Briarwood? Not after her stepbrother's hateful words.

With an effort of sheer will, she shook off the dismal gloom and busied herself with writing an entry in her journal.

Only sheer desperation will cause me to return to England, though I vow to never step foot in Briarwood Manor again. Reginald Fitzhugh, be damned.

A shudder rippled through her as the bloated, piggy-eyed face of Baron Wishingham floated before her eyes. She closed the journal and inserted the small key into the lock, securing her words from prying eyes.

She drew out a sheet of parchment and a charcoal pencil, then bent her head to sketching. As she envisioned Mautagh in its current state, she drew until satisfied that she had captured the fire-scorched walls, the collapsed third-floor roof, the overgrown hedgerows, the shamble of outbuildings, and all of it set against ominous gray clouds.

Every now and then she would catch a faint melody drifting up from below, where Mada lent her voice to song. From one of the lower rooms, Cait, the youngest of the daughters-in-law, added her own harmony to the tune. The sounds reassured Adel, and yet the weeks since Liam's departure grew long, and she became aware she was losing the vision of his fine features. She had hoped to paint him in the privacy of her own solarium at Mautagh. It seemed that day might never arrive.

She was puzzled by the feeling of emptiness that pervaded her conscience, as if she needed his presence to give life to her existence.

Though she struggled to deny the evidence of her own emotions, she was beginning to realize that in their days of travel together she had grown accustomed to Liam's company and actually missed him now he was gone.

Tilde had divulged few secrecies about the intimate moments she shared with Edwin, but it was clear she pined for her husband. Adel desired to know those feelings. She vowed that when Liam returned from India she would share his bed and his life as a proper wife should.

She stood and stretched to relieve her cramped muscles, then laid her drawings on the bed. When a knock sounded at the door, without looking up she simply said, "Enter."

Mada was quick to spot the collage, and her mouth lifted into a smile. "These are amazing. I envy your talent."

Adel, pleased with the compliment, watched as the girl lifted each picture. "You have your own talent. I admire your baking skills. I fear nothing I prepare will ever taste as good as your sweet confections."

The girl stood quiet, staring at the drawings, so quiet that Adel asked, "Is something troubling you, Mada?"

As if embarrassed, the girl placed her hands against her cheeks. "I've made a fresh apple tartlet with warmed honey, and a pot of tea. Would you join the other sisters and me? I believe Tilde needs a bit of cheering. It has been ten days since her Edwin's departure."

"You've tantalized my taste buds all morning with those wonderful aromas. You won't have to ask me twice."

As she turned to leave, Mada touched Adel's arm. Her voice soft and uncertain. "It is Eveleen and Ahern's anniversary soon. We sisters have labored over what gift to give them. Now that I've seen your drawings, a portrait of Eveleen and Ahern would be the perfect present." She cut her eyes toward the drawings on the bed. "We've collected enough coin to pay."

"It's a wonderful idea, and no, I will not accept money from you. The gift will be from all of us. But you must promise one thing."

The skepticism in Mada's eyes almost caused Adel to laugh. "Yes…I think."

"You must promise that none of you will peek at my work while it is in progress."

A sigh of relief escaped Mada's lips. "Aye, 'tis done, if you promise to accept payment. Otherwise, the gift is only from you."

"That is fair. I will give thought to my price and let you know. How long do I have?"

"When the next full moon rises—one month."

Adel hooked her arm through Mada's. "Such a short time. I think I shall charge you dearly."

She followed Mada into the great room. All the women were seated around the fireplace. While spring was in full bloom, the great stone house remained in need of warmth.

The laughter and conversations helped lift Adel's mood. When she was seated, Cait stood, a pretty girl with skin the color of wheat, eyes that seemed to dance when she laughed, and hair that reminded Adel of spun silk. Today she seemed to glow more than usual, married for half a year, and still a child at the age of seventeen.

Cait cleared her throat. "I have news to share."

Mada's voice was jovial when she said, "Did you go to the village without us and hear a juicy piece of gossip? For shame."

Adel joined the women's laughter.

Cait lifted her sweet gaze toward Mada, and smiled. "I have not been to the village, and my news isn't gossip. Shall I keep it to myself?"

A merry round of protest rose up, and then a hush fell over the room. Even the children seated on a cowhide rug in front of the fireplace quieted.

"Very well, then." Cait pressed her hands to her middle. "I didn't want to break the news until I was certain…about September—"

Eveleen rushed forward and gathered the girl in her arms. Adel wondered if she had missed something important. Cait hadn't been given an opportunity to finish telling her news.

And then everyone was asking questions at once. *Are you sure? When did you know for certain? A baby…another O'Neill. Have you told Lunn?*

A heaviness settled in Adel's stomach. She tried to ignore the questions and hopes that dashed through her brain, just as she tried to ignore whether she would be too old to conceive a child when Liam returned from India.

Outside, the dogs set up a disturbance. With all the men away, the women were alone in the house. Mada moved to grab the longbow from its place by the hearth. She loaded it with an arrow. Eveleen instructed Adel and Tilde to take the children to the cellar.

Adel said, "Cait is with child. I will stay." She turned to Cait. "I am so happy for you and Lunn; and I'm also sorry your special moment is spoiled."

"Do not fret yourself, Adel. I have not yet told Lunn. When I do, we shall celebrate with a feast."

Tilde stood next to Adel. "Send Peigi to help Cait. I will not leave Adel."

Eveleen flicked her hand. Understanding the command, the two girls gathered the children and headed for the cellar beneath the kitchen.

Adel picked up a fire poker and held the pointed end forward, while Tilde chose a stout log as her weapon.

Mada narrowed her eyes as she stepped toward the large window. "Do you think it be hooligans, Mother Eveleen?"

Eveleen joined her daughter-in-law. "We shall soon find out. Let us be ready for what may come."

The beating of Adel's heart vibrated inside her ears. Both she and Tilde joined the others at the window.

A dark shadow moved in the mists, becoming the ghostly form of a man on horseback. Behind him another appeared, little more than a grayish haze in the fog. A larger apparition came behind them, taking on the shapes of people. Behind them came a cart loaded with a loom, a blacksmith's forge and bellows, rakes, and scythes. On the seat beside the driver sat two women, each huddled in tattered quilts.

A small gasp escaped Eveleen's lips. "Adel, look, it's Shamus." She counted aloud. "Twelve...twelve workers. I hope they are all Mautagh folk."

Adel peered through the fog. "He's been gone ten days. Whoever he's brought, they must be cold and hungry, and tired."

Following in their wake came a veritable entourage of animals: a lone cow, a small flock of sheep driven by a droop-shouldered man carrying a tall staff, and a shaggy-haired dog that scampered along beside the chap.

Shamus dismounted and handed the reins to a man astride a rangy pony. He approached the steps and walked to the opened door. He paused before Adel and bowed. "As me ledy 'as requested." With a grin he swept a hand to indicate the strangers. "I have brought my father, a cook, a weaver, a gardener, a herdsman, and others who wished to return home, all honest and good folk ready to faithfully serve the new O'Shea."

They were a band of ragtags, their expressions filled with despair and hope. Adel wanted to squeal with delight, to jump up and down like a happy child who had just received wonderful gifts for Christmas. A flood of warmth for the lad filled her. "Well done, Shamus. Lady Eveleen will instruct you where to bed the animals and the people. When they are settled, bring them to the kitchen for a hearty soup, with bread and ale. They are to take their ease for the rest of the day. Tomorrow, we shall go to Mautagh and begin our lives anew."

Shamus stood straight and tall, his gaze taking in Adel as she spoke. "We be thankin' ye, mum." He turned to those waiting. "Come, let us follow Lady Eveleen for a bit of food and rest."

Adel watched until the last person had disappeared beyond the garden. She walked to the hearth and stretched her hands toward the heat. The memory of Liam's face warmed her more than any fire, and the idea of making a home of Mautagh Manor was settling comfortably within her mind. In the meantime, and until he returned home, she vowed to make it a nurturing haven for Mary Kathryn.

Chapter Eighteen

Spring had faded into summer and summer had given way to winter. Adel's second year in Ireland had come and gone. Cait had borne a healthy son and was pregnant with her second child. Mary Kathryn was an energetic six-year-old who loved her pony and would rather play with the farm puppies and kittens than recite the alphabet or practice her numbers.

Mary Kathryn.

Adel tried to remember the first time the child had stopped referring to her as Del and had called her Mommy. The memory evoked a smile.

She stared out the massive window. It seemed as if the December winds had paused to take a breath, allowing a still, breathless morning to descend, but soon wafts of air stirred from the north, bringing a bitter cold that sucked away the dregs of warmth the sun had managed to instill. A dust-fine snow began to fall. Inside every pane of glass an intricate and ever-varied pattern of frost began to form, spreading its crystals in an intricately elaborate array. The air grew brisk, and the white bearding deepened on every surface that would hold it.

A weak gust found its way between the solid rows of buildings and became a snow eddy that danced dervish-like, whirling up the middle of the long empty lane that led to the house, there dissolving abruptly in a puff of white that slowly settled with the rest.

Adel squinted at the canvas propped on the easel before her. She had chosen as her studio the turret on the third floor overlooking the sea. In the distance she could see the waves breaking against the cliffs. The light here was best, and so here she worked.

Dozens of charcoal sketches lived on the walls. She'd painted Liam from the shoulders up. It should have been an absolutely proper portrait. But it seethed with sensuality. She had captured him on their walk the day he had proposed their marriage arrangement. The wind had tousled his hair. And then when he'd kissed her in the hotel atrium, his eyes were slumberous, his mouth relaxed. She'd gotten every detail, even the deep dimple in his cheek, the scar that parted his right eyebrow, and the slight crook of his nose—broken during a sparring match, he'd said—a likeness so precise one would think it had been painted from endless sittings. Or that the artist knew every detail of her subject intimately.

Adel rarely allowed anyone in her sanctuary. This room was her place to escape the tedium of decision-making, of settling petty differences among the tenants, and from the classroom where she taught Mary Kathryn and the adults who wished to learn to read and write.

Once Eveleen, visiting, had commented that not a grown woman on the face of the earth could view Liam's portrait and not suspect its creator must have dreamed of bedding him, must be in love with him.

Sometimes, when working on it, the memory of their one passionate kiss gripped Adel so strongly her hands shook and she had to stop and do something else to distract herself.

There were half a dozen other sketches and portraits around the room, in various stages of completion. Mautagh Manor in each phase of construction, Ahern O'Neill, fierce with his beard and plaid tartan, Eveleen as she sat at the spinning loom, and a blooming Mary Kathryn in soft pastel colors in a field of heather, the sky and billowing clouds, and the magnificent Arabian stallion Adel had purchased.

She painted for the joy of it, something she had lost in her years at Briarwood. She reveled in having it back. But painting wasn't always enough. During the day, yes, she worked furiously at overseeing the running of the farm, visiting with the families who had returned to Mautagh. For the most part, she considered herself happy.

At night, and despite her best efforts, her mood turned pensive and lonely. She wondered how long it would be, if ever, before she could drop off to sleep without feeling as if something was wrong. As if something tragic was about to happen. She dreamed of Liam, and she dreamed of Robby Beck. Often, when she awoke from the dreams, her pillow was wet with tears.

Outside, the wind blew in off the sea, rattling the windows that stretched from floor to ceiling, the entire circumference of the room. Two small fireplaces on either side of the space heated the turret. Now she set her brush aside and lifted from a shelf a small box carved from applewood, then settled on the chaise longue next to a cozy fire. Inside the chest, tied together with a blue ribbon, were Liam's letters. The mail ship arrived once every three months. Afterward, there was the wait for postal delivery to the village. No matter, she cherished each bundled parcel containing his news from India.

She selected the latest note, written nearly twelve months prior, and carefully set the envelope aside. Settling her gaze on Liam's portrait, then closing her eyes, she remembered their kiss. She embraced it, longed for it, recalled it with a sweet and piercing clarity.

She held the letter tilted toward the window's light and imagined Liam's voice, a soft and gentle tendril, as she silently mouthed his words.

My Dearest Adel,

Your letters and miniature portraits sustain me. I hope you do not mind that I share with my fellow officers and even the men of lower rank, many of whom receive no mail from home. I have tacked the sketches of the cliffs, the heather fields, cattle and sheep, and the magnificent Arab stallion along the walls of my office. Of all the pictures, the collages of Mary Kathryn are the favorite. She has become a symbol of hope for all us. Your small gesture of giving me a piece of home has lifted the morale of my men enormously. For this, we all thank you.

The picture of you, I keep private. On the nights when it is impossible to sleep because of the oppressive heat or the incessant humming from the mosquitoes, I look at you and the world seems to right itself.

I wish I could say the situation here is routine and even dull. That is not the case. I fear the British forces are facing a rebellion among the Sepoy soldiers. You see, our British rifles use paper cartridges that come pre-greased with animal fat. To load the rifle, the Sepoys have to bite the cartridge open to release the powder. The grease used is tallow from beef, which is offensive to the Hindus, and the lard from pork is offensive to the Muslims. The Indians believe if they break their sacred code, they will lose their caste.

To further complicate matters, there is also prejudice amongst the castes. I shan't bore you with the details, but the situation is unstable enough that the British East India Company is sending wives and children back to England.

I was heartened to hear the fate of Fiske Barclay. Serving a life term in Newgate is no easy task, even for the most hardened criminal. You did well to rout him out.

There are so many words I wish to say, Adel, and I say them not because I am a long way from home, or because of the dire situation my men face if worse comes to worst. These words come from the truest part of my heart. I hope you will trust me when I say I believe I fell in love with you the moment I saw you in your stepbrother's library. I admired the way you stood your ground and refused an arranged marriage to Wishingham. You are a vivacious and independent woman who had the courage to marry a man she didn't know for the simple sake of preserving the welfare of a child that you didn't birth. I would be a foolish man not to recognize these wonderful traits in you.

I also have my regrets—deep regrets. On the night of our wedding, I should have scooped you into my arms and whisked you into my bed. I am a hungry man, my love. Hungry to sample all of the fruits of your sweetness. Do not think me forward, for I am a husband who longs to bed his wife.

Although I cherish our one kiss, it is my promise that when I return to Mautagh, and to you, I will not stop with one kiss.

Three years in Meerut has seemed a lifetime. I am awaiting word to see if my company will be deployed to Dum Dum, where rebel activity has been reported. Either way, two more years left on my commission. I am counting the days.

Robby sends his love, and thanks you for the package of scones. He praised Mary Kathryn's fine stitchery of his initials on the handkerchiefs you sent.

> *Hold us in your prayers.*
> *Your faithful husband,*
> *Liam*

Adel swallowed hard as she folded the letter back into its envelope. She tenderly laid it with the others and retied the bow. Then, shutting the lid to the chest, she placed it on the shelf.

Her throat ached, and she blinked rapidly to contain the tears. Wind rattled the windows, there was a chill in the room, but her heart was warm.

She picked up the brush again. His eyes were cool,

dark and controlled. A bit more warmth in the eyes, she decided.

Noise burst at the front of the house. Loud thumps on the solid oak front doors, and Mary Kathryn frantically calling, "Mommy, Mommy, come quick."

Adel's stool tumbled over as she sprang to her feet. She peered through a window to see who was causing the disturbance. A horse stood slack-hipped, the reins dangling in the snow.

Halfway down the stairs, she nearly collided with Tilde. "What is it? Why all the disturbance?"

"God's lamb, Adel. 'Tis the sheriff from Clifden."

"Is one of our people in trouble?"

"'E wouldn't say. Just that 'is instructions were to see only you."

A foreboding washed over Adel. Disjointed fragments of last night's dream flashed behind her eyes. Her heart pounded frantically in her chest. Sucking in a shaky breath, she clasped Tilde's cold hand. "Come, we will greet the sheriff together."

Mary Kathryn stood before the burly man. "Did you come to arrest somebody, Sheriff? We ain't got no bad people here."

Adel corrected the child. "We haven't any bad people here, Mary Kathryn. Why don't you go to the kitchen and ask Mrs. Bliss to heat a cup of cider for the sheriff, and a buttered scone."

She directed the man to sit by the fire. "I'm as curious as my daughter. What brings you all the way from Clifden, and in this weather?"

"Nothing would pleasure me more than to sit before this warm fire and participate in lovely chit-chat with you, Lady Adel. The truth is, when the courier brought the mail from the ship this morning, he stopped by my office with a special delivery package. His instructions were that I should deliver it to you posthaste."

The cook hastened to the hearth with a tray of cups and a kettle. She set the tray on the table between Adel and the lawman. Adel held up her hand. "Thank you, Mrs. Bliss, I'll pour." And then, "Mary Kathryn, why don't you go to the barn and see if the kittens have enough straw to keep them warm."

A grin spread across the child's face as if she'd been given a reprieve from some dreadful fate, and Adel watched her skip toward the kitchen, then turned her attention to the pouring of cider. She forced her hand to remain steady as she handed the cup and saucer to the sheriff. Decorum dictated that she wait until he had finished his refreshments before questioning him about the parcel.

Decorum be damned, she decided. "May I examine the parcel while you enjoy the food?"

He set the cup on the table, reached inside his heavy woolen shirt, and withdrew a large leather pouch. Oh, how she wanted to open it in privacy. She felt his and Tilde's eyes on her. Her last letter from Liam was nearly a year ago. What made this letter so important?

She opened the portfolio. It contained several envelopes bundled together. She up-ended the oilskin pouch and a single envelope fluttered to her lap. It was dated five months ago—July, 1857. In red letters, the word "Important" was written across the envelope.

Tilde's face had puckered in concern. "Who is it from, Adel?"

Adel touched her fingertips to her temple, willing

her brain to function. "Lord Oxley."

"God's lamb, you don't think that bloody Barclay escaped prison, do ye? He bain't decided to do us harm, is he, Sheriff?"

As if she were correcting Mary Kathryn's language, Adel said, "He hasn't decided..." before realizing her error. She offered Tilde a contrite smile.

She unfolded the letter. The words on the page were direct, staid, and to the point. No empathy. All business.

Her brain cleared in stages, like a fog thinning in uneven patches over a marsh. She was angry at Liam. She knew it, felt it burn in her belly, but couldn't locate the reason why.

"The letter is from Lord Oxley. It simply says, 'My dear Lady Adel, I regret to inform you that while performing his duties, Lieutenant Robert Beck was killed in a mutinous uprising in West Bengal, India. Liam is reported missing. I have ordered that all efforts are to be made in locating him. Before his quarters were ransacked and burned, these letters were rescued and smuggled out. I hope they bring you peace. I will keep you informed.' "

"God's lamb." Tilde crossed her arms over her breasts. The concern in her eyes touched Adel, who expelled a lengthy sigh.

After a moment's hesitation, she ordered, "Except for Ahern and Eveleen, we will not speak of this. Mary Kathryn is too young to understand, and the burden too heavy for a child to shoulder." She looked at the sheriff and then shifted her gaze back to Tilde. "We must have faith Liam is alive and believe his rescue is imminent."

Her attention went to the gaily decorated Yule tree.

How would she get through the Christmas season? She wanted to protest. Wanted to hold on to her fears. And didn't want to be touched by the fact that she might be a widow before having the opportunity to be a wife.

India

Part III
The Rebellion
1857

Loretta C. Rogers

Chapter Nineteen

Liam removed his pith helmet and hung it on a wall peg as he raked a hand through his sweat-soaked hair. Salt rings stained the armpits of his tan uniform blouse. He allowed his eyes to adjust to the dim interior of his quarters. The darkness provided a brief respite from India's intense heat.

He walked straight to his desk, opened the bottom drawer, and pulled out the small cedar chest. He found the tiny key in one of the pigeonholes and unlocked the box, then lifted out the miniature portrait of Adel.

For a long time, he stared. He tried to catalog each feature, score them into his brain where he could keep the memories safe. The color of her eyes, lilac, which reminded him of the fields of Irish heather, the angle of her nose, the way the corners of her mouth turned up when she smiled. He realized he already knew them all. She'd found her place inside him a long time ago.

He carried the picture and cedar box to his sleeping quarters and laid them on the side table while he removed his boots, turning them upside down on the boot rack. It was not uncommon for a scorpion or an asp or some other poisonous creature to nestle in the dark interior of a soldier's boot. In this forsaken country of sand and heat, negligence could bring death as quickly as the Indian talwar saber or a tongue swollen black from lack of water.

He reached for the letters in the box, and though he'd read them numerous times, Adel's words continued to intoxicate him.

He mused over her earlier letters, formal and businesslike, as if she were sending him daily reports. He stopped to think when their letters had become more intimate, sensual, loving. She no longer addressed him as "Dear Captain O'Shea."

He opened her last letter and hurriedly scanned the news about the estate, Mary Kathryn, the workers, and the animals.

My Darling Liam,

How I regret the way we parted. If I could redo the few hours we spent in the atrium after we had spoken our vows, I would have insisted upon sharing your bed. How very naïve of me. Listening to the conversations of Mada, Cait, Peigi, and Tilde lets me know how immature I was. From the glow on their cheeks when they speak of lovemaking with their husbands, I am envious of what I missed experiencing with you.

I have nearly fallen to my knees with longing to feel you next to me when I watch the stallion mount his mares. I dream of the day when you come home and teach me how to love you. My heart belongs to you, always.

The sun slowly faded to an indistinct glow in the eastern sky, silhouetting the tall rock formations against the horizons. A weak gust of wind found its way through the room's searing heat.

Liam stripped down to his shorts and undershirt, neatly folding his uniform over the back of a high-topped chair before he settled on the cot and closed the mosquito netting around the bed. He lay against the pillow and held the letter to his nose to inhale the last hints of Adel's perfume. His eyes drifted shut and sleep claimed him.

He dreamed.

Adel was on fire for him. His mouth sought hers in a passionate frenzy. She looked into his eyes and, with a muffled groan, entreated, "Teach me how to love you."

His manroot reared up and fought to split the seams of the front placket of his shorts. So intense was the sensation blazing through him, he could think of nothing beyond driving himself into her and burying himself as deep as possible between the folds of her womanhood. She was wet and ready to receive him.

He moaned and, with impatient hands that slid beneath the waistband of his underwear, gave a sharp inhalation as he relieved himself.

Spent in the aftermath of his orgasm, Liam was insensate to his surroundings. It took a while for him to recover from what had just been the most exquisite climax. This was downright terrifying. Disconcerted, he pushed back the netting and lit a tallow candle before he put his feet to the wooden floor of his quarters.

He filled a basin with lukewarm water and cleansed himself. He allowed himself the luxury of a ragged breath, and longed for a drink stronger than a cup of hot tea.

In an effort to block the torrid images of Adel's roused state from his thoughts, he put the letters back in the cedar box, locked it, and placed the key safely inside a pigeonhole in his desk.

He returned to the bedroom and lay back on the

cot, staring at the ceiling and trying to blot the dream from his memory. When sleep finally came, the feel of him inside Adel chased through his netherworld and dogged him until dawn pinked the sky. He was up and dressed long before the bugler sounded "Reveille."

****

Lieutenant Robert Beck hastened into Liam's quarters. He snapped off a salute before cutting his eyes toward Liam's personal Hindi aide.

Liam folded the document before him, placed it in an envelope, waxed the closure and sealed it with his initial. "Sanjiv, take this to the courier posthaste, and if he has already left the compound, saddle your horse and ride out after him. It is urgent this message get to Colonel Sheffield."

The Indian bowed low. "Yes, Sahib."

When the man departed, Robby went to the door and looked out. His voice was fraught with tension. "It's impossible to know who we can trust these days."

Liam removed his handkerchief and dabbed his face and eyes as he motioned Robby toward a chair. "The situation grows worse every day. Thankfully, our Hindi seem loyal and not inclined to mutiny. What causes your look of undue stress?"

"It's this damnable heat and the bloody waiting, and there is already bickering among the Hindi and Muslim soldiers. It is enough to test the strongest man's durability."

Liam walked to the water barrel and filled two cups. He handed one to Robby. "I've always known it was a mistake to mix castes. And this situation with biting the bullet greased with animal fat adds to the weightiness of the situation. I've searched my mind for a solution."

In a long thirsty gulp, Robby drained the cup and set it on Liam's desk. "What if we separated each caste and placed them in their own barracks?"

Liam reared his chair onto its back legs. "I've given thought to the same idea. We already feed the men differently. Nothing to offend their basic beliefs."

"Do you ever think about resigning your commission, Liam? Saying to hell with it, and return to England?"

Liam lowered the chair. He stood and clapped his friend on the shoulder. Waiting in the shadows of battle had the entire post on edge. He felt Robby's fear as surely as he felt his own deep dreads. He commanded an outpost of fifteen hundred, which included a mere two hundred fifty Englishmen. With five days of hard riding to the next garrison, how could they withstand an attack of thousands?

He kept his voice light. "Return to England and be bored to death attending balls, listening to mundane chatter and endless complaints from the royals? I think it's not for you, my friend."

"What about Adel and Mary Kathryn, Liam? Wouldn't you give up the heat, the sand, and the god-awful scorpions and mosquitoes to be with them?"

Liam fought to keep the slump from his shoulders. He walked to the window and looked out across the yard. He shifted his gaze beyond the parade ground to the rows of barracks, the horse corral, and along the sentry walls. Brown, a sea of brown, save for the red and white colors of the flag that dangled lifeless on the flagpole. Bloody hell, yes, he'd give it all up to return to Ireland and the two loves of his life.

While he pondered his answer to his best friend, guards running along the sentry wall's catwalk forced his attention. Shouts rang out, "Open the gates. Lone rider coming like the hounds of hell are nipping at his heels."

Another voice shouted, "Get the captain."

Liam snatched his helmet from the wall peg and settled it on his head. "Grab two rifles from the case, Robby. Stay alert. It could be a ruse to catch us off guard."

Shoulder to shoulder, the two men raced down the steps. Liam ordered, "Sentries, rifles to the ready. Open one gate, then shut it immediately behind the rider."

A sweat-lathered, heaving horse barreled through the narrow opening, bumping its side against the heavy wooden gate. The rider slumped forward, arms dangling on either side of the animal.

Liam sprinted across the yard. "Blast, that's Sanjiv's mount. But who's riding it?"

He raced to grab the reins of the wall-eyed animal. The gelding reared and danced in a circle. It took both Liam and Robby to bring the animal under control. The wounded rider moaned, "Private Perkins, sir. Courier from…" And then he fainted.

A medic and two soldiers rushed forward with a stretcher.

Liam followed the bearers to the infirmary. "How bad is he, Doctor?"

Grinding his teeth, he watched the doctor cut away the soldier's blood-soaked blouse and then cleanse the wound. The physician's voice was gruff but soft. "I'm surprised he made it this far. If you have any questions for the man, you'd better ask them quick, Captain."

With Robby standing nearby, Liam pulled a chair close to the cot and leaned forward. "Private Perkins, can you hear me?"

He patted the man's cheek to rouse him.

"Blimey, sir, I thought the angels 'ad come to take me 'ome. I 'eard 'em singing."

"What messages do you carry, and from whom?"

The private coughed. Bloody spittle dribbled from the corner of his mouth. His eyes rolled back, and then fluttered. He seemed to rally. "Captain, can ye send me back to England to be buried with me mum and father?"

Liam knew the impossibility of the request. "I'll see what I can do, son. Now, can you tell me about the messages you carry?"

Private Perkins lifted his hand and pointed. "In me saddlebags." Breath sighed out of the man like air escaping a balloon, and his hand fell limp.

"God rest your soul, Private Perkins." Liam turned to Robby. "Come. We need to see what's in those saddlebags."

"Liam, what do you suppose happened to Sanjiv and our courier?"

"Dead, most likely."

In his office, Liam laid the saddlebags on his desk, then unbuckled the straps and reached inside to remove a leather pouch. He emptied the contents—letters from soldiers to family members, and then one from Colonel Habersham, from the town of Lucknow.

He unfolded the missive and read aloud, "*Captain O'Shea—Urgent! We do not have the strength to hold our besieged garrison. Our twelve hundred are fortified against twenty thousand mutineers. The caste soldiers have turned against us. Send reinforcements. We must evacuate the women and children. The threat of death looms near. Pray God have mercy on us, and that Private Perkins escapes through the lines to deliver this plea for help."*

Robby's expression hardened. "Do you think our Hindi and Muslim soldiers will fight with us or turn their rifles against us?"

Liam stood motionless in the center of the room, trying to subdue the dread that was spreading through him like an insidious vine. Following closely behind that dread was a heavy dose of dangerously frustrating sense of helplessness.

His eyes steady, solemn, met Robby's strained features. "We will know the answer soon enough."

Chapter Twenty

The dawning sun rose, with dire crimson hues above ragged shreds of clouds, and spread its warmth across the land, forcing the last dregs of morning coolness to retreat to the lower hollows, where with reluctant lassitude they would eventually turn to waves of shimmering heat.

It was still in the sweet hush of morning when the alarm rang out from the watch tower, shattering the tranquility of the compound and snatching its occupants to their feet in quick response.

A voice beyond the gate yelled, "British dogs, I, Jemadar Ishwari Prasad, have come!"

Quick strides carried Liam across the compound yard. He ascended the ladder to the overlook. Concern filled him with worry as he took the rungs two at a time to see what fiend plotted rebellion.

"Prasad!" Liam spat the name as if it had a foul taste. Near the middle of the road where it breached the ridge a mutineer leader, known for unlocking the jails and freeing criminals to join his ranks, had come to a halt astride a prancing mount. On either side of him, his army spread out in double ranks, preparing for an attack.

Lieutenant Beck and Sergeant-Major Thompson crossed the parade ground in leaping strides and climbed the wall to where one of several cannons awaited their attention. The sergeant-major manned the second gun, while one of the Hindi soldiers gave him aid.

Prasad raised a white flag, and a pair of mounted escorts rode forward on his signal until he was within hearing distance of the wall.

"Captain O'Shea!" he bellowed. "Surrender the fort. You are out-manned and cannot hope to hold this garrison against so great a number. I have three score men behind me. What do you have behind you? Give yourselves up, and we will let you British go free with your promise to leave our country forever."

Liam scoffed. "Why do you think I would believe the murderer of innocent women and children? My soldiers, no matter their caste, are loyal to the Queen of England. They will stand and fight, as I will stand and fight."

"Do not be so sure of where loyalties lie, Captain." Prasad raised his talwar and pointed it toward Liam as if he silently vowed to crush him and his forces. Spurring his mount around, he raced back to the middle of his army. Taking a position in the center of the line, he lifted his arm high with a roar of command.

Liam asked the Hindi soldier standing next to him, "What's he doing, Corporal?"

"Sahib, he is showing his power."

"How many within these walls will turn their weapons against us?"

"I am a loyal soldier, Sahib. I can only speak for myself."

Liam did not miss the subtle answer to his question, nor the nearly imperceptible blink of the Hindi's eyes. In spite of the morning heat, a chilly premonition wrapped its icy fingers around Liam's heart.

He glanced to his right and then his left at the line of soldiers who had pledged their allegiance to the Queen and England. The somber group waited in silence.

A long moment passed, and then Jemadar Ishwari Prasad, sweeping his arm downward with a shrill yodel, sent his forces forward. His own mount danced with impatience, but the Indian commander held the animal with tight restraint as he watched the two lines of mounted soldiers move forward toward the garrison.

Liam waited until the advancing line was almost to the ranging mark and then gave his own signal to light the wicks of the cannons. The sparks lit and touched off a loud explosion that sent a volley of iron balls hurtling forcefully through the air to land in an eruption of earth and flailing bodies. Lieutenant Beck and Sergeant-Major Thompson shook their fists in triumph, and the lieutenant called out, "By the bloody hell, Captain, we sent a few to kingdom come."

Liam replied, "Give the order to reload the cannons."

The gun crew leapt forward to swab and reload as soon as the smoke cleared, and when the heavily laden vapors lifted, Liam assessed the damage.

It seemed as if a broad hand had torn a gap in the line, but this did not stop the enemy.

A report of iron missiles from the attackers came hard on the heels of the British bombardment, shredding a section of the fortress walls. As the devastation became apparent, cries within the compound turned hostile. Liam's worst nightmare was realized. The Hindi and Muslim soldiers who had pledged their loyalty to England and her Crown had turned on each other.

Another volley of cannon fire whistled overhead. Plumes of brown dust spewed up around him, eliciting loud guffaws and hearty laughter from those on the wall.

The repercussion of the blast left Liam momentarily deafened, and his mind rebelled as he watched Robby Beck's body move through space in slow motion before landing on the ground below. Robby writhed briefly in a dusty swale, then lay still. In his heart, Liam knew his best friend had not survived the impact. Before he could feel a moment of regret for Robby's death, rifles barked their say, and the blood of more lifeless humanity stained the brown earth.

The noise was shattering. Metal clashed with metal, ringing with ear-piercing intensity. Screams of agony mingled with shouts of victory.

Like droves of locusts, the attackers scaled the stone wall. With no time to reload their rifles, British soldiers fought with nothing more than sabers and bare hands. More screams rent the air.

Liam shouted orders to the Hindi and Muslim soldiers. Fury filled him when they laid down their weapons, refusing to bite the tallow-greased bullets. With horror and disgust, he watched his forces crumbling around him. He called for the British soldiers to regroup beyond the ridge, and as they fled toward the safety it promised, the cannons commenced their destructive reports again, successfully striking where they would do the most damage.

As night fell, he marked time while bolstering the

courage of the men he had left and rallying their spirits with promises of great rewards. He was himself devastated by their losses.

He used the few hours of rest to scribble a note to Lord Oxley about Robby's death. It grieved him to know his friend's body would rot in the infernal heat, shrouded in blowflies instead of receiving a decent Christian burial.

When he thought exhaustion would overtake him and his eyes protested his will to keep them open, a whisper sounded close to his ear. "Psst, Sahib. It is I, your faithful servant, Sanjiv."

"Sanjiv, thank God. We thought you were dead."

"I was shot in the head, but it did not kill me, as you can see. I have come to assist you. Tell me what to do?"

"Lieutenant Beck was killed. I must let his family know. Also there are important papers in my desk that must not fall into the hands of the enemy. Use your stealth to retrieve my cedar box. You know which one I speak of?"

"Yes, Sahib, shall I bring it to you?"

"No. Make your way to Delhi." Liam removed the signet ring from his finger. "Give this to Vice Chancellor McNamara, along with the box of letters. Tell him to send my personal letters to Lord Filbert Oxley in London. And tell him we are in dire need of reinforcements."

"What if he does not believe me, Sahib? What if this man thinks I cut off your finger and stole your ring?"

Liam recognized the reasoning behind his faithful aide's concerns. "If this should happen, then tell Lord

McNamara that when I was sixteen, his son broke my nose in a sparring match. This is a fact no one but he and I would know."

"Saah, Sahib. You are a wise man to give me such secret knowledge."

"Go now. Don't delay."

"Will you not come with me, Sahib?"

"It is my duty to stay until the last soldier in my command is no longer standing."

"Then what should I do if something happens to you, Sahib?"

"Among the letters, I have written one extolling your fluency in both written and spoken English. I have told of your loyalty, and I have asked Vice Chancellor McNamara to find a place of esteemed employment for you."

"I am most honored, Sahib."

The two men clasped hands. Even in the darkness, silent emotions spoke louder than words.

"Be off. Make haste. And may your god travel with you, my friend."

No other words were spoken. Liam sensed more than heard the little man's departure.

In the wee hours before night and dawn, canteens were passed around to quench the men's thirst. Liam passed the word for the soldiers to count their ammunition, and he commanded them to rest as they waited for another attack to begin.

In the early morning, Liam and his force of one hundred witnessed the devastation of the buildings, blackened scars reaching upward over the glowing ash heaps of the compound. He prayed Sanjiv had found a way to skirt around the enemy to safely carry out his request for aid.

The charred remains of several soldiers who had not been swift enough to escape the flames was a gruesome sight for those who had to face the prospect of rallying for another onslaught from a massive force.

Liam could only wonder what the rogue Prasad had planned for them now.

"Maybe that heathen devil will turn around and leave. He did what he came to do, didn't he, Captain?"

A pair of frightened blue eyes stared at Liam. The young private was surely no more than eighteen. Liam drew a sleeve to wipe the sweat that trickled down his cheeks. The hot, sultry morning had become almost unbearable. "When the bloodlust grips a man, it doesn't let go so easily, Private."

He gave the private a reassuring pat on the shoulder. "No need to worry, lad. I've sent for reinforcements."

"Captain?"

"Yes?"

"Does it make a man a coward to admit he's scared witless?"

The hopelessness in the younger man's expression tugged at Liam's heart. He mustered a smile. "What's your name, Private?"

"Willie Carter, sir."

"You have a special girl back home, Private Carter?"

The boy blushed until his ears matched the red of his uniform jacket. "Aye. Her name is Iris, like the flower."

"Well, Private Carter, it takes a brave man to admit when he's scared. Why don't you think about Iris. It will help settle your nerves."

The private drew in a deep breath and released it slowly. "Thank you, sir."

After a moment, Liam said, "I need to see to the troops."

Private Carter snapped off a salute. "We'll give 'em bloody hell, won't we, sir?"

Liam answered with a simple nod. His body bent low, he walked among the soldiers, giving encouragement. "Take heart, men, for we've not yet come to the end of our resources. Prasad may have caught us with our breeches down, but we Brits are made of iron. Hail the Queen!"

In rousing unison the men chorused, "Hail the Queen!"

They were far from home, these men. How many would survive, how many would leave sweethearts or wives and children to mourn for them? These questions weighed heavily on Liam.

Adel and Mary Kathryn. The names flared through his brain. He knew what the men were feeling in these long desperate moments. He, too, wanted to go home, to lie in bed with Adel in his arms. He wanted to smell her, to taste her, to never leave her again. Then there was his precious daughter. He longed to feel her little arms around his neck, and to hear her say *Daddy.* The ache of never again seeing the two loves of his life pierced him deeper than any saber.

The whinnies and stamping hooves of restless horses shattered the daydream and brought Liam back to reality.

He drew his service revolver and rechecked the loading. "Time draws near. Make yourselves ready, men."

The straggly force took their places and braced themselves for the inevitable invasion. Some whispered prayers, others hummed, most clenched their jaws against what was to come.

Prasad's harsh voice carried across the distance as he ordered a troop of mutineers to fire the cannons.

Liam ordered, "Make every bullet count."

Explosions deafened Liam. His nostrils filled with the acrid odor of gunpowder. He drew a sleeve across his eyes to clear them from stinging particles of sand. He looked to his left and to the right. He wanted to shut out the screams of dying men.

Those who followed Prasad did not even pause as they leapt over their fallen companions and surged forward with sabers. Liam found himself confronted by three of the enemy. His rifle and revolver empty, his saber broken to the hilt, he drove the boldest man to his knees with a kick to the groin, then eased the man's pain with his own dirk. In the next instant Liam blocked the thrusting attack of another's blade and gallantly stood against the two until one of them heaved a gurgling sigh and sank to the sand, clutching the blade of a talwar which protruded from his chest. Liam had no time to express his gratitude to Corporal Halim, a Hindu, as another force of rebels surged forward.

Snatching the dirk from the dead enemy's hand, and a talwar from the ground, Liam held the bloody sword, fending off an attack from the left while he thrust the long dagger forward with the right.

One of Prasad's soldiers lunged, his sword raised against Liam. There was a crazed look glazing his eyes as if he had passed the point of knowing what he was doing. Liam buried the dirk deep into the man's chest.

Though many of the enemy fell, Liam and his companions were forced ever backwards in the blistering sun. He stayed with his men, hurling orders and sharp commands while pushing others back into the fray. He shouted, "There are no cowards in the Queen's army."

With no weapon, Liam snatched up an empty rifle from the ground and held it by the barrel, using it as a cudgel. An insurgent swept forward with a vengeance, grazing Liam's shoulder with enough force to send him reeling backward into a boulder. A cry of pain was wrenched from him when a slug shattered his kneecap, giving evidence to the depth of his injury, but as the rebel stepped forward to finish his work, he was jostled aside by the sprawling form of a soldier who had fallen victim to a bullet.

"You spineless coward!" Liam chided, deliberately distracting the agent from his goal. "You are not a man, you are a cock-sucking halfie. You hide behind the saris of old women and have the courage of a braying ass."

He paused his heckling and canted his head as if hearing a sound close behind him. A shadow fell across him, and a weapon discharged with explosive force.

Liam blinked at the sudden wetness in his eyes and thought he saw Adel. Her expression was sad as she leaned down and pressed her lips to his brow. His mouth found its way to hers, and he kissed her farewell. Then, raising his head, he had little time to feel the sadness that was waiting to overtake him, for in a moment the red rage of pain assaulted him and the world turned dark.

Chapter Twenty-One

Liam lifted his head from the hard pallet and blinked away the hazy film from his eyes. Tiny flames from a myriad of squat candles frolicked in a lively dance before him. Surely Satan had carried him deep into the bowels of hell.

Nausea clawed at Liam's insides and burned the back of his throat from the overwhelming stench of rotting flesh. He retched.

Disjointed shadows hovered, then disappeared. Hushed whispers spoke to him in a language he did not understand. One moment chills chattered his teeth, and in the next his body convulsed from a raging fever.

All about him there was nothing but darkness and desolation, and pain so fierce that he pleaded for the Angel of Death to swoop down and release him from life—if he was, indeed, alive.

He tried to raise himself to view his surroundings. In his much-weakened condition, the effort proved too much, and he collapsed back upon the hard earth.

A long, panic-filled moment passed in an attempt to take air into his lungs, and he feared he was on the verge of dying.

He couldn't feel his tongue moving in his mouth. His brain was a frozen wasteland, and the cramps in his stomach were brutal.

He forced a whisper from his parched lips.

"Water... Is there someone who might give me a sip of water?"

He waited, turned his head in the direction of a slight shuffling sound. He squinted through the darkness. A candle flickered. The outline of a man knelt beside him and held a cup of water to his lips.

"Captain O'Shea, praise be to Vishnu, you live."

"Wh-Who is it?"

"It is I, Corporal Halim. You have been very ill, Sahib."

In drifts, the screams of dying men echoed in Liam's ears as he recalled the attack from Prasad's rebels. His voice rasped from lack of use. "Robby— Lieutenant Beck, did he...did he survive?"

"I am sorry, my captain, only a few of us escaped. Do not think about this now."

After a lengthy sigh, Liam spat the words. "Aye, I remember now. The infidels killed him. A bright light snuffed out, and for naught. Poor Robby didn't deserve to die."

"Do not exert yourself, my captain. You must rest."

Halim spoke in his native tongue, as if he were giving orders, and then he turned back to Liam. "You have been many days without food, and only a few drops of water. I have asked for some rich lentil soup."

Liam was weak in body and torpid in mind. "Where are we?"

"We are safely hidden in a cave, Sahib."

Liam closed his eyes as he spoke. "I am forever in your debt, Corporal Halim. I shall recommend a medal for you for your bravery, and your honor."

The Hindu soldier lifted Liam's head and spooned broth from the soup to Liam's lips until he said, "No more."

As Halim turned to leave, Liam touched the man's arm. "How long have I been here?"

"Many days. I would not risk trying to carry you to New Delhi. Your leg, it is bad, and we have only a few herbs, but no real medicine. I am sorry, my captain. Besides, many rebel forces still patrol the roads. We are safe here until help arrives."

"Help?"

"Yes, my captain. Private Jahnu and the pock-faced sergeant who tended the horses, I pray Vishnu give them both safe journey to deliver the message that you are alive."

The pounding at the back of Liam's skull eased after a time, and he sighed at the release.

A brief smile touched Halim's lips as he rose to leave. "I am sorry we have nothing to relieve your misery."

Liam's red-rimmed and swollen eyelids lowered slightly to mask the grueling pain. Bile rose in his throat, and he forced himself not to vomit. "I fear I can smell the stench of our brave soldiers' rotting bodies. All good men—British, Muslim, and Hindu alike. None deserve to have their sun-blackened remains picked clean by vultures."

Halim said without preamble, "The stink is from your leg, my captain."

Liam felt a hollowness inside, an emptiness that merged and overflowed with hurting and fury. For the first time in his life he felt utter defeat.

He tried to keep his voice steady. "Gangrene?"

"Do not think about it, Sahib. Think about the one you call Ah-dell. You have called for her many times in your delirium. Help will come soon. Vishnu has ordained it."

Liam sighed deeply. He closed his eyes and tried to recall Adel's face.

Chapter Twenty-Two

Another week slipped passed, and the cave remained secure from all outside interference. In the sun-blistered world beyond its mouth, there was a hushed stillness, as though the faraway surroundings and all inhabitants there held their collective breath in expectant dread of the furor yet to come. Small birds flitted in and out of the cavern. Liam surmised they were seeking temporary respite from the heat.

He sat propped against a large boulder, sipping tea, when the earth beneath him vibrated. He listened, certain he heard the sound of many horses' hooves drawing nearer and nearer. Then there was the thud of running footsteps.

His thoughts gathered in a dark cloud of agony as he tried to lift himself to gain a better view.

"Corporal Halim, who is it—friend or foe?"

The Hindu rushed to squat next to Liam. He placed a dagger in Liam's hands. "I am waiting to hear from the lookout. We do not have rifles to spare. You comprehend, my captain?"

Liam nodded his understanding. He shuddered as a cold knot of dread formed in the pit of his stomach. If it was Prasad or another enemy, Liam would use the weapon on himself before being captured and tortured. What difference did it make how he died? With the gangrene slowly rotting his flesh, he was already a dead man inside a living shell.

A pointed silence fell over the cave. Not even the wind whispered. While he waited, his mind drifted back to a haunting recollection of towering cliffs that were also punctuated with caves. Eternally lapping waves washed over the beach, and an exhilarating sense of freedom filled him as he remembered racing barefoot along the stretch of sand as a child, with his father giving chase. A memory drifted back of misty moors dotted with wooded crests, a large manor house, and grassy meadows whereon they had lain and leisurely pondered the gamboling clouds high above. He had loved that place and had treasured the many times he had gone alone to wander the moors, to explore the caves, to enjoy the damp breezes on his skin, even the time a giant wave had swept him off the rock he sat upon. He lifted his head as he listened to a voice speaking to him from the past. It seemed to echo in his mind. *Live. Live. Live.*

A distant shout rang out from the sentinel point, and Liam turned his head as another answered from afar.

The low rumble of horses seemed to reverberate within Liam's chest. He wiped a gaunt hand across his mouth as he gripped the dagger with the other.

A loud fervor of voices filled the cave's great chamber, and for a brief moment, Liam thought he detected the mangled speech of Sanjiv amid the chatter, but the words buzzed in his ears and his vision blurred.

And then the voice was speaking to him. "Sahib, it is I, your faithful servant, Sanjiv. I have come for you. Do you see, I have brought Colonel Wainwright?"

Liam reached out and the colonel clutched the

bony hands between both of his.

Liam blinked to clear his vision. Kneeling on one knee, the officer removed a handkerchief from his sleeve and pressed it to his nose as if to keep out the putrid stench emanating from Liam's gangrenous leg. "My God, he is little more than an emaciated skeleton."

Liam made an attempt to smile, but the effort was too much. "I am very happy to see you, too, Colonel. Forgive me for not saluting."

His face contorted suddenly as a spasm of pain seized him. Dapples of sweat popped from his pores.

Hands fussed over him. A spoon of bitter liquid was poured between his lips. He remembered saying, "My men, Colonel, they fought valiantly. Prasad—"

"Prasad is dead, Captain O'Shea. The rebellion is near its end. Rest now. The medico has given you laudanum to ease the pain while we travel."

"H-how…far?"

The officer patted Liam's hand. "Let me do the worrying about that. You close your eyes and rest."

Liam said, "With much respect, sir, if I should die before reaching the fort, would you see that Corporal Halim and the rest of the men receive medals for bravery in the face of the enemy, and for saving my life?"

Colonel Wainwright's answer was earnest. "Your faithful aide, Sanjiv, has filled me in on most of the details leading up to Prasad's attack. I have sent a company of men with a burial detail to the garrison and to collect as many identities as possible. Consider your request fulfilled, Captain O'Shea. I will see to it personally."

"My leg. Can it be saved?"

"I'm no doctor, Captain. My guess is you need to think about retiring from the service."

A chill coursed through Liam's veins as the laudanum worked its magic. "Aye. A one-legged soldier isn't much good on the battle lines."

****

After a week of grueling, torturous days on the road, Liam was ready to wish he had died back at the cave. Every dip and jerk of the wagon brought some part of his body into a rage of white searing agony.

And when he thought he couldn't hold on much longer, hands were lifting him onto a stretcher and then running with him toward a building. There was a stripping of his clothes and someone washing his body. The water was blessedly cool and refreshing.

More laudanum followed, and he drifted in and out of consciousness, grabbing snatches of conversation.

"The leg will definitely have to come off."

"Bloody damned shame."

"His days of serving in the Queen's service are over."

"Don't know how he survived this long. Poor devil would probably prefer death over living life with one leg."

"Strap his arms and good leg tight. Can't have him flailing about."

"Loaded with puss. Damned well makes me want to chuck up my breakfast."

"Yes, yes. I'll have to make the cut above the knee."

"Did you hear how he practically fought off an army of thousands with a handful of men?

"Blood and guts. That's what he is. Deserves all

the honors he'll receive."

"My guess is he'd rather keep his leg than get a handful of medals."

"Here, boy, bring a bucket to catch the blood."

"Wonder how his wife will react to a one-legged husband?"

"I wager she walks out on him."

Liam searched for courage. He turned his head. A ray of sun glinted off a meat cleaver and the serrated blade of the handsaw. He reached toward the white-gowned surgeon. "No. Don't take my leg. I'd rather die than live as an invalid."

The doctor commanded, "Strap his hands." Then he offered a lopsided smile. Without further words, he nodded. Someone placed a cloth over Liam's mouth and nose and directed him to take deep breaths.

Liam's head swam with the heady intoxicant, and as his eyes closed his world spiraled into nothingness.

Loretta C. Rogers

Ireland

Part IV

Homecoming

1858

Loretta C. Rogers

Chapter Twenty-Three

The military dispatch stated simply that Captain Liam O'Shea would arrive at the port of Galway on eleven December 1858.

Through correspondence with Lord Oxley, Adel had learned morbid details of the severity of Liam's wounds, the days he and his men had hidden inside a cave from the enemy, his rescue, and of the subsequent amputation of his leg.

No matter how many times she read the letter, her eyes still blurred with tears.

I fear, my dear Adel, that our Liam has suffered and survived an unspeakable ordeal. The communication through my liaison with the East India Company assures me Liam was given superior medical care. Though the wounds to his shoulder and back were extensive, they are healing well. It appears the amputation of his leg is what has taken a toll on his mental state, however. I write this as a caution that the Liam we once knew may no longer exist.

He will need the tenderness of your hand and the compassion of your heart to help heal his tortured soul. How long he will remain in this state of instability, only God knows. I have not forgotten that your marriage is without consummation. Although it is my fervent hope you will not invoke the annulment clause until you have exhausted all measures to restore Liam to health, I will hold you without fault for your devotion to Mary Kathryn, and to the new lifeblood you have breathed into Mautagh Manor.

My resources are at your disposal. Do not hesitate to utilize them.

Adel had read the letter often enough to recall the words from memory. She shivered as the chilling gusts whipped her heavy woolen cloak and invaded the billowing hood to snatch her hair from its sober mooring. She had donned plain, warmly serviceable clothes, preferring to meet Liam without ostentatious fanfare.

She allowed her gaze to linger on the Claddagh wedding ring for a second or two as she raised her hand to look at it. A ring that Liam had placed on her finger as a token of friendship and love. What was love, she wondered. Were they mere words written in letters from a lonely man far from home? She knew she loved Mary Kathryn. But the love between a husband and wife was surely different from that of a stepmother and her child.

So eager had she been to escape from an arranged marriage to a despicable cad that she had hastily married a man she barely knew. And now he was coming home—broken in body and mind.

She felt as if a vise were gripping her heart, crushing it, and she closed her eyes searching for the strength to meet this new purpose.

Not knowing the extent of Liam's incapacity, she

had packed warm blankets and a fur coverlet. It was but a day's journey to home. Still, she was thankful that Ahern had insisted his brawn might be needed.

Seeking a place beyond reach of the mist, Adel climbed inside the brougham and kept wary eyes alert for the arrival of the ship.

Edwin's shout from atop the coach brought Adel to full attention. She opened the carriage door and stood for a better view. Looking out beyond the breakwater, she spotted the dot of white and knew it was the ship's sails.

"Is she...is it the ship that brings Liam?" Adel was almost fearful of asking. She fretted in anxious worry.

Edwin lifted the spyglass. He called down, "Aye, milady. 'Tis the HMS Clarence."

"How long before she docks?"

"The wind is right and her sails be full. 'Bout an hour, me thinks."

Tears clouded Adel's eyes. She struggled to keep her composure from cracking.

Ahern came to stand by her side. "Take heart, lass. Ye've only the word of the magistrate about Liam. Might ne'er be as bad as it sounds."

She clasped her adopted uncle's hand for strength. "I pray you are right."

It was some time before the sailing ship halted at the river docks of Galway. Passengers descended and baggage and crates filled with gabbling geese were unloaded.

Adel stood on tiptoe and strained to watch each passenger descend the sloped gangplank. "Perhaps he decided not to come. What if...what if something happened to him? It will break Mary Kathryn's heart.

Oh, what will I tell her?"

Ahern's voice was quiet as he folded his beefy arms over his broad chest. "Still yourself, Adel. You fret for no reason."

She gathered a calming breath, and continued her search until it seemed no others were left onboard. And then she spotted a scarecrow draped in a navy blue jacket and dingy white trousers. She placed a hand over her mouth to stifle the gasp. Her heart broke a little at the sight of him.

She drifted toward him, nervously smoothing the folds of her woolen cape.

It pained her to see him struggle to manage the crutches down the wet, slippery plank. And when the wooden stick seemed to snag on one of the plank cleats, Liam lost his balance.

Adel cried out, "Oh, Ahern…Edwin!"

In two long bounds the giant Irishman was there and gathered up his nephew as if he weighed no more than a newborn foal.

Edwin rushed to assist Ahern, calling out, "Don't worry yerself, milady. I'll manage the captain's baggage."

Adel opened her mouth to reply but closed it again as she found herself assailed by uncertainty. She pressed a trembling hand to her throat and heard her own indrawn breath rasping there.

****

Close above the ship's white sails, dark clouds scudded past, chased by strong breezes from the north. Salt spray hurled itself over the bow. Sea terns soared aloft on widespread wings and cried their strident song as they followed the vessel's progress toward the port.

Liam stood by the rail and lifted his face to feel the fine spray of spindrift upon his face as he looked out to sea toward the distant horizon. Somewhere beyond that vague, grayish murk that blended with the sky was home. He felt no joy at returning. He had no assurance of how Adel would receive him, or if she even knew he was alive.

He had not slept and cared not for his appearance. When he closed his eyes, he was confronted with the visions of mangled bodies and found himself choking on the acrid smoke from gunpowder that seemed eternally embedded inside his nostrils. He continually waged a desperate battle that threatened to utterly rend his sanity.

He was tired to the point that there were times he was certain his bones were melting. The wind stirred his hair and tugged at the edges of his jacket. What desire had possessed him to return to Ireland? A one-legged man was useless. Useless to himself and especially to a wife.

How could he run a farm when he needed both hands to manage the crutches? He couldn't hitch a team of horses, he couldn't ride a horse... Bloody hell, would Adel expect to share his bed?

Liam sucked in a breath that felt as if he were inhaling shards of glass. For one agonizing moment he didn't know who he hated more—himself or the doctor who had kept him alive.

And then he spotted her. Dressed in a dove gray cloak, the hood billowing out, the wind teasing her hair. She was flesh and blood, and beautiful. There was no sign of the girl he had married. This woman stood with the elegant grace of someone in control of herself.

"Adel!" The word was barely a whisper, but in his mind it was a shout of acclamation as he recognized the slender form. Though he could not see her face or discern the movement of her lips, he knew it was she.

She lifted a hand to brush an errant tress back from her face. He saw the fine delicacy of her cheekbones, the fullness of her lips. The sight evoked memories that he preferred to keep at bay.

Heaviness the size of a large stone settled in his stomach. Seeing her standing there, searching along the bowline of the ship, he had to remind himself that whatever he had fantasized during the long months in the hospital and during the ocean crossing was just that—a fantasy. He and Adel were strangers. There was nothing between them. *Nothing.*

No, it would not do him any good to think of her in a romantic way. He had to stifle these reactions. He'd experienced the repugnant glances of the nurses when they gazed upon his scarred body and the red puckered end of his stump. He closed his eyes briefly, searching for the strength to face Adel.

His voice, hoarse and ragged, commanded a passing sailor. "My box of letters. Bring them."

"Aye, sir."

As the crew secured the bowlines and lowered the gangplank, Liam made up his mind. He would write his uncle, Lord Oxley, and request him to enforce the annulment. He would send Adel back to England. And then he planned to cocoon himself in the comfort and warmth of a mistress named Irish Rose, a fine blended whiskey, brewed especially for gentlemen. He harrumphed as he looked at the shabbiness of his uniform. *A gentleman, indeed.* And he would live out the remainder of his days alone.

He deliberately waited until the last passenger had left the boat. Unsure of how he would traverse the steep and slippery slope of the gangplank, he hefted the cedar box under his left arm. He gripped the crutches and, by the time he'd taken two steps, one of the tips caught on a cleat. His balance upset, he tumbled down the gangplank much the way a ball would roll down a hill.

In a vexatious temper, he snatched his arm away as a bearded giant came to his aid. His voice was sharp. "Unhand me, you blackguard."

Ahern stiffened at the affront. "I spanked your arse red when ye was a wee lad. I give not a care if ye are a grown man, I'll do it once more if ye insult me again."

Liam raised a querying brow at the huge red-bearded man, sensing a familiarity.

He collected his scattered wits and accepted the crutch. Situating it under his arm, he said, "Do I know you, sir?"

"Aye, ye do, laddie. 'Tis your Uncle Ahern O'Neill I be."

A stinging shame whipped through Liam's heart. "My apologies, Uncle."

Edwin stepped forward. He extended his hand. "Edwin Trumble, Capt'n. I don't know if ye remember me? 'Tis good yer home, sir."

Liam returned the handshake. "It's been a while, but I do remember you."

"If you will point out which is your trunk, I'll load it on the carriage."

Liam cleared his throat. "All was lost when the Sepoy rebels burned and looted the garrison at Meerut. The ruling Indian government was kind enough to leave me with my life, the clothes on my back, and *that*"—he indicated the cedar box at his foot—"is my only possession."

Edwin lifted the small cedar box from the wet ground. He used the end of his heavy coat to wipe away a spot of mud clinging to the container. "Most dreadful, sir. Come, Lady Adel awaits."

Liam's heart thudded against his ribs. He wanted to drink in her beauty, to drown in the sweet aroma of her perfume. Instead, he searched the depths of her lilac eyes. Searched for signs of pity. What he saw was compassion. Blast! He didn't want compassion. It made living all the more difficult.

****

Adel eyed him warily, as if unsure of his identity. The emaciated man approaching bore little semblance to the portrait hanging in her studio. Finding herself face to face with Liam, she could not draw a deep breath into her lungs. His haggard appearance brought back memories of yesteryear and the stoically proud soldier who had danced with her, whose passionate kiss had left her weak-kneed. It was a terrible shock to see how he had wasted away.

She was horrified by the sight standing before her. There was a haunted look in Liam's eyes, a look filled with pain and despair.

She collected her scattered wits and reached out to embrace him. He drew back, his sharp distaste obvious. "I fear, madam, that I am besieged with lice." He held a crutch upward. "If it were within my power, I would ride atop the coach and not expose you to infestation."

As if to make his point, he scratched beneath the armpit of his stained jacket.

A smile traced Adel's lips. "Welcome home, Liam. Mary Kathryn wanted to come, but I cajoled her into staying to help Tilde prepare a sumptuous dinner for you."

He tilted his head sideways as he contemplated Adel. "It will tear me apart for the child to see me like this."

Adel shrugged confidently. "Mary Kathryn is a beautiful seven-year-old with a compassionate understanding that belies her youth. She is aware of your...your physical condition. And cares not a whit less for you. Now come. It is cold, and I see the tiredness in your eyes."

He stood before the open carriage door. Determined to enter under his own steam, he handed the crutches to Edwin and then reached up to grasp the insides of the door. His strength failed him.

Ahern stepped forward. "You're an O'Neill to the heart, laddie. Too stubborn to ask for help. Well, the chill is causing me bones to ache. So your stubborn pride be damned." He grabbed Liam around the waist and with ease lifted him inside the conveyance.

Ahern offered Adel a hand. He gave her a wink of reassurance as he assisted her, then secured the door shut.

Inside the dim interior, Liam lay propped in the corner, his arms tightly crossed over his chest. Adel thought he looked feverish. She reached for the fur coverlet and tucked it around his shivering body.

"Thank you, madam."

He seemed cold and distant, as if he hated her presence. Adel's eyes lifted and she stared at him in puzzling question. "There is no need for such formality,

Liam. 'Adel' will do just fine."

Outside, Edwin cracked the whip and clucked the horses into motion. The sharp sound caused Liam to flinch. The look on his face suggested he was ready to do battle.

That surprised her. "I can't imagine all you have suffered, Liam—"

His voice, soft and menacing, cut her off. "No, madam, you cannot."

She was too stunned to respond, at first. She gave her husband a soft smile. "I will try to understand, if you will let me."

As soon as the carriage settled into a gentle rocking rhythm, Adel reached beneath the seat and withdrew a wicker basket laden with sandwiches. Deciding he needed warmth rather than food, she removed a decanter filled with Irish Rose and poured two fingers of the amber liquid into a cup.

"Drink this. It will help warm you."

Without hesitation, he chugged down the contents and held the cup for a refill. He grimaced as the whiskey burned itself down his throat and into his stomach.

"Are you hungry? I've brought sandwiches."

"I don't remember the last good meal I've had. Sometimes my memory plays tricks on me. With your permission, I would prefer whiskey over bread."

She had read everything at her disposal about how the tragedies of war affected soldiers. Patience, love, and strength were advised. She hoped she possessed all the requirements.

Her voice was gentle, but determined. "Too much alcohol on an empty stomach is detrimental to your health—so I've read. Perhaps a mild libation after you've had a hearty meal?"

He scowled as he pulled the fur wrap tighter around his shoulders. His tone derisive, he told her, "When you've lived in hell, it isn't a hearty meal that holds the demons at bay, my good lady." After that, Liam remained quiet for a long while. He closed his eyes, and Adel thought he had drifted to sleep.

It was as if he sensed she watched him. He opened his eyes, his lips lifted in a sad smile, and he confessed in a hushed whisper, "It pains me to know I have failed you."

Adel opened her mouth to reply but closed it again as she found herself assailed by uncertainty.

"How horrible it must have been, all you have endured. It is enough that you are alive, Liam. That you have returned to Mary Kathryn…and to me. I do not count that as failure."

His gaze found hers. His voice hitched. "Robby—"

Adel leaned forward. She soothed his cheek with a feathery touch. "Lord and Lady Beck held a beautiful memorial for Robby. We shall always hold him in our hearts."

Liam nodded as if further words escaped him.

She longed to wipe away the tears clustered on his thick, dark lashes. She longed to wrap him in her arms and croon to him the way she did when Mary Kathryn was afraid. She longed to know how much it would take to heal her husband's broken soul.

Chapter Twenty-Four

The wind slashed a spattering of snow across the silent yard. Adel had watched the muscle tics in his face, the twitches of his body as he slept. He'd spoken of demons. She wondered if they visited him now.

She reached forward to give the sleeping man a gentle nudge. "We're home, Liam."

He bolted forward, wild-eyed, the confusion on his face evident. She resisted the prodding prongs of fear when his hands reached toward her throat, as if seriously contemplating doing her harm.

Her heart trembled inside her chest. "I-I'm dreadfully sorry. I didn't mean to startle you."

Liam lowered his hands to his lap. His gaze troubled, he looked directly into Adel's eyes. "I could have killed you."

"Y-yes, I believe the medical books call it battle trauma. It was my fault. I shouldn't have startled you."

Liam gave a slow, deliberate nod and then swung his legs around to look out the coach window and drink in the scene unfolding as the horses trotted up the driveway and onto the circular drive to stop in front of the house.

It took a moment before he spoke. "All the drawings you sent were destroyed in the attack. I can't seem to recall them."

"No matter. When you are stronger, I will take you

to the room I use as my art studio." She pointed. "It's there, on the third floor. I have copies of each phase of the rebuilding. I hope they will please you."

The coach stopped. Edwin opened the door. "Captain, may I assist you?"

Liam seemed to deliberate how he would descend the coach. "Let's pray I don't make a fool of myself by spilling to the ground."

Ahern stepped forward. "I picked ye up when ye were a lad and tumbled from your pony. Don't worry 'bout falling. I'll catch you."

Liam lowered one crutch to the mounting step and then the second crutch. Those watching did so holding their breath. He lifted his good leg over the coach's floor sill. When his boot settled on the step, all breathed a sigh of relief, and another as he repeated the process to stand firmly on the ground.

Ahern clapped his nephew on the shoulder. "I'd give ye a bear hug, but I'm afeard of breaking your bones."

Adel didn't try to contain her smile. "Bravo, Liam."

He turned to find Adel standing close behind him. "Come inside," she urged. "We'll sit by the fire and warm ourselves with a pot of hot tea and a plate of Mrs. Bliss's wonderful scones."

Ahern said, "This is a private time. I will ride home and share the news of Liam with Eveleen. Send word by Shamus when Liam is ready to receive his family."

Liam turned. "It was your letters which sustained me in my darkest hours, Uncle. Yours and Adel's."

Ahern blustered a bit as he doffed his tam. "Come, Edwin. I'll help unhitch the horses."

Liam lifted his face to the snow. For several minutes neither he nor Adel spoke. A fierce shivering wracked his body, and then, with the forward-swinging motion of his crutches, he made his way toward the house, allowing Adel to stabilize him as he maneuvered the steps.

When he entered the great room, he stood for a long moment near the door as he watched a girl with hair the color of burnished autumn leaves and eyes that reminded him of the bluest depths of the ocean as she stood staring at him.

"Mary Kathryn?"

"Oh, Daddy!"

The cherished title was like a tender caress softly soothing him, and tears welled in his eyes as he whispered, "My beautiful...beautiful daughter."

A sigh of relief escaped Adel as Liam faced her, but she realized by the pained look in her husband's eyes that he was hurting inside. She laid a gentle hand on his arm. With the other, she motioned a lad forward from beyond Mary Kathryn.

"This is Gaffney. Like so many of our people, he needed a family. He helps in the kitchen garden and tends to errands for which I haven't the time. He is schooled and intelligent. He also enjoys a good game of chess. Gaffney will serve as your valet."

The boy's limp was obvious when he stepped forward and bowed. Liam expelled a derisive snort. *Very appropriate. A cripple helping a cripple.*

"How old are you, lad?"

"Sixteen, sir."

Young, thought Liam, so very young. "When I was your age, I was attending military school."

"Yes, sir. Milady has told me much about you. I've heated water. Shall I draw a bath for you?"

Liam's eyes went straight to the stairs. "The water will need reheating by the time I manage to get all the way up there."

Mary Kathryn said, "Oh, no, Daddy. Mommy and I have prepared a room on this level." She reached out to lay her hand on his arm. "I will show you."

He flinched as if her grip had sent shock waves through him.

The tearing blue eyes lifted to Liam in a worried stare. "I'm sorry, Daddy. Did I hurt you?"

He wanted to wrap her in his arms. The cords in his neck tensed as he suffered from several moments of confusion. "It is I who owe you an apology. I seem to have lost all sense of decorum."

A worried smile tugged at Mary Kathryn's lips as she glanced from Adel to the man she only knew from pencil sketches. "It's all right, Daddy. Mommy says you need plenty of care."

"I suppose a good scrubbing wouldn't hurt." He plucked at a hole in his jacket. "What will I do for clothes? These have seen their better days."

Adel said, "My apologies, Liam. We did not know what to expect. I'm afraid I didn't think about clothing."

Tilde stepped forward. She curtsied. "Beg pardon, Captain. If it wouldn't offend you, Edwin is about your height. Though a little larger in the girth."

His look of confusion clearly stated he didn't remember the woman. "This is Edwin's wife, Tilde."

"Ah, yes, your maid."

"Did I not write to tell you I had adopted Tilde as

229

my sister?"

He looked from Adel to the tall woman standing next to her, obviously trying to recall the letter she spoke of. "Forgive me for forgetting. It was a long time ago."

Adel said, "Mary Kathryn, perhaps you might ask Mrs. Bliss to prepare a pot of tea."

She smiled as the child curtsied. "May I read to you sometime, Daddy?"

"I should like that fine."

As soon as the child had skipped from the room, Liam thanked Tilde for loan of her husband's clothing. "I shall welcome the exchange of clean attire for the stench of these rags."

A smile lifted the corners of Adel's mouth. "I will have one of the ladies in the sewing room come straight away to take measurements, and Gaffney will ride to the village in the morning to bring the cobbler."

Liam's good leg seemed not to remember what its duty was, and he sagged against the crutches.

Adel screamed, "Gaffney, catch him!"

Liam didn't know why he was furious. Anger welled like an overactive volcano. He wanted to lash out. To scream that he didn't want their coddling. He wanted to crawl inside a whiskey bottle and drown. Instead, his gritted teeth allowed out the words, "I'll take that bath now."

****

Mary Kathryn set the tray of tea and biscuits on the side table and then pounced on the large bed. "I hope you like it, Daddy. I helped Mommy stuff the comforter with down from our geese. And I helped with the stitching, too."

230

Liam scanned the room. "Why do you call Adel Mommy?"

The child scrunched her face at the question. "I know my real mother is with the angels, but I can't remember her. Del is my true mommy."

She looked up at him, and in all her innocence, asked, "Does your leg hurt?"

The question caught him off guard. Breath seemed to whoosh out of him. Most people avoided looking at the pinned-up trouser leg that covered his stump as much as they avoided asking about it. Not wanting to alarm or patronize the child, he kept his voice quiet. "Sometimes it hurts, like a toothache. Other times it feels as if the bottom of my foot itches."

Mary Kathryn offered a puzzled frown. "But you don't have a foot."

Adel scolded, "You mustn't wear your father out with questions."

"She meant no harm, Adel. I admire the child's honesty." He looked at Mary Kathryn. "It's true. Sometimes I forget that I have no foot, and I try to walk. The doctors call it phantom limb sensation."

"If you fall, Daddy, I will help pick you up."

Her comment staggered his heart. He fought against the chill invading his body and gripped the bedpost for support. "Leave me while I freshen myself and rest a bit."

Taking Mary Kathryn by the hand, Adel complied. Before stepping from the room, she sighed softly. "If you need anything, tell Gaffney."

With some disgust for his lack of civilized manners, Liam kneaded his icy palms together. A pang of anguish stabbed him as he turned to see his image reflected in the cheval glass which stood a short arm's length from him. He felt like smashing the mirror to destroy the repugnant reflection staring back at him.

The flames in the hearth burned low. "I will add more logs, sir."

"As you wish, lad."

Liam took in every element of the room. A large four-poster bed, a chaise, luxurious wool carpeting on the floor, and the heirloom tapestry. He remembered it from his childhood. A highboy for his clothes, and heavy drapes to shut out the cold. No softening contours or feminine embellishments. A masculine room that smelled of polished mahogany.

He pointed toward a door. "Where does that lead, Gaffney?"

The boy opened the door and swung it wide. "'Tis the water closet, sir. Be ye ready for the hot water, now?"

A small fireplace heated the compact area. A large copper tub sat in the middle of the room, where an oak cabinet with a copper ewer adorned one wall, a mirror above it, and facing it a closed stool. Liam had heard of the chairs with a hole in the center and a porcelain chamber pot underneath. Such contraptions had not made their way to India. It seemed Adel had spared no expense in modernizing the house.

Liam answered with a nod. While he waited for the boy to return, he puzzled over the best way to enter the tub. He could straddle it with his stump and hope not to lose his balance and risk cracking his head.

Gaffney and Edwin, each carrying two buckets, entered the room and filled the tub. The boy laid a towel, a washcloth, and a bar of lye soap within easy reach. He hung a heavy green robe on a wall peg, then placed a matching green slipper next to the robe. "Shall I remove your boot, sir?"

Liam sat on the closed stool and offered his booted foot. The boy straddled Liam's leg and, with a hard tug, removed the worn footwear.

"'Tis none of my business, sir, but I can see getting in and out of the tub may present a challenge. With your permission, tomorrow I will ask Master Murphy, the smithy, to devise a bar of some sort so you do not hurt yourself."

Part of Liam wanted to scold the lad for brash impertinence; the other part admired his simple yet ingenious solution to an everyday trial. "A good valet always looks after his master. Now leave me."

"Shall I help with your undress, sir?"

Liam's temper flared. He did not wish to share his scars with anyone. "Blast it, boy, do you not have ears?"

Gaffney retreated as if he feared a cuffing.

He called after the boy, "I'll have no further use for this uniform. Burn it."

As soon as the lad left the room, Liam removed the tattered jacket and under-blouse, then stood and slid the suspenders over his shoulders, allowing the dingy white trousers to fall around his ankle. He sat back on the chamber seat and bent forward to retrieve the pants from his foot.

Pondering the best way to get into the tub, he first tried bearing his weight on the crutches and lifting his good leg over the edge. When that didn't work, he tried a different approach. His crutch skewed aside and he crashed to the floor.

He lay for a moment, stunned, before reaching up to grasp the tub's rim. Using upper body strength and his muscled arms, he lifted himself from the floor and sat on the tub's cold copper edge, then swiveled until his good leg was in the water. Waves undulated over his naked body as he submerged to his shoulders. Liam expelled a contented sigh as he reached for the bar of soap. He lathered every inch of his body and scrubbed away layers of grime. He rubbed his scalp with vigor and hoped the harsh soap would kill the lice. He hoped the boy Gaffney would have sense enough to burn the infested uniform as ordered.

He couldn't remember the last time he had enjoyed the luxury of a complete bath.

Chapter Twenty-Five

At first Liam didn't know what had awakened him. His quarters were dark and quiet. He shivered beneath the downy quilt. He felt hot and cold at the same time. After several seconds, his eyes adjusted to the darkness. He perceived the presence before he heard the movement at the side of the bed.

His head snapped in the direction of the sound. A vision of the Sepoy attacking his men flashed before his eyes. The deafening roar of gunfire and the horrific screams of men engaging in combat filled his ears. For an instant, he hovered between confusion and terror before recognition set in.

Adel.

His head rested against the hunter green brocade bolster. His fevered mind tried to rationalize her presence there but couldn't quite make the enormous leap from the heat of battle to the luxurious room. He could only lower his head back onto the pillow and watch her silently, his gaze drifting along the shadowed contours of her face. There was a certain vulnerability in her moonlit features that made her appear childlike.

Through the sooty night, he tried to focus on her. He spoke through parched lips, his voice a soft rasp. "Water. May I have some water?"

Like the ghost of the men who flitted in and out of his dreams, Adel was out of sight before he fully comprehended she was gone. Light suffused the room in a dim glow. The slosh of water filled the silence. She returned to his side with a glass in one hand and a candle in the other. She set the taper on the table beside the bed. Awash in the flickering radiance, Liam could now see the fatigue on Adel's face. Her tiredness did not, however, detract from the beauty of her features. Even in his illness, he clearly saw that and felt the inexorable pull of her femininity.

Instead of handing him the glass, Adel sat on the edge of the bed. He flinched when she gently slid her hand beneath his head and lifted the glass to his lips. "Here, drink."

Liam automatically parted his lips at the softly spoken command. The water was neither cold nor warm, but it refreshed his parched throat. He drank the glass's entire contents before slumping back against the pillow.

Adel didn't remove her hand immediately. He felt the pressure of her palm, the weight of every finger, with a keenness that had his skin tingling—a sensation not caused by his body aches or fever.

She stared at him with a quiet intensity. "Would you like me to get you anything else?"

"No. I'm feeling much better now."

She placed the back of her hand against his forehead. "You are feverish. I'll get a cloth to cool your brow." She removed her hand from beneath his head. Liam felt the loss like a flower would miss the warmth of the sun on a frigid winter day. He wasn't bereft of her touch for long.

"There is no need to concern yourself over me. This ague will pass."

"You've survived so much, Liam. Perhaps the malaise is from all you've suffered. Nonetheless, in the morning, when Gaffney rides to the village to bring the cobbler, I shall instruct him to seek out the doctor for a tonic."

Perhaps tomorrow he would tell himself his weakened state had left him vulnerable to a bedside manner that every physician should emulate. But it wasn't tomorrow, it was tonight, and his heart thumped erratically. Her nearness, the feminine scent from her every pore had him dragging in air as if it were the very essence of life.

His throat was no longer dry, and he wasn't feeling as poorly as he had been earlier. Yet it appeared he suffered from another bout of illness—one that could be every bit as dangerous as losing his leg. The woman he had vowed not to love. The woman he had vowed not to obligate to an invalid. Adel.

"Do not trouble yourself. I am already much better."

Adel removed her hand from his forehead. "You look somewhat distressed. Are you not comfortable?" Her gaze skimmed the length of his body outlined beneath the plane of the bed covers.

He clasped her wrist. "Leave me, Adel. All I need is rest." *And I need you to leave so I can regain my senses...my sanity.*

She gave a slight gasp in response to his vise-like grip. "As you wish, Liam." At the softly spoken words, Adel stood, the shift in the mattress slight from her weight. Her face was immediately cast in the shadow, the candle's light illuminating the tumbled curls around her shoulders, and the puzzled confusion in her eyes.

"Rest well, Liam. I will visit you in the morning." Her gaze seemed to linger on him before she turned and slipped quietly from the room.

Don't go, hovered on his lips as she softly closed the door behind her.

****

Adel was relieved Liam's fever lasted only a few days. Despite its brevity, she instructed him to remain in bed and to take a teaspoon of tonic until she determined he was fully recovered. He could fret and moan about it all he wanted—which he did. Adel's position didn't waver.

In addition, she instructed Gaffney to cater to Liam's every need, to ensure his every comfort. She herself made it her duty to check on him twice during the day—visits she limited to the times she knew he was asleep.

By the fourth day of his confinement, and much to Adel's satisfaction, Liam did appear restored to full health. Only then did she finally grant him leave to venture beyond his bedchamber walls.

She spent the better part of her days cloistered in her studio, designing a drawing for an artificial leg. When she wasn't working on the drawing, she was down at the stables with her latest purchase, a majestic black thoroughbred. She wanted a tall horse, a horse with spirit but also an even temperament, a horse who might heal the broken nature of a once magnificent man. Onyx possessed all the traits she desired, despite the fact he had several imperfections she didn't wish passed along to the pure lines of her breeding program.

"Onyx has a gentle nature about him, don't you agree, Shamus?"

"Aye, miledy. Too bad the horse is cow-hocked." Shamus laid a gentle slap on the animal's rump. "No racing for you, me laddie. He'll need gelding, for certain."

Adel remained pensive for a moment as she walked around the tall, jet black stallion. "Agreed. I can't risk passing on this affliction to any foals he would sire. Still, it is too bad, because otherwise he is a splendid animal."

She offered a deep sigh as she gave the animal a gentle pat on the neck. "Shamus, walk with me. I wish to speak with both you and your father."

"'Tis serious, I'd judge, by the look on your face. You are not unhappy with our work, miledy?"

Adel spotted the concern on the lad's face and rushed to reassure him. "I have no concerns about the way you and your father help run the farm. No, this is a matter that requires special workmanship."

At the smithy shed, Adel pulled the drawing from the deep pocket of her woolen cape. It pained her to watch Liam struggle with a pair of crutches that were not suitably built for his height. She also knew that, as his healing continued, it was only a matter of time before he completely salved his pity in a bottle. Although he had not voiced as much, instinctively she knew he considered himself less than a man—useless.

"Master Murphy, I wish you to use your skills to build this." She tapped a finger against the pencil sketch.

Patrick Murphy leaned over the drawing. He reached under his woolen tam to scratch his head. "It don't look like any wooden leg I've ever seen, mum. 'Tisn't much like the peglegs of yore." He pointed at the swiveled joint. "What be this?"

She tipped her head to one side. "I've heard the stories of the old peglegged pirates and how they stumped around, often unable to perform simple things like climbing stairs or maintaining a good balance." She traced her finger along the sketch. "I thought about how the knee works. I know the drawing defies anything we've all seen, but we must try. And it must fit comfortably, so as not to rub abscesses on the captain's flesh."

Patrick Murphy looked at Adel, his eyes serious. "I only know what Gaffney has passed on to me son Shamus. The captain be a proud man, and not one who will admit kindly to such a contraption."

Adel didn't immediately respond. The elder Murphy was correct in his assessment. She knew she walked a fine line between pushing Liam deeper into his melancholy and helping him regain a new lease on life.

"Sometimes a person either doesn't know how to help themselves or would rather wallow in his misery. It is my intent to help the captain realize that he is still the man he always was. So, my question is, will you use your skills to build the captain a wooden leg with a hinged knee?"

Without hesitation, Patrick Murphy said, "Aye, milady. You do me a great honor by placin' yer confidence in me. I won't let ye down."

Adel expelled a sigh of relief. The tone of her voice grew even more serious. "Shamus, as with your father, I am charging you with a dire task. The captain has always been a true horseman. In time, he will ride again. I trust no one but you with the training of Onyx.

The animal must stand perfectly still when the captain climbs into the saddle, and again when he dismounts. And further, the horse must not move until given the command. I will not risk injury to the captain."

While she spoke to his son, Patrick Murphy had been studying the drawing. Adel caught his scowl and heard him say several times, "Hmmm" and "Well, let me think."

She was more than hopeful when he looked at her again and smiled. "'Tis an odd contraption, that be for sure. Aye, miledy, aye, it'll pleasure me much to make this for the captain."

He then shifted from one foot to the other. Adel didn't miss the unasked question on the elder Murphy's face. "What disturbs you, Patrick?"

"Well, miledy, 'tis the stirrup that be worrying me, 'tis."

"What stirrup, Patrick?" And then she grasped his meaning. "Oh, that stirrup. I hadn't thought about it. What shall we do?"

"Not to worry, mum. I'll think of something. Can't have the captain's leg dangling. Need to think of a way to fit the end o' the peg in the stirrup so 'tis easy on 'is balance, don't you know."

She turned her attention toward Shamus. "You've no doubt you can train the horse?"

"Aye, miledy. You can count on me. By the time I am finished, a wee child will be able to sit under the horse's belly and rest against 'is hind legs without 'im flinching a muscle or flicking 'is tail."

"Can you accomplish this feat before Christmas?"

Adel feared she was asking the impossible. However, she knew it would take the impossible to rebuild Liam's confidence in himself. She watched Shamus use his fingers to count the days.

"With only fourteen days 'til the 'oliday, 'tis a tall order ye ask of the 'orse, mum. But I'll do me best."

"It isn't your best I want, Shamus. It's assurance."

"Then ye 'ave it. I'll train Onyx as if I were training 'im for Mistress Mary Kathryn. 'E'll be ready. Ye 'ave me promise."

Adel clasped her hands together. She smiled at father and son. "Thank you both. I can ask for none better."

Chapter Twenty-Six

Liam swore under his breath. He was sick of being sick, and though his suite was spacious and comfortable, there were times when he felt as if the four walls were his prison. Vivid memories of the darkened cave shuddered over him. His palms suddenly turned damp. He closed his eyes and fought the nausea that assailed his stomach. It was his memories of Ireland, fields of purple heather, the sounds of the waves crashing against the cliffs, and Adel that had helped him survive those claustrophobic conditions. He smiled. Adel would blister his ears, for sure, if he decided to leave the confines of his room. But he needed to feel the brisk air in his face, to breath in the purity of it. He needed to assure himself that he was home, at Mautagh, and not in a dream.

He situated the crutches under his arms and stumped across the space to fling back the heavy drapes. The rug beneath his bare foot was thick, plush wool that tickled his toes.

He viewed the outside surroundings. A barn, corral, smithy shed, and farm hands all engaged in their daily work. Little else except the fields dotted with sheep.

And Adel. The shapely length of her stretched on her tiptoes to touch the cheeks of a long-legged black horse, a thoroughbred, no doubt.

During his deployment to India, and in his illness, he'd certainly spent a fair amount of time dwelling on Adel. He could not pretend that his passion for her didn't exist. He loved the way he felt when she was near, the way his blood thrummed in his veins, and how his senses came alive. As a matter of survival, during all the weeks hidden inside the cave and after, he'd kept a tight rein on his emotions, until now. Smell and taste and touch—oh, aye, touch. His skin heated. He needed to ignore his feelings, his emotions. Adel deserved someone more appropriate, who would fit into her life. Someone to love her as a woman should be loved.

As he watched, he saw her walk around the animal, smoothing her hands over its withers, along its sleek black body, and down its hindquarters. He knew by the set of the animal's ears that Adel spoke to it. He envied the horse her touch.

A thread of fury ran through Liam, a strong and detectable anger. No use. He was a one-legged man. What could he offer Adel? The sound of the wind outside seemed to whisper the answer. *Nothing.* He decided to shut off his emotions. He would not allow a relationship to grow between them. No, he would not. He tugged the drapes shut.

Two sharp raps sounded at the door. He recognized the knocks as Gaffney's signal. Good, Liam thought. The boy could help him dress. Come hell or high water, today he planned to escape his room and seek the outdoors. "Come. Gaffney, I…"

"G'morn, Captain. As Lady Adel instructed, I've brought Mistress O'Hurley. She is a fine seamstress, and is here to measure you."

"But, I—"

"Sure, an' good morn to ye, Captain, sir." An overly plump woman who looked as if she'd sucked a sour lemon marched forward. With a slight grunt, she set a wicker basket on the floor as she knelt in front of him. She removed a coiled cord from the case and announced, "Don't think me fiddling with yer private parts, 'cause I ain't. 'Tis necessary to measure the inseam to know how long to sew yer britches. Wouldn't want to make one leg longer than t'other."

She gasped the moment the words were out of her mouth. "Oh, crap. Yer Lordship, 'tis sorry I am for me wayward tongue. I-I…"

Not waiting for a reprimand from Liam, she raced on, "My, 'e's a tall one, ain't 'e? 'Ere, Gaffney, be a good laddie and write down 'is measurements when I call 'em to you."

Clearly as flustered as the woman, Gaffney fled to the mahogany secretary and opened a drawer to remove pen and paper. He scolded, "Be careful you don't go knocking the crutches out from under the captain. Lady Adel wouldn't like it if he fell and hurt himself."

The seamstress swiveled her head carefully, almost as carefully as she chose her words. "Look 'ere, yer lordship. I can't get a true measurement wid ye all hunched over like that. If'n I'm truly careful, can ye let go one of them sticks so ye can stand tall?"

Liam growled his annoyance. "Can't this wait? I'd rather get a spot of fresh air."

Gaffney cleared his throat, and in his most tactful voice said, "Beg pardon, Captain, but it wouldn't do to be seen walking around in your morning robe. Your borrowed clothes are in the wash."

"Blast it all." Then as if to prove he could stand

without assistance, he handed both crutches to Gaffney. "How long will this nonsense take?"

The seamstress didn't bother to look up from her measuring. "If ye'll stop fidgeting, I'll be done in two shakes of a lamb's tail."

Gaffney hovered like a protective mother hen guarding a lone chick. He wrote the measurements as the seamstress called them out. Then, as if she needed reminding, he ticked off all of the garments Adel had ordered for Liam.

"Listen, ye young upstart, I know me business, and I don't 'preciate you reminding me. I sew all the time. I'll 'ave 'is lordship's clothes ready before Christmas."

Liam closed his eyes and willed away the sounds of the two bickering voices. *Christmas.* The word ran through his mind. He tried to remember the last time he'd thought about the Yule season, or any holiday. He sighed inwardly.

Forgetting about his ability to walk without the crutches, he moved to take a step forward, lost his balance, and fell sprawling on top of Mrs. O'Hurley.

She squealed and wriggled under his weight. "'Pon my word," she exclaimed.

Liam opened his eyes and looked straight into the plump seamstress's leering smile. He sucked in a breath through his teeth as though he had to struggle to bring in enough air before he rolled to one side and gave an inelegant snort. "Gaffney, stop flitting around like a drunken chicken and help me off the floor. Mrs. O'Hurley, I hope you have all the measurements you need, because we're finished here."

Pressing her lips together, she sat up, her legs splayed apart. She reached up to adjust the topknot on her head. Her eyes widened a little. "Gawd, yer 'ung like a bleedin' stallion."

Liam realized the front of his robe had come untied, fully exposing his nakedness. He sat up and rolled to his good knee, at the same time fumbling to pull the front of his robe together and retie the sash. "Damn it to hell, Gaffney, get that blasted woman out of here."

The scarecrow of a lad huffed as he struggled to help the fleshy woman from the floor.

When Liam thought the boy would lose the battle in trying to lift the seamstress, the bedroom door banged opened. Adel, followed by Tilde, burst into the room.

"We heard a scream, and a crash." Adel cut a startled look toward the struggling pair on the floor. "Tilde, I fear we need Edwin to help poor Gaffney."

Just when it looked as if the boy were making a bit of progress, Mary Kathryn entered the room, chasing after her kitten. Without warning or malice the child careened into Gaffney and caused him to lose his grip on Mrs. O'Hurley.

Four legs seemed to tangle in a mass of skirt and petticoats. Indignant squeals, cursing, and hilarity filled the room. Adel held her sides. "I-I'm so sorry, Mrs. O'Hurley. It isn't you I'm laughing at. I-It's—" A new round of laughter bubbled forth.

With her topknot listing to one side and a length of hair escaping its combs and dangling over one eye, Mrs. O'Hurley reminded Liam of a mime in a play he'd long forgotten. In spite of himself, he laughed.

Edwin and Shamus, a breathless duo, skidded into the bedchamber. Edwin was the first to speak. "'Ere,

Shamus, let's get the captain off the floor."

With no time to think and only a second to react, Liam was lifted to the edge of his bed.

The room fell quiet. Waiting. Adel finally clapped her hands together. "Mrs. O'Hurley, I trust you have all the measurements you need?"

"Aye, that I do, mum."

"Good. Then there is no need for you to tarry. Everyone, the captain has had enough excitement." Adel thanked Edwin and Shamus for coming to Liam's aid.

He ran a trembling hand over his jaw, feeling feverish in spite of the room's chill. "Leave me, Adel. I wish for Gaffney to help me with my wardrobe. One does get tired of being cooped up for any length of time. I'm going for a walk."

"You should rest, Liam. I fear the exertion will cause your fever to return."

His gaze flickered over her, briefly, his expression inscrutable. "I'm not a child, woman. My mind is made up. Now do as I say and leave me."

She nodded curtly. "Of course. Perhaps a bit of fresh air will cool your foul mood."

Adel turned, her skirts swishing as she made her way out the door. Like a wayward child, she placed her hands over her mouth to hold the laughter at bay.

****

A morning walk had been a mistake. Liam realized it the moment his stomach contracted in a second wave of pain. He should have heeded the signs when he awoke feeling queasy from the night before. A mug of steaming mint tea and dry bread at breakfast had not settled his stomach. And when he had started feeling warm again, instead of getting himself back to bed, he had decided fresh air—cold though it might be—and a walk about the estate would be the thing. But then there was the dreadful fiasco with the seamstress, Mrs. O'Hurley.

The truth was he had been all too eager to escape the confines of the house and Gaffney's incessant hovering. He also hated being sick. Most of all, Liam hated the worthlessness of being a one-legged man. Memories of fevers wracking his body, and worse, the bloodletting use of leeches, could still elicit the odd niggling sense of dread.

A weakness wafted over him. The phantom pains in his right leg increased. He was ill, plain and simple.

Liam gripped the handles of his crutches until his knuckles ached.

As he turned to go back to the house, the tip of his crutch slipped on a stone and, unable to maintain his balance, sent him careening in the yard's wet sludge. He swore a shot had rung out, not realizing the dried wood of one crutch had snapped.

The cold, moist ground felt good against his fevered cheek. The sprawling fall did more than soil his freshly washed and pressed clothes; it damaged his already fragile ego.

He rolled to his back and looked up, squinting against the glare until a giant shadow blocked out the sun. His heart thudded against his chest, and an automatic reflex sent his hands searching for a weapon. His fingers stretched toward a crutch, broken and splintered from the fall. In his fevered state, the face bending toward him was that of Jemadar Ishwari Prasad, the rebel leader who had overrun the garrison and was responsible for the slaughter of so many loyal soldiers. For a paralyzing fraction of a moment, all he wanted to do was crawl into a small dark hole and hide.

He bit off a vicious oath. "Come on, you bastard. What are you waiting for?" His voice rose with authority. "Lieutenant Beck, give the command."

Adel's breath escaped in a shuddering sob. "Oh, dear God, Ahern, I fear the delirium has taken over his mind again." Her hands darted over Liam's body like a pair of frantic birds searching for broken bones. Her voice raised in alarm. "Merciful heaven, he's burning with fever!"

Liam sat up. His voice was matter of fact. "It's all right. I'm not shot. Sound the alarm."

She looked into his fever-glazed eyes. She spoke softly. "Liam, you are home, at Mautagh Manor. This is your Uncle Ahern. There is no enemy here."

In his weakened condition, and he did indeed feel weak, he couldn't gauge whether she was toying with him or not. He briefly closed his eyes to fight the dizziness threatening to engulf him. "I-I'm fine, Adel. I must have bumped my head when I fell." The last thing he needed was sympathy.

Despite the dampness penetrating his borrowed woolen coat and seeping through to his flesh, he chuckled. "Damned cold."

He stretched his hand upward. "It's been a while, Uncle. We have much to talk about."

Liam closed his eyes against the weakness in his limbs. "Blasted ague."

With a swiftness that left Liam gasping, Ahern hoisted him into his arms.

"No," he said, a feeble protest. "I can walk just fine

on my own. Hand me my crutches."

"'Fraid not, laddie." Ahern gave the broken crutch a swift kick. "Wood is dry-rotted. Can't be mended. Lucky you didn't break your fool head."

Another roll of Liam's belly had him wincing against breath-stealing cramps.

Ahern's black brows drew over narrowed blue eyes. "Besides, laddie, broken crutch or not, you don't even have the strength to hold your head up, much less walk fifty yards to the house."

Liam struggled to recall the last time he had seen his uncle. It bothered him that he didn't know. His eyes grave, he looked at Ahern. "I'm not much of a man anymore, Uncle."

Ahern's mouth formed a tight line. "I been through a war. Watched me clansmen die all round me. Takes the heart right out of a man, 'tis for certain. But you're an O'Neill, and O'Neills are survivors."

Inside the chamber, Ahern laid his nephew gently on the bed. "Rest now, lad. Me Eveleen's brewing up a poultice. She's very good at doctoring."

Liam nodded slowly. "Uncle, if you had a plow horse that had foundered itself, and it could no longer pull its weight on the farm, what would you do with it?"

Behind his harshly bitten-out question lay a fear so distasteful Liam found it difficult to swallow.

Ahern shifted on one foot, momentarily averting his gaze toward Adel, then back to Liam. "You are not a horse, Nephew, to be put out of its sorrowful misery. You're a man who is sick in body and soul. Healing will take time." He lowered one knee to the bed and placed his beefy hands on each of Liam's cheeks. The coolness of his uncle's hands was a balm to the fevered skin.

"Do you understand me words, lad? You are no horse to be put out of your misery. In time, the devils that plague your mind will fade. You can trust me words, because...I know."

Liam harrumphed. "And how would you know, old man?"

"The Battle of Bourassa was as bloody as they come. I was there."

Liam blinked against the intensity of his uncle's gaze. They locked eye to eye for several seconds before Ahern abruptly pivoted and walked away, his heavy tread muffled by the velvet pile carpeting.

Adel lifted the cloth from the porcelain basin and wrung it dry. She crossed the room to sit on the edge of the bed. Without uttering a word, she placed the cloth on Liam's forehead. She touched his cheek, her thumb scraping over the dense beard that seemed to have sprouted overnight.

There was a catch in her voice when she finally spoke. "I read somewhere that talking is good for the soul. If you're a mind to, I'll listen without judgment."

"Why would I want to talk?"

"It will help me understand all you've suffered." She held her breath as if awaiting his answer.

"What do you want to know?"

"Everything."

Liam went still. His gaze fixed on her. And then he shrugged, shifting his focus across the broad stretch of the room.

"After a long siege," he said, "at first you think that all you want to do is sleep. Every bit of energy has been drained from you, and all you want is oblivion. But then

I would just lie there looking up at the sky, and no matter how much I begged for sleep, *prayed* for it, I could never force it to take me."

Adel's hand rubbed his arm soothingly. "I'm sorry about Robby. Did he...he didn't...suffer?"

"Don't ask me, Adel." Liam's voice was barely a whisper. "Don't ever ask me again."

****

His faint smile told her he appreciated her attempt to comfort him. He wasn't without flaws. He was human, someone who'd survived long enough to have his body start to show the wear of the years he had spent in the military.

He studied her, regret etched into his handsome face. He didn't want her to worry about him, she knew that. She interlaced her fingers with his.

An ache hummed within her. It wasn't physical, the grinding drive that compelled bodies together, the simmering heat that had kept her awake so many nights. His look settled in her heart, piercing deep, the tenderness more devastating than any passion.

She felt her throat clog and her eyes burn with the tears she didn't dare release. She battled them back. Her emotions were fragile, as if she might shatter at any moment.

His blue eyes met hers, and she stared at him, wanting desperately to say something, anything, to narrow the gulf that stretched between them. In the end, she didn't know what to say, and he seemed unwilling or uninterested in meeting her halfway.

Finally, he removed his hand. She saw the flare of regret in his eyes.

"Don't pity me, Adel."

"Never," she whispered.

So he would ignore her careful overture, and their relationship would remain light and so much less than what it could be.

Chapter Twenty-Seven

Liam lurched up in his bed, his heart racing from the nightmare screams echoing in his mind, his throat tight with horror. Scrambling, he kicked off the downy comforter. He was coated in sweat, the sheet clinging to him like an extra layer of skin.

Eyes wide, he strained to hear anything except the wind as it moaned around the house. The sound reminded him of the air that had whispered through the cave.

He swallowed, trying to bring his rational mind to the fore. But his dream had been so vivid, with the agony of seeing Robby take the full brunt of a cannonball blast and his body trampled by a brigade of horses. Then the enemy was on Liam, savagely attacking.

His skin felt as if pecked by hundreds of tiny birds, and anxiety pierced his heart.

The nightmares were not new to him. In his dreams he was always reaching for Adel, trying to protect her from terrible danger. It was the feelings that went along with the dreams that always left him shaken. Crushed by frustration and fear and a terrible sense of impotence, Liam would call out, and then he'd awakened.

****

Liam haunted her sleep. What little sleep there

was. Adel lay on her bed and stared up at the inky darkness above her. Moonlight trickled through the window so the gilding on the ceiling shimmered now and then, as if a starlit sky arched above her.

Restless, she left the comfort of her soft, downy tick and pulled the clean, sweet-smelling sheets and heavy quilt into place behind her to preserve what warmth she could for her return. She slipped a long silk gown over her naked body and donned a pair of slippers, giving little heed to the luxuries she now enjoyed. What did they matter when her husband preferred the privacy of his own rooms?

The fire had burned low, and she placed a few more logs upon the glowing coals before tugging a chair close and propping her feet upon the raised hearth. She could find no comforting home for her thoughts to rest.

Finally she forced herself to review the past weeks with meticulous detail and deliberation, and memories of Liam quickly overshadowed the gloom.

For most of the time, she had kept busy with the tasks of running the estate. The seamstress had sewn almost all of an entire new wardrobe for Liam, and new hangings for his bed, heavy enough to keep out the drafts. Rugs had been placed over the stone floors throughout the house, and woolen lap robes were furnished for chairs everywhere.

Adel's own chamber had taken on a coziness with the draped velvet on her windows. The new bed hangings added an inviting warmth to the haven, and it was almost a pleasure to curl beneath the down comforters as she drifted off into a restless slumber. In its separate bathing room, the copper tub gleamed from its weekly polishing.

Liam was home. He was alive. Still, Adel found the passing weeks had chafed hard against her emotions. She was very much a stranger to the growing yearnings that assailed her and more than a little cautious of the desires that enflamed her. Never in her life had she felt the smallest urge to seek out a man's company as she now was inclined to do with Liam.

He seemed casual enough about touching her, but he had yet to respond in kind to the yearning she had; it was not yet appeased. She had been totally amazed by the attack on her senses the morning she came upon him bereft of a shirt, and she had been hard pressed to drag her eyes away from that well-muscled expanse. From simple to sensuous, her mind was ever wont to wander when her hungering gaze touched upon the man.

During the dark days of his illness, she had allowed no one but herself to care for him, to bathe him, and to hold him when the delirium ravaged his mind.

She had memorized every shape, every swell, every bulge, every leanness, every firmness, every flowing muscle that had all been wonderfully combined to create that tall, handsome torso. Quite often her lashes would flick down, brushing burning cheeks as she tried to hide her growing fascination, but her imagination refused to halt on the outer garb of the man. She had seen all, and, wanton maid that she was, all was what she desired to see again.

Stepping away from the hearth, Adel slowly paced about the chamber. Her longings were by no means a singular problem, for Liam had made it known that he did not desire intimacy with her.

A sound caught her attention. She stilled herself and listened. Liam had cried out in his sleep.

She lit a candle with purposeful intent, then slipped from her room and down the corridor. The house was quiet as she descended the stairs and crossed the hall to Liam's quarters. She was determined that nothing would dissuade her from her resolve. Not even when a yawning Gaffney appeared in his nightshirt at the bottom of the stairs. "D'ye think the captain's fever has returned, milady?"

"I pray not, Gaffney."

"You want I should see to him?"

"Go back to bed. You need your rest, too."

"I could brew you and the captain a pot of tea, mum."

Anxious to be rid of the boy, she said, "It's a bit late for tea. If I need you, I'll pull the bell cord."

He hugged his arms around his shivering body. "As you wish, mum. G'night."

Gently Adel worked the latch. The door opened smoothly without the slightest sound, and as she stepped over the threshold, she caught the slow, steady breathing of the slumbering man who occupied the bed. The low fire cast more shadows than light, while the heavy velvet hangings held the heat within the room.

Adel's nerves stretched taut as she crept to the canopied piece. There was no mistaking Liam's tousled tawny head. He lay on his left side, facing away from her, and the down comforters barely preserved her composure, for they provided only a meager covering over his narrow hips. An ugly purple scar marred the smooth symmetry of his back, lending her an understanding of those brief times she had seen him grimace and stretch, as if some twinge of pain plagued him.

A sudden pang of compassion stirred within her as she thought of the agony he must have suffered all those long days inside the cave before Colonel Wainwright rescued him. Liam had said he had been close to death, and that a large part of him died with the amputation of his leg. His despondency greatly saddened her.

Adel held her breath as he stirred restlessly in his sleep and rolled onto his back. A long sigh slipped from him as his flung an arm up over his head and turned his face slightly away.

Though she dared not move or breathe, her eyes wandered where they would, while a warming blush suffused her cheeks at the forwardness of her inspection. Slowly her gaze passed down the furred chest and lean waist and moved on to the firm, flat belly with its light tracing of hair. A dark shadow of a scar traced upward across his ribs from his left side. While the imperfection was not new to her, she leaned over the bed as her eyes followed the line of it. She shuddered at the pain Liam must have suffered with such a wound.

Liam sat up, and with brute force his strong hands reached out and grasped her upper arms. He shouted, "Die, infidel!"

His agility, for a one-legged man, surprised Adel. He flung her down on the bed as if she were a mere rag doll and straddled her body.

"Liam…no…it's—" A glance up stilled the words in her throat, and her heart gave a terrifying thud. Adel had never seen a sapphire burn, but the blue eyes staring down at her looked exactly like cobalt sparks, akin to a raging fire.

Liam didn't breathe a word. He simply retained a firm hold on Adel's arms. Ignoring the quaking of her body and the violent churning of her stomach, she swallowed hard. The words squeaked out. "Liam—it's me—Adel. Wake up. Oh, please, wake up."

It seemed time stood still. An eternity passed before she felt his muscles relax and the grip loosen on her arms. He gave a small start and regarded her with dull, impotent eyes. He lowered his mouth to her ear. "What the hell do you think you're doing? Do you have any idea how easily I could have snapped your pretty little neck?"

He issued his threat in the kind of dangerous soft tone that undoubtedly had men, or in this case, a lady, hoping the punishment would be carried out swiftly and with minimum fuss. Then with great deliberation of purpose, he hefted his body from hers to prop against the massive headboard of tufted green velvet.

"Answer me, Adel. What brings you to my room at this hour?"

"Y-you cried out. I came to see if you were ailing again."

He snorted. "Are you certain, or did you finally get the courage to enter my room while I slept to sneak a peek at my mangled stump?"

He flung back the sheet to reveal the horribly scarred remainder of his leg. The leg had been removed above the knee. The skin was a blackened char of ridged scars.

"Take a good look. Is it what you envisioned?" When she offered no comment, he sneered, "Not exactly all neat and pretty, is it?"

She glared at him. "Why do you think to shock me, Liam, when I have tended you, bathed you, and seen all of you? What remains of your leg isn't a vision of beauty, but I am not repulsed by the sight."

He lay back and flung an arm over his eyes. "God, sometimes I can still hear the saw grinding through the bones, and smell the searing stench as the quacks that called themselves doctors set a hot iron to what was left of my leg to cauterize the flesh. There was no laudanum, and the pain...and then the bloody leeches."

Liam's hands flailed as if he were trying to remove the bloodsuckers from his body. The sounds coming from his throat reminded Adel of a wounded animal.

In desperation to comfort him, she straddled his lap and pulled his body to hers. She gathered him into her arms and crooned soothing words as she held him tight. Tears spilled from her eyes.

"You're safe, Liam. I will never let anyone hurt you again."

He pulled from her embrace to rest farther back against the massive headboard. Her eyes met his, and her breath seized in her throat. A fire burned in his eyes, and for a moment its heat focused on her. She felt it deep in her bones, in her chest, and in places that had no business feeling anything, as far as she was concerned.

Alarm bells rang in her ears. She shouldn't be looking at Liam this way. Then she reminded herself she had every right. She was the O'Shea. No, Liam was the rightful O'Shea.

She couldn't help the glowing heat inside her; her traitorous body longed to know him...as a wife should know her husband.

She swallowed, her mouth suddenly dry. Inwardly, she cursed the fires that had been lit by this virtual stranger. She felt like a warming oven that, once lit, was unable to burn out.

If only he weren't so breathtakingly handsome. What woman wouldn't want to kiss that chiseled jawline or run her fingers through those golden tresses? What woman with blood in her veins wouldn't want to feel his broad chest against her or have her body crushed beneath his?

****

Before Liam could fully absorb what was happening, Adel had nestled her cheek against his shoulder. Trying to find a more comfortable position, Liam swore softly beneath his breath.

She curled one hand around his upper thigh, and he went still. Her rosebud lips curved into an innocent smile. She had no way of knowing that her bliss was his agony. The caress of her warm breath against his neck was a taste of both heaven and hell. He rolled his eyes to the bed's canopied top. He was forced to clench his teeth against a moan.

He'd had no problem maintaining celibacy in the desolate region of his outpost. Controlling his lust had not been a problem, especially through the long months of hospitalization and with the loss of his leg. What woman in her right mind wouldn't be repulsed by the appalling sight, after all. Yet now his manroot surged to life, growing hard beneath the sheet.

"Stop moving." His voice was harsh, his control slipping as her soft, womanly flesh moved against him.

Adel stilled. She stared up at him, her lilac eyes

wide and uncertain as if she feared even a breath would draw attention to the way their bodies meshed from shoulder to hip.

Blood, hot and thick, coursed through him, pulsing strongly between his thighs, his erection near to bursting. Impatient and hungry, he took her mouth. A shudder ran down the length of his frame when his tongue touched hers. He tried to temper his need, but it required only one delicious swipe of the cavern of her mouth before she eagerly, and almost helplessly, joined in the sensual tongue play.

Lust had him in its grip, making his mind merely a vehicle of his physical needs. Mewling sounds escaped her lips when he angled his head for a more thorough access to her mouth.

One hand inched down and palmed the firm thrust of her breast, his thumb swiping repeatedly across the nipple, causing it to pebble against the pale yellow bodice of her gown before he moved to the other breast to repeat the caress. He didn't only want to feel them in his hand, he wanted to feast on them with his eyes and taste them with his lips.

A guttural sound emerged from his throat as he lifted his mouth from her to gaze into her shadowed, flushed face. Taking in her swollen lips and closed eyes, he stared at the silk ribbons neatly tied down the front of her gown, then deftly released them to reveal her breasts and firm, smooth, creamy skin. He grew harder than he thought possible.

Slowly her eyes drifted open, dark with desire, and she gazed up at him. It took only a few moments for her to lose the look of a woman lost in the deepest regions of passion. Her fingers were reaching down the remaining length of his amputated leg when her eyes widened in alarm.

He could not bear the revulsion in those two lilac orbs. He realized in that moment exactly what he had to do if he was to escape this woman with his heart unscathed.

He shoved her from him and barked out harshly, "Get the hell away from me."

Adel immediately bolted to a sitting position and jerked both edges of her bodice together in a desperate attempt to cover herself. There was no time to struggle with the bows, not with his gaze blistering her.

"Liam, I-I…beg your pardon?"

He watched her silently, a derisive smile twisting his lips. "You're no better than the street hoochies brought to the garrisons for their monthly visits to satisfy the men's urges."

A dry laugh emerged from his lips. He grabbed her hand and forced her to touch the permanently blackened, puckered skin of his leg. "Looks like a burned tree stump, doesn't it, Adel? Don't worry. It's not a disease. You can't catch it; and you're not the only woman repulsed by its ugliness."

"No, you misunderstand, I-I—"

He didn't allow her to finish. What was the use? He'd heard all the excuses—*didn't want to hurt him; didn't feel right humping a one-legged man; mi gawd, 'tis plumb freakish; no decent woman will ever want to bed you.*

"You disgust me, Adel. Get out of my sight. Take Mary Kathryn and go back to England; just leave me the bloody hell—*alone.*"

****

Without uttering a word, Adel scrambled from the bed and threw open the door. In her hasty exit, she caught the hem of her nightgown on the sharp edge of the door jamb. The fragile material rent under her impatient tug. She would have gladly shredded half her wardrobe to get away from Captain Liam O'Shea and every wretched emotion he elicited in her.

Safe in her own room, she climbed beneath the heavy covers and gathered the pillow close, hugging it as if seeking comfort from the misery welling inside her. Tears leaked down both cheeks. She had made an utter fool of herself, and now Liam had ordered her back to England. She had spent so many happy days in this house. Her heart sank even further. How would she explain to Mary Kathryn that she must leave the only home she'd ever known?

Staring into the darkness, Adel blinked away the tears and tried to concentrate on anything except the man she loved so deeply. Her safe and secure world was about to be turned upside down.

Chapter Twenty-Eight

The next morning, Adel crumbled a particularly large hunk of soda bread to one of the house dogs. She flinched under Tilde's long and hard stare.

"Ye didn't sleep well, Adel. Ye look unhappy, and your eyes are all dark-circled. 'Tis the captain, isn't it?"

Adel wiped her eyes with the backs of her hands, then sat there worrying her thumbnail. "Yes, but if you don't mind, I'd rather not talk about it just now. We have much work waiting for us."

"There is always much work to do." Tilde sighed. "When yer a mind to talk, I'll listen."

Though she felt sick, Adel smiled at her adopted sister. "I know you will."

What on earth was she going to do? She rose and gathered the woolen cape around her shoulders. For a moment she stood at the kitchen door and looked out over the grounds. She would have to face the situation head on and do her best to keep up appearances.

In a spate of feverish activity to distract herself, she helped dump lime down the outdoor privy hole. She ordered lime scattered around the sheep pens, and behind the barn and corrals. She spaded a small garden area to ready for spring planting. She watched the women sewing, always sewing, and she praised them, and joined them for an hour, hemming a new gown for Mary Kathryn. Mrs. O'Hurley ran her fingers over it and gave Adel a satisfied smile.

"Mrs. O'Hurley, have you sewn all the trousers for the captain?"

"No, mum. 'Tis busy I've been with 'is shirts and jackets, and special coats. Be there a problem?"

Adel reassured the woman with a sweet smile. "Your stitchery is impeccable, as is that of all the seamstresses you oversee." Adel tapped a cheek as she thought for a moment. "Actually, I wish you to sew the trousers with both legs long."

The topknot on the woman's head bobbled as she cocked her head in surprise. "Blimey, both legs...long, ye say?"

Adel leaned forward in a conspiratorial manner. "Master Murphy is constructing a special peg leg for the captain. So you see the necessity of uniformity in the pants?"

The seamstress clapped her hands together like an excited child. "Oh, aye, I do."

Adel placed a finger to her lips. "Shall we keep this our secret? I want to surprise the captain."

"Oh, tick-a-lock, milady. Me lips are sealed." The seamstress set her hands against her ample hips and faced the other women in the sewing shed. "Ye hear that? Not a peep from any of yer bleedin' lips. I done give the mistress me word."

A giggle riffled amongst the women, and all agreed to keep the O'Shea's secret.

Her spirits lifting somewhat, Adel visited Patrick Murphy at the blacksmith shed to check on his progress in constructing the special leg.

"Good morning, Master Murphy. I've come to check your progress."

"Oh, aye, miledy. 'Tis a fine leg, if I do say so. And me son, Shamus, 'as done a grand job of workin' with Mrs. O'Hurley on the measurements for the leather casing and waist straps, without givin' 'er a clue. The boy 'as tanned the leather so 'tis soft as a babe's bottom." The older Murphy's face reddened to the tip of his ears. "Forgive me tongue for misspeaking, miledy. I meant no disrespect to ye."

Adel laughed and patted the man's arm. "No offense taken, Patrick. I place great value on you and Shamus."

She lifted the contraption. "It's very light, and the knee bends back and forth almost as good as a real leg. You're certain the captain will be able to straddle a horse when he wears this?"

Patrick called out, "Shamus, bring the saddle."

The once scrawny lad had matured into a well-built man of twenty-one years. He had taken a wife, and, as the O'Shea, Adel had helped with the christening of his firstborn. She trusted Shamus's loyalty and expertise and would allow no other to train her Arabians.

Shamus settled the saddle over a sawhorse. He lifted the stirrup. "Look 'ere, miledy. I've put a leather bonnet round both stirrups, but on the right one, me father made a flat surface so the captain can rest the end o' the peg without fear of it slipping through and hanging the leg. 'E can use this saddle on the feistiest of 'orses, and no worry 'bout losing 'is balance."

Shamus' cheeks pinked then as he mentioned his wife. "Me Noreen 'as spun the finest and softest woolen sock to fit o'er the captain's stump. 'is new leg will fit him comfortable."

Without thought of propriety, Adel hugged the

young man. "You've both brightened my day considerably." Her smile widened. "There will be extra coin in your stockings come the Yuletide. I could not have asked for more from both of you."

The voices of the men drifted out of earshot as Adel crossed the yard to the house. Tension built in the pit of her stomach. The yard dogs scrambled for her attention, and she called each of them by name and spoke endearing words to them before hurrying up the steps and through the kitchen. She stopped long enough to ask Mrs. Bliss to brew a pot of tea and send it and a plate of scones up to her room. Passing through the great hall, she stopped long enough to admire the fireplace mantel, adorned with holly, fresh yew boughs, and tall candles, but soon called, "Tilde…Tilde, where are you?"

A voice answered. Adel lifted her skirts and hurried up the stairs. Tilde met her in the corridor. "By the look on your face, I can tell ye be on a mission."

Adel grabbed the woman's hand. "Come to my room, Tilde. I am ready to talk."

Once inside and behind closed doors, she met Tilde's probing gaze without flinching. Adel sat on the velvet divan and invited Tilde to sit in the wingback chair facing her.

Tilde rose to answer the knock at the door. When Mary Kathryn appeared with a tray of fruit tarts and a pot of tea, Adel lifted her brows. "Where is Mrs. Bliss?"

"Oh, it's all right, Mommy. Mrs. Bliss burned her finger and a big blister popped up. I offered to bring the tray for her."

Adel set the salver on the table. She hugged the

child. "I'm truly blessed to have you as my daughter. Have you spoken with your father today?"

Mary Kathryn's pretty face scrunched into a pout. "I don't think Daddy likes me very much."

Adel huffed. "Whatever gave you such a notion?"

"He always frowns, and he mostly grouches at me and Gaffney."

Though she seethed inside at Liam's treatment of his daughter, she gathered the child to her with a hug. "Oh, my sweetness. Your father has been through a terrible war, and the sickness still plagues his body. He loves you very much, but you must give him time to heal."

The child's face brightened. "Do you think he'll like the scarf I knitted for him?"

"I'm certain of it. Now, why don't you ask our Mrs. Bliss to heat you a cup of honey milk, and you may have a fruit tart, too." She stroked the little girl's ginger hair. "Aunt Tilde and I need to talk in private."

Mary Kathryn clapped her hands together. "Oh, Mommy, is it about a surprise for me?"

Adel kissed the top of the little girl's head. "Shoo, be off, and no eavesdropping. You wouldn't want to spoil a surprise, would you?"

Mary Kathryn skipped across the room and out the door. She opened it again, and with an impish giggle blew Adel a kiss.

Adel settled on the divan and accepted a cup from Tilde.

Tilde said, "Is there a surprise for Mary Kathryn?"

"Truly, there is. I've made her the most beautiful gown of green organza. But now I must tell you what's troubling me."

She filled her lungs and proceeded to relate the bedroom incident she'd shared with Liam last evening.

Her face felt as if the sun had scalded it when she told about touching him—down there. "I've seen the length and size of a stallion's shaft, and I saw Liam's when he was deep in delirium. He wasn't even aware that I saw it, as well as every inch of his body. But his shaft lay limp, like a lifeless eel, at that time. When we were...uhmm...in the heat of the moment, I reached down to touch him and was shocked that his manhood was engorged and the size of a stallion's. He mistook my surprise as revulsion at his leg."

Sadness, sharp and penetrating, pierced her heart. For the first time since the encounter, she considered Liam's demand that she leave Mautagh Manor.

Tilde inhaled sharply. "Didn't you explain?"

"I tried, but he was beyond reasoning. He said I was no better than a street hoochie." Adel set the teacup on the table. Her voice a husky tremor, she said softly, "He's ordered me to take Mary Kathryn and return to England."

Tilde's composure visibly snapped. "Look around you, Adel. This place was a burned-out shambles less than five years ago. Ye've rebuilt it and provided 'omes and livelihoods for the very people he shunned for so many years. Yer the O'Shea, and yer loved and admired. God's lamb, Adel, yer not purposing to go...are ye?"

"What other choice do I have, Tilde? To become a slave to a man who hates me as much as he hates himself? I've Mary Kathryn to think of. I won't subject that dear, sweet child to Liam's meanness. To eventually have her spirit broken is cruel beyond measure."

Tilde spread her hands wide in obvious consternation. "Adel, where will we go? 'Is lordship yer stepbrother banned you from Briarwood, lest ye've forgotten."

Silence settled across the room as Adel watched the play of emotions on her adopted sister's face. "Though it's been these many years, Reggie's last words about not giving me charity are burned into my brain. Besides, there is no *we,* Tilde. Just *me.* I will not ask you and Edwin to uproot your lives and leave Mautagh."

"God's lamb, Adel. Have ye gone daft in the head? Ye've loved me like a sister. Ye've *made* me yer sister. Do you think I'd choose this place over you?"

Tilde stood and gathered her skirts. "I've a mind to give 'is lordship a good tongue-lashing. He has no right to use the loss of 'is leg and him being unwell to act like a bleedin' bugger."

"No, I beg you, no. We cannot blame Liam for that over which he has no control. His soul is sick. I don't know if it will ever heal, but God help me, I don't have the wherewithal to give more of myself than I've already given."

She and Liam were strangers, with only a marriage certificate to prove otherwise. Their union had not been consummated, and under the contract Liam had had his uncle draw up, she could file for an annulment. Her shoulders shook violently from all the years of struggles and pent-up longings. Tilde folded her sister into her arms. Her voice filled with quiet compassion. "I'll tell Edwin."

Adel pulled from Tilde's embrace. She brushed the

tears from her eyes. "Don't worry, Tilde. I'll send a message to Liam's Uncle Filbert Oxley, the magistrate, and ask him to procure a furnished rental for us."

"What will ye tell Mary Kathryn?"

Now that she had verbalized her commitment to leaving, without hesitation she said, "It's time Mary Kathryn attended a proper school. I'm certain Lord Oxley can arrange admission to London's Academy for Young Ladies."

"Sounds like ye've figured it all out. How soon do we leave?"

"After the Yule feast and the exchanging of gifts."

"Ye have no qualms about yer decision?"

Adel slumped into the chair. She closed her eyes and rested her head on the high back. A hundred thoughts, a hundred concerns, rushed through her mind. "Of course I do. I love Mautagh, and her people are our family. I worry what will become of them. Tell me you understand, Tilde."

Tilde released an audible sigh. "You've always done right by Edwin and me. I've no reason to doubt you. We are sisters, after all. I will begin packing immediately."

Adel clung to the silent affirmation that leaving Liam to wallow in his misery was the right thing to do. "Tilde, we will take little more than we brought with us when we first arrived at Mautagh Manor. Let us be as discreet as possible. I don't relish any wagging tongues to spoil the Yuletide ceremony."

Tilde lifted the corner of her apron and wiped a tear from the corner of her eye. She gave one quick nod. "So be it."

****

Adel had no way of knowing that Liam sat in his room, in self-imposed isolation, staring into the fire. He finished the whiskey and, with a careless tilt of the bottle, poured another.

He took a deep breath and shook his head, lifting his shoulders in a helpless shrug. He was in pain—not physical pain but a kind of incriminating hurt. He lifted his glass toward the portrait hanging above the fireplace, of a Celtic ancestor. "Today…" he started, and the rest of his words just dried up, unwilling to be voiced. He sighed and then slogged down the whiskey, allowing a shudder to wrack through his body. He cleared his throat. "Liam, old chap, last night you proved you are a royal asshole of the worst kind."

He'd cut the heart out of the woman who'd kept him sane during the endless sun-bleached days of monotonous routine in India, and even when the nurses tended him and whispered that the angel of death lurked over him, he had focused on Adel.

He beat the heel of his hand against his forehead. He'd wanted to ask Adel to stay in his arms. He'd wanted to give his heart to her. Intellectually, he knew it wasn't his leg that had caused her eyes to widen. She was a virgin, an innocent. Of course she'd been surprised at the size of his lust-engorged shaft. But as much as he wanted to relinquish his heart, he couldn't reconcile saddling her with a cripple, a man who would spend the rest of his life pulling her down until it destroyed them both.

Suddenly all the anger in him seemed to ebb. He heaved a dejected sigh, and again lifted his glass toward the painting. His words slurred. "Aegnus Conall, brave warrior, you are the only one to know this secret. I have to love my dearest Adel enough to force her out of my life. She will never know how much I adore her. Never!"

He chugged the amber liquid; then, in a paroxysm of disgust, he threw the glass into the fireplace.

Chapter Twenty-Nine

Christmas with family and clansmen was different from the large gala affairs Adel had known in London, or even at Briarwood. There was less glamour and pageantry certainly, but a gathering of the O'Shea and O'Neill clans and people from the village for the Yule season was old-fashioned and special.

Each house was decorated with holly and candles and religious figurines. On Christmas Eve the traditional loaf of bread laden with caraway seeds and raisins, a glass of milk, and a lighted candle was left on the kitchen table. Kitchen doors were left unlocked. In this humble and gracious way, Irish families extended hospitality to the traveling Holy Family and to any travelers with a need to stop for food and warmth.

Knowing she would see old acquaintances, many of whom she hadn't visited for several months, Adel dressed with care. She wore a gown of the palest lilac velvet to match the color of her eyes. The long sleeves flared at her wrists, and a sash of black, embroidered with threads of gold, set off her small waist. Her skirt was unusually narrow, with the excess material gathered in the back to form a train.

Adel greeted Ahern and Eveleen, and each of their sons and daughters-in-law. Gaffney, in his suit of new clothes, stood behind Liam's chair. Liam sat before the fireplace, a mug of eggnog in hand. Mary Kathryn, holding her favorite calico tabby, sat on a tufted stool at her father's knees.

He looked handsome and well kept in his new gray jacket of brushed suede with deeper gray trousers. Calm and self-assured, he gave Adel a reserved smile even as his eyes noted every change in her.

She flushed, remembering his passion, sweet and stormy and violent.

His expression altered subtly as he stared at her. She wondered if he were remembering days long past— the day he had proposed, the night they had spoken the marriage vows, the kiss as he said goodbye. It felt strange to know that she had come to love him through the impassioned letters he'd written from India, while now the distance between them could never be traversed except in memories. She felt a quick stab of sorrow, and shifted her gaze to Mrs. O'Hurley.

The seamstress had perfectly tailored the pants to Liam's tall stature, and she had discreetly basted the one leg shorter than the other so that, when the time came, the threads could easily be removed to allow both pant legs to drape neatly down the length of Liam's height.

The seamstress rewarded Adel with a knowing wink. Adel gave her a smile and glanced around the great room. She made no distinction between the workers and the kinsmen. To her, all were equal. Shamus stood next to his lovely wife, Noreen, who had spun the wool and sewn the sock to fit over Liam's stub. Patrick proudly held his first grandson and crooned softly to the babe.

Adel smiled again when Tilde jabbed Edwin in the ribs for the scowl he was bestowing on Liam.

An Irish Christmas. Her first Christmas with Liam; his first Christmas home. The picture was too perfect. It would all have been perfect, if only he hadn't ordered her away.

Mary Kathryn had said something funny to Liam. The dimple in his cheek deepened. His laughter was soft and lazy, eliciting a delicious chill from the pit of Adel's stomach. Then his expression became disgruntled as he bade Gaffney to refill the empty mug.

At Adel's slight nod, Ahern stepped forward. His deep baritone voice filled the spacious grand hall. "Friends and family, 'tis good to have me nephew home. Let us all raise our cups and drink a toast. May peace and plenty be the first to lift the latch on your door, and happiness be guided to your home by the candle of Christmas."

A round of boisterous cheers and good wishes were offered. Adel turned away and stared out the window. Nerves tensed the muscles in her stomach. All gifts had been given except those for Liam. Misgivings filled her. The slight headache she had fought all morning threatened to blossom into throbbing pain. Ahern's voice startled her. "What troubles ye, lass?"

She twisted her hands together as she cast a cautious glance toward Liam. He seemed lost in his own private world.

She spoke softly and with trepidation. "Oh, Ahern, what if Liam takes offense when I present him with the peg leg? Master Murphy has created a masterpiece. But, Liam is surly and overly sensitive where his stub is concerned. I fear he will cause grievous embarrassment to Patrick, when building the peg leg was my idea. And then, to rub more salt into his wounds, I dread his reaction when Shamus brings the thoroughbred to the front of the house. Oh, whatever was I thinking?"

She stared out the window. The world of white outside did little to calm her anxious heart. "You've been more of a father to me than Liam's uncle. Tell me what to do, Ahern."

"Aye, battle does terrible things to a man's mind, I agree. I can see by the color of his cheeks and the way he fills the new suit of clothing that my nephew's body is healed. 'Twill take a while longer yet before his mind blocks out the horrors of war and the stench of death, mind ye. All this I understand, for I, too, carry my own dark wounds from doing battle. But I will not tolerate rude behavior, not on Christmas Day, and not in front of our kinsmen."

Ahern clasped his beefy hand around Adel's. He led her to stand next to Liam's chair. Ahern cleared his throat as he collected an object from the massive wooden mantel above the fireplace. He tapped the end of an elegantly hand-carved and highly polished shillelagh against the stone floor, then thrust the stout walking stick toward his nephew. "Merry Christmas, Liam. This shillelagh belonged to yer grandfather. He wanted you to have it once ye returned to Mautagh Manor. It has passed from mighty warrior to mighty warrior of the Mautaghs and O'Sheas."

An expectant hush fell over the room. Voices seemed to ebb into silence like a wave returning to the sea. A shiver laced down Adel's spine.

Liam's hands curled around the shillelagh. "My God…"

Adel could hear the familiar growl building in his throat. Her eyes flashed to Ahern, who gripped Liam's shoulder with a huge hand. The O'Neill leaned and whispered words heard by none of the guests. Liam paled and sank back into the chair.

"Family and friends," Ahern's voice boomed, "my niece, Lady Adel, has commissioned two special gifts for her husband." He pointed to Shamus. "Our Shamus has trained a fine thoroughbred to stand perfectly still and not move until commanded by his rider. Shamus has also devised a saddle with special stirrups so Liam will have no trouble mounting the horse."

Liam shifted a reserved smile between Adel and his uncle. His eyes held no warmth to soften the moment, and Adel, feeling his glowering regard, thought she had never seen his eyes so cold and angry before. "You seem to forget that, no matter how well trained the horse, a one-legged man cannot master the saddle, Uncle."

The chastisement was clear. Ahern did not quail under it. "I've forgotten nothing, Nephew." Ahern beckoned Patrick Murphy forward.

Clearly pleased with his craftsmanship, the elder Murphy reached beneath the chair in which he sat and crossed the room to stand in front of Liam. "The mistress designed a good leg for ye, Captain." He held it forth and used his free hand to move the jointed knee back and forth. "'Twon't replace the leg ye lost, but 'twill do ye well." He reached inside the hollow wooden leg and removed the stocking Noreen had knitted. "Me daughter-in-law made this to fit around…" He suddenly seemed lost for words.

Adel, seeing the near panic in Master Murphy's eyes, took the artificial limb and placed it in Liam's lap. "It's truly a wonderful gift, Liam. It's from all of us."

She was thankful for whatever Ahern had whispered in Liam's ear, for his savage mood was concealed, though barely.

She forced a smile. "Shamus, I believe the captain is tired from all the excitement. We will look at Onyx tomorrow."

The disappointment in the lad's eyes was unmistakable, though he smiled and offered a gracious nod.

Liam's voice was soft and harsh at the same time. "Get this damned contraption away from me. Gaffney, help me to my room."

He used the strength of his arms against the sturdy wooden sides of the chair to push himself to a standing position. He grabbed the shillelagh and, with his young valet's help, hopped toward his suite. He turned, his voice a harsh whisper. "It's a good thing you're leaving, because I will never forgive you for this, Adel."

A long pensive sigh escaped her lips. When he had gone, her eyes moved sadly around the room at all the happy faces, hearing the laughter and chattering voices as her mind recalled Liam's words, *Get the hell out of my sight. Take Mary Kathryn and go back to England.*

Ahern gazed at her through a frown. "Adel, what did my nephew mean, that you are leaving?"

She raised a hand to massage her throbbing temple. "Liam has ordered me to leave Mautagh and to take Mary Kathryn with me. He has ordered me back to England."

"The devil ye say! Why that young upstart pup, I'll thrash him a new hide—one-legged or not. 'Tis weary I grow of him whimpering like a wretched coward."

A weariness threatened to send her into a faint. She needed to escape to the quiet confines of her room. "Please, Ahern, leave it be. You know the terms of Liam's marriage to me. It is clear that I have earned no place in his heart. I will honor his wish and file for the annulment. Keep this between us. I do not wish our people to heap malice upon Liam. It is my prayer that in time he will find his lost path and return to his true self."

She wavered, and Ahern signaled for Tilde. "See to yer sister. 'Tis time for all to ride to Cathmor to make merry. I'll have me Eveleen and daughters take charge."

Adel touched his arm, her slim body trembling. "Thank you."

All in all, Christmas Day had gone better than she'd expected, and for that she was thankful.

****

Liam once again rested in his chair before the fireplace, a whiskey in his hand. His temper foul, he was in no mood for company, least of all Adel's. "Gaffney, whoever is making that incessant pounding, send them away."

The young valet opened the door. "His lordship is indisposed and doesn't want company."

Ahern pushed his way into the room. "I don't give a horse's arse what me nephew wants." He waggled a finger at Gaffney's nose. "Laddie, if I were you, I'd go to the kitchen and visit with the cook for a while."

The boy stammered, "A-aye, sir." He made haste and slammed the door behind him.

Ahern cuffed his giant hands against his massive thighs as he sneered at his nephew. "If ye could stand,

I'd knock ye flat on yer sorry arse. It must be yer mother's weak blood wot makes ye a bleedin' coward, 'cause we O'Neills are fighters to the very end. We never bred no quitters, and that's wot ye are—a bleedin' quitter. Why, ye ain't fit to scratch fleas with the yard dogs."

Liam sat forward. He pointed toward the door. "Get the hell out of my room, old man."

"Shuddup, lad, before ye make me lose my temper. Do ye know what ye've done? Do ye even care that ye've ripped the heart right out of Adel?"

His anger mounting, he reached out and grabbed a handful of shirt, twisting the material until Liam's face suffused red, and then Ahern slammed him against the back of the chair. "Ye embarrassed her in front of her people. Ye spurned the best gifts she could give ye—a leg for walking, not just any peg leg, but one that comes close to a natural one, and a fine thoroughbred, especially trained for you. Are ye so stupid and blind that ye can't see the love the lass has for ye? Not to speak of yer wee daughter? I'm that ashamed of ye, lad."

Liam ground the words between his teeth. "You know nothing about what it's like not to be a man. What good am I with one leg?"

"Pah, nothing but excuses." Ahern shook his finger under Liam's nose. "When the lass leaves, the people will leave, too. *She* is the O'Shea. Ye'll have no love, no loyalty. Ye'll get your bloody wish to be left alone. And eventually poor Gaffney will get tired of your whiskey-sotted tirades, and he'll leave you, too."

Ahern grabbed the whisky bottle from the side table and thrust it against Liam's chest. "'Ere, drink yerself to death, because yer already a dead man."

Liam leaned over the side of the chair and grabbed the shillelagh, but when he swung it at his uncle, Ahern caught the sturdy cane, jerked it from Liam's grip, and tossed it to the bed.

"This place was naught but a burned-out shambles. Ye din't know 'cause ye din't care to know. You was being robbed blind by a crooked solicitor cause ye din't care enough to keep track of where yer money was going. Ye din't care about the people left 'omeless. All that ye see, all that ye 'ave, is because of Adel."

With one last disgusted look, Ahern strode from the room, the sound of his heavy footfalls echoing his anger.

Liam felt someone standing behind him. He turned enough to look over his shoulder. Gaffney stood wringing his hands. "Will you be needing me the rest of the night, Captain?"

He gave the boy a long hard look. "No. I have a balm to soothe my bruised soul." He reached for the bottle of whiskey.

Gaffney nodded and withdrew from the room, quietly closing the door.

Liam lifted the bottle to his lips, then, with a second thought, placed it back on the table. He couldn't help feeling a certain despair. Heaving a deep sigh, he stared dolefully into the firelight's flames. He felt the prodding of his uncle's words, and murmured in hushed tones, "You are more right than you know, Uncle."

Chapter Thirty

For the first time in two days Adel left the house. She had completed her midday chores and decided to reward herself with a ride to her favorite spot on the cliffs. She galloped along the ridge top and stopped to look at the sea below, a brisk wind blasting her in the face all the while until she turned the horse and dashed toward the forest.

She couldn't run far or fast enough to escape her own folly. A strangled sob caught in her throat. She had wasted five years of her life loving her idea of a man who had never even existed. She had fallen in love with the portrait she had drawn of Liam in his starched uniform. She had been blinded by an illusion, and now she was left with nothing to blind her but her tears.

It was incredibly mortifying to remember how she had entertained any number of fantasies that involved kissing her hand and pretending it was Liam's lips, and when she'd received the letter saying he had been injured and was coming home, she'd imagined dabbing a cool cloth on his wounded brow and spooning broth between his lips while he recovered from his injuries and fell deeply and irrevocably in love with her.

She could easily forget that she had truly ministered to his needs, even cradled him in her arms during his darkest moments of delirium. But she didn't think she could forgive him for deliberately trying to break her heart—for denying the truth she'd tasted on his lips the night he had so passionately kissed her. It wasn't the cold that sent shivers splintering through her, but the memory of how his hands had caressed her breasts. How his touch to her most womanly core had heated her body and left her yearning for more.

In her haze of hurt, she pushed the gelding to a faster pace. Stray twigs lashed painfully at her cheeks as she raced over the rough track, the horse's hooves crushing the thin crust of snow. She dodged the outstretched claws of a tree and plunged down a long, stony hill furred with moss and mottled lichen. She turned the gelding to race to the summit of Diamond Hill. Somewhere in the distance she heard a burn rushing over the rocks of a creek bed when she stopped to give the horse a breather. After only a few seconds of inactivity, she began to shiver with both exhaustion and cold. It was far too easy to wish she had worn a warmer coat. And easier yet to wish she had Liam's strong, warm arms wrapped around her.

She gigged the gelding forward, scrambling up a steep hillside, and held tight when the horse leaped over exposed roots that jutted from the rocky soil.

She burst over the top of the hill, only to find herself teetering on the brink of a dizzying precipice. The gelding skidded to a halt, falling to its knees in its panicked state.

Adel's arms cartwheeled wildly as she flew over the horse's head. She snatched at the air, her hands searching for anything to grasp, and a shrill scream tore from her throat as her momentum sent her plunging over the edge of the cliff and into the icy waters of the burn below.

The cold dug its razor-sharp claws into her with brutal force. For a terrifying flash of time, she couldn't scream, breathe, or think.

The creek would shrink to a lazy trickle during the summer, but at the moment its banks were swollen from the recent storms, as well as icy rushing water pouring down from the mountains. By the time Adel surfaced, sputtering and coughing and gasping for breath, she had traveled a good ways downstream.

Bobbing like a cork on the open seas, she tipped back her head and screamed, *"Help!"*

The faces of everyone she loved flashed before her eyes. She opened her mouth to scream again but was only able to drag in a single desperate gulp of air before the weight of her skirts dragged her beneath the water and into the merciless arms of the current.

****

"Whoa, horse! Whoa! 'Tis Lady Adel's gelding! There be blood on its knees!"

Liam sat bolt upright, his heart thundering like a cannon and the beseeching cries of his gallant soldiers being struck down in battle still ringing in his ears. He cocked his head to listen, but all he could hear was the rasp of his own breathing in the silence of his room. He ran an unsteady hand over his jaw, haunted by that hollow echo.

He must have been dreaming.

God knows his dreams had been vivid enough. He had been roaming the bewildering labyrinth of a darkened cave—one minute a small boy, the next a man. He would catch a glimpse of flowing skirts down a shadowy passageway and hear a haunting echo of Adel's laughter. But when he tried to follow her his legs grew shorter and shorter with each step and he would soon find himself all alone again.

He had finally turned a corner inside the cave, only to come face to face with a chilling apparition of Adel holding out her hands in supplication, rose petals streaming like blood from her pale fingers.

Shrugging away a shudder, he slowly climbed to his foot, his limbs so stiff with cold he was surprised they didn't creak. The fire had died in the fireplace. *Where the hell is Gaffney?*

The inside of his mouth tasted vile. An empty whiskey bottle lay on the floor a few feet away, as if it had been flung there in a fit of temper. Burying his face in his hands, he groaned.

He was answered by an excited Gaffney bursting through the door. "My Lord…Captain…ooh…" He entered wringing his hands and hopping around like a dancing chicken.

With a snort of irritation, Liam said, "Stop that confounded blabbering. My head feels like it's ready to fall off my shoulders."

"B-but, it's Lady Adel, sir. Her horse came back without her, and its legs are deeply gashed and bleeding."

Liam drew himself up to his full height. His brain forgot to tell him he couldn't walk. He fell forward, reaching out to grab hold of the bedpost.

"Slow down, Gaffney. What's this about Lady Adel's horse?"

"Sh-she's been terribly upset about returning to England, so she w-went for a ride right after she had finished her noonday tasks."

Gaffney lifted Liam's arm over his shoulders and

helped him to the window. "Look, her horse came back without her. She's an excellent rider. I-I fear the worst has happened."

The young valet turned, his eyes filled with concern for his lady, but blazing with anger toward the man responsible for sending her away. "It is only because of Lady Adel I've catered to your every whim and endured your insults. I believe you are a man without a heart. When my lady returns to England, I will no longer play your fool, Captain."

Liam braced his hands against the window sill. He gazed down at Shamus lifting the gelding's leg, running his hands over the sweat-lathered body. A small crowd was congregating in the yard.

Gaffney wore the expression of a servant who had overstepped his boundaries and feared the consequences. "Calm yourself, Gaffney. Anger has a way of making a fool of a man. Believe me, I know, because I am a first-class horse's ass."

A cold knot of dread pooled in the pit of Liam's stomach. "Where was Lady Adel's favorite place to ride?"

"On the cliffs. She said looking at the sea calmed her." As if he read Liam's mind, the young valet's fist flew to his mouth. "Oh, bless my bones, you don't think... No, no... It's too horrible to think that she... Ooh!" He ended with a mournful sob.

A moment of silence passed as Liam debated the boy's concern. It was obvious the lad cared deeply for his mistress, to risk speaking his mind as he had.

Liam envisioned Adel's broken body lying on the beach far below the cliffs. He had to reach her before the tide swept her out to sea.

This was his fault. All his fault.

He snapped his fingers. "Where is that contraption?" His eyes searched the room. "The peg leg…where did you put it?"

"As you commanded, in the closet, out of your sight."

"Well, don't just stand there gawping. Get the damned thing."

It took a split second for Gaffney to fetch the artificial leg. "Let me help you, Captain."

"No, you run down and tell Shamus to saddle the horse."

"You mean, Black Onyx?"

"If that's his name, then aye. Now, be off with you."

"You'll need my help, sir. Give me a moment, and I'll be right back." Gaffney disappeared out the door.

By the time the boy returned, Liam had pulled the sock over his stub and had slipped it into the hollow of the wooden leg. He was testing his balance while struggling with the strap around the waist.

He looked up as Gaffney re-entered the room. "I thought I told you to—"

"I sent Edwin, Captain. It's my duty to help you with the straps."

Between the two, they managed to buckle the belt around Liam's waist and secure the straps around his thigh to hold the peg leg tight.

Using the shillelagh for balance, Liam made a full lap around the bed without falling. His voice was fraught with dismay. "It works. I'll be damned, it works."

None too gently, he ushered the valet out the

bedroom door. His heart quickened to a staccato rhythm. Step by step, he crossed the floor of the great hall toward the kitchen. His mind whirled, trying to recall the places of his childhood—places where Adel might have ridden.

At the kitchen door, Gaffney helped Liam down the back steps. With a stumbling effort, he walked across the yard, the shillelagh and his wooden leg tapping a tempo against the ground.

He hadn't been near a horse in over a year. The sight of the magnificent black thoroughbred nearly stole his breath. What was it Adel had said? *Shamus has trained the horse to stand still until the rider issues a command.*

His mouth was thin and tense. In spite of the cold, a bead of sweat trickled down the side of his lean cheek from the exertion of lifting the wooden leg and trying to adjust to the back and forth motion of the hinged knee, after months of sedentary inactivity.

He closed his eyes, trying to conjure Adel. Her image sprang up immediately, the details of her beauty perfectly clear. He could almost forget his fear of falling off the horse when he concentrated on her and the sweet scent that always drifted from her skin. He needed to find her. He needed to explain his feelings to her.

By the time he reached the place where Shamus stood holding two saddled horses, exhaustion threatened to overtake Liam. He fought to still the trembling in his hands, a trembling not from trepidation, not from fatigue or lack of activity, but from the long days of substituting whiskey for food. He needed a drink in the worst way.

When he'd left India, he'd been heralded a hero. He didn't consider himself a hero; in his mind he was a bastard and a coward who would never be worthy of so much as a smile from a woman like Adel.

Shamus said, "I trained Onyx meself. He's used to a gentle hand and responds well to commands. He'll do you good, Captain."

"Lady Adel often praised your talent with horses."

Shamus accepted the compliment without a smile, only a nod. "I see you've taken well to the leg me father made for ye."

Liam heaved a shaky breath. An odd mixture of relief welled up inside him. "It's easy to see the father is as talented as the son."

Shamus handed Liam the reins. "You want me to hold his head while you mount?"

"My uncle said you'd trained the horse to stand until given the command to move."

"Aye, and his name is Black Onyx. Onyx for short. He answers to it."

Liam noted the flick of the horse's ears at the mention of his name. "Once, I considered myself a fair horseman. Let's see if I still am."

He accepted the reins, drew in a deep breath, and lifted his left boot to the stirrup, wincing as the tender end of his stub pressed against the solidness of the peg leg. He was glad for the sock and made a mental note to personally thank Noreen for her fine handiwork.

He needed that little bounce to help him swing his hip and the peg leg over the saddle. It didn't happen.

He'd be damned if he'd make a fool of himself in front of the onlookers. He'd done everything to lose their respect, and nothing to gain it. Another point to work on.

He secured the reins in his left hand and grabbed hold of the saddle's pommel, then with his right gripped the cantle. When he bent his left knee, he found that the hinge on the wooden knee moved almost as if it had a mind of its own. He crouched on his right thigh and used the strength of his left leg and his arms to hoist himself into the saddle.

The horse stood still in total obedience.

Liam adjusted his weight in the saddle and, without thought, settled the peg of his artificial leg into the stirrup. He reached forward and petted the glistening black neck. He glanced over at Shamus, who had mounted his own horse. "I'm indebted to you and your father."

"We did it for Lady Adel."

Shamus had said it without malice, but Liam knew that in his own subtle way the lad was letting him know that he didn't give a tinker's dam for Liam's gratitude. Payback was hell, and Liam knew it.

Chapter Thirty-One

"Gaffney said Lady Adel's favorite spot was the cliffs. We'll ride there first. If we don't find her, we'll split up—cover more ground that way."

Shamus nodded his agreement.

The shillelagh securely lashed to his saddle, Liam turned his mount and nudged the horse in the flank, feeling the first cold drops of snow against his cheeks as he reined his horse directly into the wind and galloped across the storm-soaked field, closely followed by Shamus. The mists and vapors caused by the cold air roiled in the low glades and hung over the copses, but Liam rode on with one purpose in mind— find Adel.

At the cliffs they could see where a horse's hooves had churned up the grass. Liam gauged the position of the sun and determined the time well past four in the evening.

Without giving caution to his new peg leg, Liam dismounted like an expert horseman, allowing the horse to stand ground-tied while he loosed the shillelagh and used it to aid him over the rough ground to the edge of the ridge. Steeling himself against the possibility of seeing Adel's lifeless body being battered by the waves below, he fervently hoped she had landed on a ledge partway down and was still alive. Thoughts crowded his mind—if she were hurt, how would he rescue her?

His mind refused to believe she was dead.

He raced over the rough and rocky terrain in a curious hopping lope, once losing his balance and struggling with the awkwardness of a wooden leg to push back to a standing position, unmindful of the mud, grass, and leaves that clung to his new jacket and the knees of his pants.

His gut twisted with dread. He steadied himself with the stout cane as he looked down at the sea. He scanned the beach line, back...forth...back again. No Adel. The tide was rising. He felt the spray on his face as the waves crashed violently against the cliff's solid stone walls.

He lifted a hand and shaded his eyes against the waning sun. He worried whether he had arrived too late.

An odd mixture of relief and frustration welled up. He heaved with a shaky breath as Shamus returned from his foray in the opposite direction shrugging his shoulders and spreading his hands wide to indicate no sign of Adel.

Clenching his jaw, he tried to keep his voice low and controlled. "Shamus, has she ever mentioned riding anywhere other than the cliffs?"

"No, Captain, she has not."

Liam recognized the concern in Shamus's voice, saw the flash of panic in his eyes, and knew the lad's feelings for Adel—like Liam's own—were genuine, for Adel was indeed a treasure.

Wearily, Liam rubbed his eyes. "Even if the horse simply threw her and she were walking, we would have spotted her."

The young man persisted. "Her being on foot,

maybe she decided to cut through the forest. 'Tis a short way to the house. If that's the case, we would have missed her."

Liam lifted the reins. Almost too tired to lift his good leg to the stirrup, he managed to swing himself into the thoroughbred's saddle. "This storm is getting worse, Shamus. Go back to the house, and if she's not there, then she has to be stranded somewhere. Get a dozen men with torches to search for her. I'll want you to ride to my uncle's house. Tell him we need as many to search as possible."

Shamus mounted his horse. "Aye, I will. I'll also search the hay barns on the marsh. She might have taken shelter in one of them."

By now the slashing snowflakes came in a furious bombardment. Splashing through ice-crusted puddles and squinting through the driving wind and snow, Liam gathered his coat tighter around his neck and urged his horse to the forest.

Chill traveled down his spine. What if Adel didn't meet with an accident? What if it was a ruse to punish him for ordering her out of his life? He quickly dismissed that thought. She might abandon him without a backward glance, but she would never leave Mary Kathryn nor the people she had claimed as her kinsmen.

He entered the forest, so much more dense than he remembered as a lad. He shifted around in the saddle, his wary eyes scanning the underbrush.

The wind whispered through the swaying boughs of pines, but its secrets were not meant for his ears. He halted the thoroughbred and dismounted. He soon had Onyx tethered to a tree. The horse had proven to be all Adel had acclaimed, and more, and now gazed at him accusingly over a mouthful of grass.

"Stop looking at me like that," Liam ordered, glaring back. "I know she's pampered you like you were her own. Though she's not your mistress, I'll find her." He pointed the shillelagh at him.

The horse flicked its ears backward and forward, and gave a series of squeals. Liam swore the animal had understood every word he'd said.

Leaving the horse munching on grass, Liam plunged into the woods. Although he felt as if his hip and stub were ready to crack wide open, he paused every few steps to call Adel's name.

He thought upon his actions at the Christmas Eve gathering. He deserved the punishment he'd earned, of her ignoring him. It wasn't as if he didn't. For a man who always prided himself on treating the fair sex with the most tender consideration, he had certainly behaved like a bastard the past weeks.

A chilling breeze from the east carried in snow and filtered it over the tightly coiled buds on the naked tree branches, stirring Liam's hair.

He leaned heavily on the shillelagh as he climbed a steep hill. He hesitated at the top, the hairs on the back of his neck prickling. Haunted by the sensation that he was being watched by eyes even more ancient than the towering evergreens, he looked behind him. Despite feeling he was being followed, he had never felt more alone in his life.

"Who's there? Show yourself."

Only the wind's moaning answered him.

He began to feel as if his nightmare was pursuing him into his waking hours. He half expected to catch a glimpse of a flowing skirt in the distance or hear a woman's echoing laughter. Growing ever more fearful that his path was taking him farther away from Adel instead of closer, he swung in the direction of where he'd left Onyx. But the faint murmur of water lapping at rocks lured him to a spacious glade occupied by a deep, dark pool. He closed his eyes and tried to recall if he'd visited this place as a child. Twenty-five years was a long time to recall a place.

The pool's serene waters were fed by a natural waterfall that bubbled over a jagged shelf of rock on the far side of the pool. He closed his eyes again. He'd never explored this part of the woods, he was certain. He wouldn't have forgotten this magical place.

Liam was bone-weary tired and promised himself he would linger just long enough to rinse his mouth and splash the remaining fog from his brain. He struggled to his knees to bend over the edge of the pool.

He splashed handfuls of water over his face, welcoming the icy sting. The man gazing back at him from the pool with beard-stubbled jaw, haggard cheeks, and desperate bloodshot eyes suddenly seemed as much a stranger to him as the drawings of a handsome young officer that hung on the walls of Mary Kathryn's reading nook in the library.

He plunged his whole head beneath the water, obliterating his image, then jerked it back out, flinging his sopping hair from his eyes. Only then did he notice the large flat rock crouching in the shadows on the other side of the pool.

And the raven-black tendrils of hair floating lazily on the surface of the water.

Just like that, his heart stopped. And for one agonizing moment he wasn't sure it would beat again.

But then he saw the small, pale hand curled up at the rock's edge and realized the tendrils of hair were cascading over the rock and into the water.

"Oh, sweet mother of God," he breathed the words, more of a prayer than an oath.

Without a thought for his clothes or his comfort, or his ability to navigate with his peg leg, he plunged into the water and splashed his way over to the boulder. He used the strength of his arms to haul himself onto the rock shelf, to find Adel stretched out on her back, her eyes closed, so still and pale that for one terrible moment he feared it would take more than a prince's enchanted kiss to wake her up.

But the sodden bodice of her cloak clung to a chest that was gently rising and falling with each shallow breath. Liam lifted her into his arms, shuddering to think what might have happened if she hadn't found the strength to drag herself out of the frigid water. Her flesh was damp and clammy, but he could feel the precious warmth radiating from her body.

He gazed down into her face, desperately missing the roses that usually bloomed in her cheeks. "Adel, my darling girl, will you open your eyes and speak to me?"

She slowly opened her eyes. Her voice was little more than a throaty rasp. "I've been calling for hours. I thought no one would ever hear me."

It was fate that had led him to this section of the forest. He thought he heard the whispering of men's voices—the words in old Gaelic. He jerked around. Tree branches bowed and swayed in a gentle breeze. Except for the babbling creek, the woods were silent.

Adel lifted her hand to his cheek, and, before it fell limp again, she said, "Don't worry, it's only the spirits of the old Celtic warriors. They've been watching over me, waiting for you to rescue me."

A bark of laughter escaped him as he tightened his arms around her and buried his face in the damp ropes of her hair, humbled by a grace he did not deserve. "That's right, my sweet girl, it's the ghosts who led me to you."

****

She was dead. It was the only explanation for what Adel saw when she finally managed to shake off her exhausted stupor enough to pry open her eyes.

She sighed, feeling a vague pang of disappointment. She had fought so hard to survive the tumbling in the burn. She had spit and sputtered and struggled, and snatched at every passing branch, never dreaming her deliverance would come in the form of a waterfall. When the still cold waters of the pool had sought to lure her into their seductive embrace, she had even managed to claw her way out of them and collapse on top of the flat rock. But apparently all her efforts had been in vain.

Because if she wasn't dead, then why was the ghost of all her years of passion sitting in a wingback chair next to her bed? His head rested against one of the large wings, his eyes closed. In his slumber, there was a boyish purity about him, and it added to his compelling masculinity.

His cheeks and jaws were freshly shaven, his tawny hair drawn back and bound neatly in a queue by a leather thong at the nape, his profile classically handsome enough to hang in the gallery of London's art district.

He wore a shiny black Hessian boot on his foot,

dark gray trousers, dazzling white shirtsleeves, and a…a peg leg. And he was one wicked grin away from stealing her heart, again.

Adel frowned, growing more bewildered. If she wasn't dead, then she was most certainly delirious with fever, because the Liam O'Shea she knew would never wear a peg leg. The only thing he'd use it for was firewood.

She turned her face away and closed her eyes.

Hours later, when she opened them again, Liam was standing over her, his golden hair haloed by sunlight.

Her throat hurt when she spoke. "If you're an angel, then God surely has a wicked sense of humor."

"Oh, I'm no angel, my sweet girl." He sat on the bed, bringing his devilish grin into crisp focus. "I'm Captain Liam O'Shea, recently retired from Her Majesty's Service. For the rest of my life, I'm here to serve you."

She pressed the back of her hand to her brow, striving to be brave but failing miserably. "I must be delirious with fever. I'm dying, aren't I?"

He tugged her hand into his own and pressed it to his lips. "On the contrary, my love. There is no trace of fever, no congestion in your lungs, no chills. You've slept like the dead for two days. Though you gave all of us a scare, I think you just might survive."

The teasing sparkle in his eyes faded to a somber glow. "I must confess that when I first saw you lying on that rock, I thought—"

"That you would be rid of me, once and forever," she finished softly.

A shade of crimson spread across Liam's cheeks.

"I regret, more than you'll ever know, the day I spoke those words. I hope you can find it in your heart to forgive me. I need the only woman I will ever love. I need you, Adel."

Her mind struggled with his words, her heart quickening in response. "What…what did you say?"

"I love you, Adel." His voice softened.

Her gaze skimmed his somber expression. She had struggled against her dreads for weeks, with only one goal—to become strong enough to face the future.

As she struggled to a sitting position, Liam's arm went around her shoulders. She wanted nothing more than to slip into his embrace.

With his hand lifted to her cheek, he gently cupped her jaw while his thumb feathered gently across her lips, coaxing them to part of their own accord. As she stared into those fathomless blue depths, a shiver cascaded through her. He must be wrong. She was suffering from a fever. A fever that raced through her veins and burned away all traces of common sense, leaving an unbearable yearning for this man.

She closed her eyes, already anticipating the tantalizing caress of his lips against hers. Which left her feeling foolish when it didn't come and his touch was removed from her entirely.

She opened her eyes to find him standing a few feet away, his hands on his hips, his back to her. Something in his stance made her shove the heavy coverlet aside and come to her feet as well.

She touched his shoulder. "Why do you turn away from me, Liam?"

A look of haunting anxiety sprang into his eyes, and then he turned away to gaze into the flickering fire.

"Liam, did I do something wrong?"

"I can't do this, Adel. I thought I could, but I can't."

"I don't understand. Are you saying you don't love me?"

"I'm saying that I can't give you what you are wanting of me."

When he looked down at her, she understood his meaning. The torment in his eyes was more than she could bear. She reached out and circled her arms around his waist. "Why, because of your leg?"

He nodded, without comment.

She smiled when he placed his hands gently over her arms, holding them in place around his middle. She closed her eyes, biting her bottom lip as her breasts rubbed against the hard muscles of his chest and hot tingles scorched a path through her veins.

She stood listening to the steady beat of his heart, and a sense of peace flooded through her. "To me, you are no less a man than when you left for India five years ago. Life is full of hurts, Liam. We've all been hurt at one time or another, but life goes on. I'm certain Ahern has told you of his experiences with battle. He said to me once, 'What doesn't kill you, makes you stronger.' I believe that, Liam, and so should you."

****

Liam's heart jolted. He knew he should back away. He wanted to step forward, wanted to press his mouth to the slender length of her neck and slowly work his way down.

Damn! Why did she have to be so pretty...so tempting?

A hot flame of anticipation torched her eyes,

mirroring his own expectations. "Make love to me, Liam."

His heart stopped at the sound of his name, as soft as a gentle breeze whispering from her lips.

"It's too soon. You're not well."

She stabbed a finger at him. "A moment ago, you said I was in good health, with no fever and no chills."

He took a step away from her. "You are the most infuriating woman I've ever known."

She drew another step closer to him. "And, I'm tired of being a virgin wife."

He was the one who closed the bit of distance between them. Before he could talk himself out of it, he reached around, cupped his hand to the back of her head, and leaned down. Her warm palms flattened against his chest and she closed her eyes as he pressed his mouth to her full, luscious lips. He wrapped his other arm around her back and pulled her closer, kissing her slowly, wracked with a powerful need as her mouth parted, her tongue eagerly meeting his in an urgent exploration.

Liam ended the kiss, forcing himself to draw back from her sweet, willing response. He stared down into her dazed expression. There was something about this kind, beautiful woman that touched his soul with a comforting sense of rightness, that pulled more strongly at his trust every time he was with her.

He admired her determination, but he couldn't help teasing her. "I believe you are the most stubborn woman I've ever met."

"Me…stubborn?" He liked the sound of her soft chuckle. Her pale purple eyes sparkled with mischief. "I've just been taking lessons from you."

He laughed. He raked his gaze over her linen nightgown and imagined the curves hidden beneath the fabric.

She smiled, a fervent glow springing into her eyes, sending hot currents of desire straight to the lower regions of his body. But Adel made no move to pull away. She trailed her fingers on a burning path around his neck and quietly drove him crazy.

He crushed her to him, running one hand up her spine and reveling in the feel of her tongue thrusting to meet his.

Blood roared through his heart at her gentle moan. Her fingers stroked the corded muscles of his back. He caressed the smooth nape of her neck, then buried his fingers in the silken strands of her hair and pressed her even closer, deepening his exploration of her warm mouth.

Pulling away abruptly, he looked deep into her eyes as if to assure himself she was really there. Then, cupping her head again, he kissed her with a fierce passion.

His body hardened. His hands itched to roam over her luscious curves. With great reluctance, he left the soft sweetness of her lips. "You make me forget that I'm a—"

Her eyes sparkled, and she smiled with a beautiful candor that seriously threatened his tenuous control. "That you're what, Liam…a virile and passionate man who is about to make love to his wife?"

Her words washed over him in heated waves and set his heart to hammering against his ribs. He loved her velvety voice, and the way she said his name, so tenderly, so passionately.

"Are you certain, Adel?"

"It's what I want," she stated in a low voice, reaching up to touch his strong, handsome face.

Liam stared at the sheer confidence that glowed in her eyes, his fired blood coursing with a deepening desire. He wanted her more than he wanted his next breath.

He lowered her onto the soft eiderdown tick. "Give me a moment while I remove my…" he hesitated to say the words.

"Say it, Liam."

"Bloody hell. All right, my peg leg."

She smiled as she arched one eyebrow. "There. That wasn't so bad, was it?"

Her velvety voice broke through the brief silence that had settled between them.

A spark quirked the corners of her lips into an impish smile. "We should name your leg. I propose we call it—Charlie, or Louie, or Roi. Take your pick. One name is as good as another."

This time, his laughter filled the bedroom. He unbuttoned the front of his breeches and slid them down over his firm hips. He unbuckled the leather strap around his waist, and the two smaller straps that secured the wooden leg to his thigh. He removed his stub from the hollow well and gave the artificial limb a pat. "My dear wife, may I introduce you to…Louie. He's a much welcomed part of my life."

The muscles in his back and shoulders relaxed as Adel crooked a finger and motioned Liam to join her under the bedcovers.

She gazed at him, her eyes repeating her desire for him. Adel, his beautiful Adel, was wearing her heart on her sleeve. How could he have ever thought of sending her away?

With aching, jubilant surrender, he pulled her into his arms. The room was dim, but he could still see the faint luster of her eyes, smell the sweetness of her breath, feel the silky texture of her skin. He needed her. Dear God, he needed her. And he intended to show her just how much.

Gently, he lowered his mouth to hers.

She rose to meet his kiss, wrapping her arms around his neck and pulling him fast against her soft heaving breasts. She parted her lips for him, and he plunged eagerly into the warmth she offered. He kissed her deeply and passionately, stopping only long enough to say, "I'm so sorry, Adel."

She laughed out loud—a happy, joyful release. "No more apologies, my love. We've walked through the fire together."

He pulled her into him and kissed her with sheer abandon until her passion seared him like red-hot flames licking his body.

She whispered, "Oh, Liam, I have dreamed of this moment for such a long time. I thought I was doomed to live without you forever."

He touched a finger to her lips. "No more of that. We are real, you and I. You love me as I am, and I love you for the woman you are. You, my sweet girl, are the one I plan to spend the rest of my life with."

"Take me now, Liam. Make me your true wife. Let us make up for lost time."

It took no more to convince him, and he rose to his knee, his entire being pulsing with need.

Moonlight shone through the parted drapes,

illuminating Adel's white gown. She looked like a goddess, lying back upon the pillows, waiting for him. Her beauty was breathtaking, her innocence intoxicating. He had not known he could ever love a woman as much as he loved this one before him.

Liam loosened his wide cravat and pulled the shirt over his head, tossed it aside, and then lowered himself upon her. His lips found hers in the darkness and he reveled in their delicious flavor.

She wrapped her long legs around his hips, and he held her tightly in his arms, pressing his body against hers. He wanted all of her. He had waited so long. And so had she.

He unbuttoned her gown and let his lips trace a path down to the mounds of her breasts. Gently his hands played from her hips down to her legs, sliding the gown up and up. He whispered, "I want to see all of you."

Without hesitation, she removed the garment, and he kissed between her breasts. His hands slid down her length until he found the moist core of her womanhood.

"You're trembling, Adel." His voice was filled with concern. "I fear your fever is returning."

"No, I'm not sick. It's just that…I want to please you, but I don't know what to do."

His hand caressed her inner thigh. "Don't apologize for being adorable."

Adel laid a hand on his cheek. "Tell me what to do, Liam."

He took her hand and guided it to his manhood. "Touch me."

With a coquettish flutter of her eyelashes, she wrapped her fingers around the length of him. He shuddered with pleasure. She moved her hand. "Like this?"

"Yes, like that."

He closed his eyes for a moment, then lowered his mouth to her breasts to kiss and suckle one and then the other. He kissed down her belly and around her navel, and then lower, until he reached the center of her womanhood, where he brought her desires to full culmination.

An urgent response blazed through her at the exquisite feel of his mouth. Shocked at the intensity of her body's sweet, throbbing ache, she clutched Liam's shoulders until the pleasure became too potent to bear. Tension coursed through her body like a riptide threatening to drown her in a sea of pleasure. Then everything exploded within.

Her muscles squeezed tightly, held fast for a moment, then relented with a titillating, debilitating release. Euphoria filled her, and for the first time in her life she experienced a pure and absolute physical contentment.

"Oh, Liam!" Her voice was a breathy whisper. "I had no idea."

He rose up to settle himself between her thighs and gently thrust into her opening. Though she was tight and virginal, she was relaxed, and the pain was insignificant compared to the divine bliss of his entry as he broke through her maidenhead. Tears of joy sprang to her eyes.

He lifted her hips to his, and they merged as lovers who were bound to each other for all eternity. Liam touched his forehead to hers while he moved within her, their bodies mating in pure, primitive harmony. It was everything she'd dreamed it would be—intimate, pleasurable, loving. She had never known making love could be so beautiful.

His head lowered to her breast, and her mouth opened in a soundless cry as his tongue caressed a soft peak. His hands moved with unhesitating boldness over her body, while her own explored the sinews that rippled beneath his warm flesh.

Liam's pace intensified, and she recognized his mounting need. He rose up on both arms and drove into her again and again until she hummed within. "Adel, my sweet, Adel," he whispered hotly in her ear, his breath sending a torrent of shudders down her satiated body.

"I love you, my wife, and I will spend the rest of my life telling you so."

The depth of her emotion brought tears to her eyes again. "Then I am yours for as long as you will have me, Captain O'Shea."

"That will be forever, my sweet girl."

Chapter Thirty-Two

Spring had graced the grounds of Mautagh Manor with an abundance of flowers. They filled every garden and bordered every walk, lavishly spreading a vivid array of colors across the spacious lawn and in the carefully tended beds of the courtyards.

Amid all her responsibilities as the O'Shea, Adel still found an hour or so each morning to spend outside at some gardening chore or another. She donned skirts, blouses, and laced bodices that copied the simplicity of peasant garb yet were themselves fresh bouquets of delicate spring hues. Wide-brimmed hats with long ribbon streamers not only framed the beauty of her face and complemented her gowns but gave service in shading her creamy skin from the sun. To be sure, she drew more admiring glances than the flowers she tended.

Liam was like a man slowly unwinding as the tensions that had oppressed him began to diminish and fade. His laughter came more easily now and was heard more often. He pleasured himself in the good camaraderie of his uncle and cousins, in the loving attentions of his wife, in the knowledge of the babe growing inside her body, and in the sheer joy of being home. Often were the occasions when he strolled through the gardens with Adel. He reveled in selecting the perfect pony for Mary Kathryn, and in the long rides he shared with his daughter thereafter.

His gaze shifted to the corral where Black Onyx bugled toward his corral mates.

The horse had proven everything Adel had promised, and more. And though Liam still walked with an uneven gait, assisted by the shillelagh, he rode with an eagerness that set Onyx's hooves flying.

Liam smiled and lifted his face to the sun, letting it cleanse away all the emotions and fears and anger that had so recently bound him up.

He watched Adel approach, her basket laden with freshly cut flowers for the house. She raised her gaze to him, and he saw all the adoration he had ever desired within those translucent orbs.

"Liam!" Her lips formed the name with a sigh. She came to him, took his hand, and placed it on her growing belly. "Our child grows stronger every day."

He lifted her hand and kissed the inside of her palm. "Come, Wife, let us walk to the house."

Adel giggled now. "Why, because the day grows warm?"

"No."

"Because you have need of a meal?"

"No."

A smiled tugged at her lips. "Hmm…because—"

Liam stood and leaned close, gazing down at her, his eyes filled with love. "A kiss."

"Just one?"

He covered her mouth with his own, tasting the sweet honey of her kiss, increasing the light that had begun to shine in his soul. Breathing a small, helpless moan, her cheeks pinked with a hot blush.

"Does that give you a hint?" he asked, rubbing his

nose against hers.

Adel looped her arm through his as she smiled into his warmly glowing eyes. "You are a wicked, wicked man, Captain O'Shea."

His tongue traced the inside of her ear, and she quivered with yearning.

Liam laughed and kissed her again. As his kiss deepened, she parted her lips, allowing him to savor her. She moaned aloud as his hand brushed the swell of her breast and his thumb slipped beneath the low-cut bodice of the white muslin blouse to stroke her nipple.

"Someone will see us," she groaned as she tried to push him away.

"And what will they see, my love? A man who passionately desires his wife?"

Now she laughed. The basket of flowers dropped unbidden from her hand as she wantonly threw her arms around him. He drew her tightly against his hard, muscular frame, pressing her pelvis to his, and stroked her hair.

She answered with a devious grin. "Perhaps you should demonstrate this passion you speak of in a more private setting."

Together they walked toward the house. She matched her gait to his. With one hand, Liam pushed the heavy mahogany door wide.

In the great hall, he lowered his mouth to her throat and pressed a slow kiss to her throbbing pulse.

Adel lifted her head and encircled his neck with her arms, meeting his mouth, her tongue flicking out to brush his. She purred, "This could be quite embarrassing if Mary Kathryn were to walk in."

Liam smiled a smile that could have brought any

woman to her knees in surrender.

"Then allow me to invite you to our chambers, where a large, lonely bed awaits."

He wasted not a moment, pushing the bedroom door open and locking it behind him.

She hugged him, and whispered, "Isn't it odd how fate brought us together?"

He chuckled. "Ah, your stepbrother was none too pleased about you offering your services as governess to a total stranger."

"Strange, I haven't thought about Reggie for years."

"Would you like to return to England to visit him?"

"My life is here with my true family. Besides, I have no wish to talk about my stepbrother."

Liam slipped an arm around Adel's waist. "In that case, you have on too many clothes."

Adel cocked an eyebrow. "And what about yourself?"

After he'd removed his clothing and wooden leg, he stretched out on top of the covers, drawing Adel down upon his chest. His desire intensified until he was aching with need. His hand moved between her legs until he found the treasure he sought. He wanted it all.

Rolling to his side, Adel turned to face him.

"Do you know how much you please me, Wife?"

"I do," she whispered. "I love you, Liam, now and forever."

Life was truly good. He had the urge to laugh out loud. Instead he wrapped Adel into his arms, smiled and said, "I have the urge to let you seduce me."

Adel sighed into his mouth as she mounted his well risen manhood and settled between his thighs. She opened her mouth, rubbed her tongue against his. She shivered in reaction to the pleasure of riding him.

She drove him to the brink of fulfillment with her erotic whimpers of pleasure. When Liam couldn't hold back any longer, he rolled over, pinning Adel beneath his length. He wanted to shout with his release. He couldn't, of course, not with his daughter and a houseful of staff to hear.

Her eyes misty with passion and her lips red and swollen, Adel lay with her head nestled against his shoulder. He listened to her even breathing, watched her eyes flutter to stay awake, and then she gave a little start. Her eyes widened.

"What is it? I didn't hurt you, did I?"

She took his hand and moved it to her stomach. "I fear we have disturbed our child, and he protests."

Liam laughed when the little mound bumped the palm of his hand. "With a kick like that, I venture it is a strong lad you carry."

Adel placed her hand over his. "I hope he's just like his father."

He pressed his mouth close to hers. She was his wife...his lady...forever.

A word about the author...

Loretta C. Rogers is an award-winning author who writes historical romance with a twist.

When not writing, she enjoys reading and traveling, especially with her husband on their motorcycle.

Loretta enjoys hearing from readers and invites them to visit her website:

www.lorettacrogersbooks.com

Author's Note

If you enjoyed *Lady Adel's Captain,* Loretta would appreciate if readers would post a review at www.thewildrosepress.com or amazon.com.

Thank you for purchasing
this publication of The Wild Rose Press, Inc.
For other wonderful stories of romance,
please visit our on-line bookstore at
www.thewildrosepress.com.

For questions or more information
contact us at
info@thewildrosepress.com.

The Wild Rose Press, Inc.
www.thewildrosepress.com

To visit with authors of
The Wild Rose Press, Inc.
join our yahoo loop at
http://groups.yahoo.com/group/thewildrosepress/